D1733443

רררז ספ

THE INN KEEPER'S DAUGHTERS

A Tale of Southampton and the American Civil War

by
Jeffery J. Nicholas

authorHOUSE™

1663 LIBERTY DRIVE, SUITE 200
BLOOMINGTON, INDIANA 47403
(800) 839-8640
WWW.AUTHORHOUSE.COM

This book is a work of fiction. People, places, events, and situations are the product of the author's imagination. Any resemblance to actual persons, living or dead, or historical events, is purely coincidental.

© 2005 Jeffery J. Nicholas. All Rights Reserved.

No part of this book may be reproduced, stored in a retrieval system, or transmitted by any means without the written permission of the author.

First published by AuthorHouse 10/11/05

ISBN: 1-4208-8564-2 (sc)

Printed in the United States of America Bloomington, Indiana

This book is printed on acid-free paper.

For Hilary and Jane

Acknowledgements

My grateful thanks to the Hartley Library, University of Southampton, for permission to use the cover illustration, *The Walk West Along the Blechynden Shore* (Cope Collection).

Chapter 1

The Clarence Hotel,
High Street,
Southampton,
Hants.
11 January 1884.

Dear Reader,

I shall never know who you are, unless in some afterlife my spirit is allowed to return awhile to see how the things one may have begun on earth have worked out. My name is Thomas Musselwhite and I am - was - the proprietor here.

Ah! To continue in this style, in an attempt to acknowledge my anticipated state of existence, will soon confuse me and possibly irritate you. So, suffice to say, at the time of writing I am the owner of this hotel; and the manner of how I, who came from humble origins, acquired such a substantial property is a part of the story I have to tell.

In this day and age, it has come to be considered not quite the thing for the successful businessman to live 'over the shop', as it were, and so my wife and I and the children live a short walk away in a new villa in Forest View, which looks across the old town walls and Southampton Water to the fields on the other side and the trees of the New Forest beyond. They say it is this prospect that inspired Isaac Watts the hymnist to write of 'Sweet fields beyond the swelling flood' and 'While Jordan rolled between', and of course his old house is just round the corner in French Street. Perhaps I

1

should add that it is a short walk for me through St Michael's Square and the alleys, in daylight... My family must go a little further round by the High Street at any time, because even the police constables only go into the alleys in threes. I shall no doubt be robbed or worse one day.

The family consists of my wife Rachel, Georgiana - the eldest girl, in her twentieth year - then Phillip, who is fifteen, and Charlotte thirteen. There is also old, old Molly, who was once a slave. Oh yes, she must be considered part of the family too, for we are not to be outdone by the *noblesse oblige* of so-called Southern Gentlemen. She is devoted to Georgiana, who is my adopted daughter and also my niece. Georgiana is the child of Judith, Rachel's younger sister, taken from us these twenty years, and whilst as my orphaned niece would have been welcome under my roof as she was, so closely were all of our lives entwined that only this closer tie sufficed.

As of now I do not feel sure that I am equal to the task I have set myself here. I can write a business letter with its 'Esteemed Sirs' and all of that and when I was young I wrote compositions at the school, which sometimes won praise. However, this will be a long piece and of events that happened to us when we ourselves were still young - and that is long ago. How the great and terrible War between the States in America, which we call their Civil War, put its tentacles across even the wild, wide waste of the Western Ocean and into our lives until everything was changed. I do not know if I can do it, nor even if I should.

Perhaps you will be a descendant, or perhaps simply some twentieth-century individual who finds these papers in a rusty old box in an attic, or from forcing a drawer whose key is long lost. I only know that I do not wish it all to pass and be forgotten, no matter what. Some might blame me now but, as I look around me, steamers get bigger and faster every year. The railways let the people travel everywhere they please. Perhaps you will even have seen airships!

With such improvements I may hope yours is a more tolerant world and less inclined to judgement and retribution than mine, and in that hope I will continue.

How we came to be here...

Behind the hotel, in French Street, is the Bell Inn. Indeed, in years gone by it was the taproom of the hotel. It is a tall, narrow house almost opposite St Michael's church. At the time of which I write, the fifties and sixties of the nineteenth century, the landlord's name was Mr Job Day, but I called him Uncle Joby. He and my father Joe were cousins who had come together from a village not far from Salisbury, looking for work. They had lived hard at first, labouring on the new Tidal Dock by day and lying by night in some of the verminous lodging houses of Back Of The Walls. Joby would sometimes laugh and tell stories about those days, but my father never would. Job's family kept a village public house, but his older brother got that. My grandfather had a smallholding so Pa knew a thing or two about vegetables. With the little money in his pocket he bought a barrow and, starting in the gutter, made his way via a stall in Kingsland Market to his little greengrocer's shop in Mount Street, off East Street.

Raised in the publican's trade, when his chance came Uncle Joby did what he knew best and, at the time of which I speak, was landlord, no less, of the Bell.

You may wonder why it is that I am not piling high the fruit and veg on the pavement of Mount Street or somewhere grander. May Pa's shade forgive me. I shall tell you how it happened.

Cousins...

If Job was my uncle then his two daughters should have been my cousins, but I suppose they must have been second cousins. Rachel and I are much the same age. Judith was about a year younger. When we were only little children, playing trains like the ones we saw puffing fiercely through their long chimneys in the Terminus Station, I thought nothing of my cousins' looks. I recognise now that of course they both grew up to be beautiful women, so I suppose they must have been beautiful children. To me then they were just girls - fortunately tolerable ones. Rachel now has the dark dramatic looks and black hair - although a little streaked with silver - with hazel eyes that flash when she is angry. She also has a voice of a lower pitch than is somehow expected, which even after all these years may catch me unawares, making something turn over within me and sending me back to the gawkiness of youth. Yet this gypsy woman who shares my life keeps no knife about her and if her anger flashes forth it is usually because she has come across some injustice or because some person has thoughtlessly denigrated another. Old Job used to declare that it was lost dogs that she collected - and I should know, for in the end I was one of them.

And Judith? Dark hair too, with chestnut lights in it around a pale, heart-shaped face. But it was Judith's eyes that once seen were never forgotten: great pastel grey lamps, which, if she turned them on you, seemingly searched the dustiest corners of your being. She was not tall but still slender and the summer sun brought out - horror! - a few faint freckles. So there they stood together, one a creature made for the daylight and the sun, and the younger a moth called from the dusk to the lamp. And for long I did not see it as we shouted and ran at play. I was this awkward young fellow amusing himself on the edge of water that was too deep. The greengrocer's boy and the innkeeper's daughters: what did they know of life?

And me? Now I am besuited and top-hatted. Then? Then I was three stone lighter, a skinny youngster, very proud of his check trousers and outsize tasselled cap.

The girls' mother, Martha, had died when we would have been about five and six. I could not say truthfully that I remembered her beyond a kind and indulgent adult figure, not always common in our world of the Protestant God and children who are to be seen but not heard. I wonder if you out there in your time will be shocked? I am not on good terms with the English Protestant God and you shall find out why if you persist with these recollections of mine.

The Bell Inn...

Years later Rachel told me that she believes they came to the Bell in a precipitate move because of their father's anxiety to get away from the setting of his bereavement, and it was a mistake. The Bell was on the edge of a bad area of town: St Michael's Parish. It was a tall, narrow house with three arched windows in the ground-floor facade. Behind those ancient crumbling town walls was a warren of streets, alleys and decayed houses, three, four and more hundred years old. Upper stories overhung and, even with the sea but a stone's throw away, kept out light and fresh air, while keeping in the soot and grime of chimney smoke. Human filth ran in open drains down the middle of the alleys. Plastering had fallen away to show rotten timber framing, areas of coarse stonework with no sense to them, and I remember noticing strange narrow bricks in the walls. There were midden heaps in courts, which were never carted away, and privies that were never emptied and oozed disgustingly towards the gutters. It stank of ruinous old age and excrement, farmyard as well as human. People kept pigs and chickens in there. The people were the poorest of the poor, a dozen, maybe a whole family, crammed into one room. And of course where seamen come and go, there went the bedraggled whores.

If you can do such a slum justice, trade and prosperity had been ebbing away from it for a long time. The decline of the old port just outside those walls had left it to rot and rot for century after century. In the days of the Spa it was an embarrassment, lying as it did between the High Street and the Dolphin and Star Inns above, and the Long Rooms below the walls, almost on the shore, when a sedan chair was not to hand and ladies' shoes were soiled in the mire of Blue Anchor Lane or Simnel Street. Such grand ladies also had to endure the hard stares of ragged women standing in their doorways, who had nothing but their pale, puffy-faced children.

The revival of the port with the coming of the railway and the building of the two new docks on the River Itchen only moved the affluence of business further away to the east. In short, not so different from how it is today, save for some slightly better drains and a few of Mr Crapper's water closets, and Mr Chamberlain's gas lights. All only a few yards, feet even, from Society shopping in the High Street.

Uncle Joby was not your Jolly John Bull type of landlord. He was a bony, balding man with a small neat beard round a mouth forever filled with a briar pipe. He walked in a strange lunging way, and would plunge upon an empty beer cup like a bird of prey, sweeping it up for replenishment with a roll of his eye. Not a man of conversation, he would listen to all, puffing his pipe the while and responding with a plangent word or two before turning away to some other task. Consequently he was not seen as one with the body of his customers but as a little aloof; nonetheless he ran a good house with good beer, was watchful for trouble and quick to quell it, and was respected. This was just as well with those clients who made their way there by crossing from the opposite side of French Street. The pub was also popular with seafarers. Perhaps it was the ship's bell of polished brass and spotless white lanyard that hung behind the bar, out of reach of exuberant customers but in moments of crisis capable of a clangourous racket that made the ears ring in their turn and was also useful sometimes in attracting any police constables who may have been patrolling nearby. By George, I heard it rung one winter's night!

He tried to keep his girls away from the pallid, dirty-faced slum children, so I was especially welcome as a playmate, and when I was older I earned a penny or two as potboy. Thus I suppose I was even then soaking up knowledge of the hard work but good living of the publican's trade. This was something of a bone of contention with the girls because he expected them to take their turn as barmaid. He used to say that he expected them to work toward their keep, but I have the idea that really he liked to show them off a little. Indeed they grew up to become the 'Belles of the Bell', an appellation that would make them turn scarlet with embarrassment whenever some boozy, late-night customer used it. But it did no harm to his trade and he would have it so. Men far away in freezing, sea-soaked forecastles, lying on sodden donkey's breakfasts, could forget the cold with memories of hot food and good drink in the lamplight with the Belles.

Ma would sometimes tut-tut over the way they were thus exposed to the seamy side of life, but Uncle Joby may have had it in his head that, while he might send his young ladies to a dame-school in rooms over a shop in the High Street by day, they should remember they were but the daughters of an innkeeper by night.

They had their own ways of retaliation. Rachel would stand, all innocence, hands behind her back, fingers crossed if I could see them, while her father grumbled that he was sure that somehow he was a pork pie or some cheese rolls short. While I would know, of course, that when he was not looking these had been delivered to grubby hands and hungry mouths from Pepper Alley lurking outside the door.

It was Judy, ah Judy, who could not come to terms with their position. She hated the place and the disreputable neighbours whom she feared, although only her sister and I thought we knew how much. If she heard herself lapsing even for a moment into the distinctive, aitch-dropping, rounded local accent, she would almost pinch herself with shame and annoyance and for a while would speak only in such cut-glass tones that it was a wonder we did not all injure ourselves. But even I knew that you teased her when she was in that mood at your peril. What we did not realise was how much she longed to be truly genteel. This was her secret dream, her passion, and how heavily the sad admission that she was 'only an innkeeper's daughter' weighed down her spirit. Of course, the old school ma'am twittering on about long gone better days at the Spa no doubt played a part. What was the use of music and embroidery to her, Judy would sometimes complain, when her lot was drawing pints? If only we had really known, for God's Sake. As it was, we looked at each other and silently dismissed Judy's dreams. A carriage and horses indeed!

It was in this manner that Uncle Joby raised his girls, assisted by sundry cooks, barmaids and maids of all work, with my Ma as the reserve for illness or disputes or shopping or whatever.

Otherwise it was an ordinary enough childhood, through games and make-believe, teasing and treats and tantrums. We were mercifully spared serious illness, apart from the childish ailments: measles, mumps and the like. Merciful indeed, when, almost across the street, death was common from smallpox, cholera and similar evils. In that time, where typhoid could carry off the Prince Consort, how did we come to be spared? Or were we? Is life only a meaningless lottery in such matters?

There was a difference from other children and other families, I suppose. How could one ask? How can one tell?

Even now. It was an utterly secret thing then. If it was sin, it visited us with a terrible retribution. Yes, it must have been sin, but how can a sin begin in the age of innocence? How old were Adam and Eve when expelled from Eden? Round and round in my head the secret has gone, decade after decade, and now at least the burden will be shared with you, even if I have long been silent. My wife knows, but that is not the same as sharing. I have had to carry the burden alone. Did I bring it into being? Did I forge my own fetters?

Playing with fire...

We must have been only nine and ten and we were bad, all three of us, we knew, for we had been disobedient. We visited forbidden territory: the foreshore beyond the West Gate. We had been sent on an errand by Uncle Joby, returning a brace of a particular claret to the landlord of the Royal Standard, which stands beside the arch. Our business concluded, the temptation to stay and play was too much. The tide was going out, the exposed mud making sucking bubbling sounds from a million holes. The smell of it was rich, strong and awful, and bore God knew what miasmas of disease from broken, trickling drains. But we knew that under the stones and muddy clumps of seaweed lurked hopping things and shore crabs, which could be prodded into motion by a stick or even a toe. We also knew that at all costs we must not muddy ourselves, or the grown-ups would find out. Rachel was left a little behind, peering into some puddle. Judy and I were almost behind Stockham's boatyard.

"You have got mud on your drawers," said I to Judy out of devilment, and of course she stopped and craned her head backward to see.

"I have not, you bad boy, Tommy," said she. "And they are not drawers, they're pantaloons."

"They're drawers," I said. "Everyone knows girls wear drawers." I was even getting a little tired of the sport, for my eye had been caught by a brigantine going out on the tide.

"They are *not* drawers, Tom, they are proper pantaloons. I should know, shouldn't I?"

"Gammon! No they ain't," said I, carefully pouring oil onto the flames. "They're drawers as sure as sure. Don't tell lies."

"*It's not lies. They are not drawers, they're pantaloons,*" she shouted at me, trying to stamp her foot, which with the mud and slimy stones did not go well. "*Look!*" and with that she pulled up the skirt of her sailor suit. I was transfixed. Indeed they were pantaloons of nice white calico and even with a little lace frill around her ankles, although I suppose I must have seen that before but did not notice. Shamefully, I will confess that I can recall every stitch, every seam, every fold, every little crease of Judy's pantaloons, and her white petticoat under her navy blue dress, to this moment. Great questions were answered. Ladies *did* have legs that went all the way up under their skirts - or girls did anyway, as Judy was not a lady yet. And there was more. The sight of Judy's underclothes was utterly new, utterly exciting. Judy would never be the same again. Life would never be the same again. There were simply no words to express this earth-shattering moment.

"Why, you're so pretty," I said, bending down to take a better look - and the God of Abraham and Isaac heard and gazed down on us. Judy stood there for a moment with a look of surprise on her face and then threw down her skirts. But it was too late. God's fury was surely in the whirlwind that fell upon us disguised as Rachel, red with anger and her dark hair flying and her hands slap-slapping - oh, my face stung and my eyes watered.

"She's *not* pretty. She's bad, she's bad. She's...*rude*," Rachel shouted at me, and how she slapped her sister's hands and her behind. Judith's face showed shock and then interest, even as her eyes brimmed. She skipped out of reach and I swear she put her head on one side and the look on her face was one that stated she might have been assaulted but she still had safe in her hand the very last sweetie.

The fury subsided and silently we made our way back with Rachel holding her sister's hand so tight you could see it hurt. And not holding mine. She flounced into the Bell with never a goodbye for me, but Judy's eyes caught mine over her shoulder before she was dragged after her sister.

When I got home to Mount Street and supper, and was at last in bed, I slowly became sure that to look at Judy's pantaloons was a sin. There was no reason, but sin often needed no reason and sin would bring punishment. Uncle Joby would surely visit Pa. Pa would summon me and I should be beaten. Yet the days rolled by and nothing happened. Rachel, that most transparently truthful of creatures, could have said nothing - but why? I did not believe that looking under Judy's skirt did not matter, although I could not think exactly why. It had been the greatest hammer blow in my life thus far. Perhaps then, it must be so awful a thing and would attract so tremendous a punishment that Rachel could not bring herself to speak of it. Or she was afraid that it would spill over onto us all. Better it had. Better by far, bread and water for supper and a behind too uncomfortable to sit on. But nothing happened and fear declined. As it declined, interest grew, and every time I thought about Judy with her skirts disarranged, the strange excitement returned as well.

However, we were children and this was but one of many experiences that were so new and so sharp. There was a first trip on the ferry to Hythe, and a walk round and tea and cake in this strange and foreign place. There was the day when all of us went into the High Street to see the soldiers marching down to the docks on their way to the Crimea. The crowd good-naturedly let us children pass through them so that we could stand on the very edge of the pavement and see it all. I think we were rather scared and felt exposed as they seemed to advance upon us from the Bargate, but we looked backward to where we could see Uncle Joby's bald head shining - for he had rushed out still in his white apron and without his hat - and there was Ma's bonnet also, so we held hands and turned our faces to the troops again. It seemed as if we could feel the steady tread of their boots through our own feet and the drums through our stomachs, even if we put our hands over our ears. There were the harsh cries of the sergeants, the fierce moustaches and the bright brass buttons on the scarlet tunics and the officers' horses' hooves clattering. And the music of the bands. It echoed back from the tall houses and bay windows and the shop fronts beneath, as the sea sounds against cliffs, with the tower of Holyrood looking down. When we were a little used to it, how strange it was to recognise in this martial guise some of the sweet old country tunes we sang at school or on Sundays round the pianoforte at home. Judy was jigging up and down with excitement and waving her pocket-handkerchief. We felt it very strange then, to discover that Rachel was silently weeping. Silly girl!

"What is the matter? Why are you crying?" we asked and she answered, "When will they be coming home again?" - I'll never forget it - "When will they be coming home again?" There is no answer to that when you are ten or eleven. No answer that we, or I certainly, really believed. I remembered her question when, a long time after, we saw what happens to soldiers.

These are but examples of the high-days and holidays for us children. More typical happenings might be going to the Grammar School and dawdling back from it again with a diversion to see what might be tied up at the Town Quay that day. Or helping Pa move out vegetable crates and sweeping up the cabbage leaves. Playing with hoops with Rachel and

Judy in St. Michael's Square. Or with whipping tops. Or conkers in their season. However, the strange, exciting secret stayed in my mind. To and fro, round and round, as I lay awake in my bed in darkness in my room, I thought of Judith with her skirt up and the white sight of her pantaloons and petticoat. Memories would come of other paltry glimpses of ankles glimpsed and dresses caught up for an instant and an inch or two on a windy day, but nothing to compare with Judy uncovered to her middle like that. I tossed and turned, wondering if she remembered it at all, wondering if she thought about it at nights like I did. Or was it just an ordinary mistake for her, not to be repeated?

A few weeks later, Judy and I found ourselves alone in the private parlour upstairs at the Bell, all mahogany furniture and red leather buttoned chair seats. We were supposed to be doing French knitting with wool and old cotton reels. The devil must have seen us and sent in sin because it was almost with surprise that I heard my voice asking if I could see her pantaloons again. In a moment I was terrified. This was all different. She had not known better before. She would run out screaming. She did indeed walk to the door and my heart was in my mouth. She was wearing a green tartan dress down to just over her knees, I suppose, with a dark green sash and the white legs of her drawers or whatever they were down to her ankles. Words bubbled desperately in my mind. I did not mean it. No, don't do it, Judy. I don't want you to be naughty. You won't tell, will you? Will you?

She put her ear to the door and listened for a long time. There were only the usual sounds of pub life but they were far, far away downstairs. Then she turned around and leant against it and looked me in the eye. She said never a word but like in a dream I watched her take hold of her dress and draw it upwards and it was as delicious as before. I can recall the small sounds that her clothes made to this very day. I bent to look and at that she held her clothes down a little lower but I could still see her legs, wholly encased in her pantaloons, of course. I must have been crazy. I might have spoiled it forever but I still heard my voice with a tremble in it explaining that it was not quite right. Could she lift a little bit higher so that I could see all of her pantaloons? She looked a little surprised once more and glanced down to check how much she was showing, then took a new hold on her clothes and got her skirts all up round her waist and bunched on her hips. She even took pains to lift folds drooping down in the middle out of the way. I also noticed that she pressed her knees together for a moment as a grown woman will, discovered in dishabille, and it was a strange thrill to see it. And then she did not, and that was good too. Perhaps Jehovah singled her out at that moment, little girl as she still might be, because her instinct to modesty was so outweighed by what? A desire to please? Something new? An inexplicable thrill that a boy enjoyed looking at her body? But that is the opinion of an adult and the father of a daughter. Then I was but a prurient small boy utterly delighted with what I - we - were doing.

"Is that better? Can you see everything now?" She spoke to me in a stage whisper, with a suppressed giggle afterward. Maybe it was simply the younger sister enjoying being the focus of attention. Maybe it was the naughty girl enjoying the defiance of doing what she had been forbidden to do. So Rachel had smacked her: she was doing again what her elder sister had been outraged to find her about. What fun! And as I stared at her body I felt quite certain that I was face to face with one of the most important things in the world.

"They look a bit like sailors' trousers."

"What? My pantaloons?"

"Yes. A bit like sailors' trousers - the ones they wear in summer. But yours are much prettier."

"Are they? I wish I could wear trousers. I'm tired of dresses. They catch on everything when I want to pick blackberries in Love Lane. I can't stand on the swing and go really high in case someone sees. I can only sit down. I can't climb trees."

"That's silly. Girls can't wear trousers. They have got to wear skirts. It's the law. And it would not be the same if you wore trousers."

"Why wouldn't it?"

"Well...it would not be so pretty, would it? I do like seeing your pantaloons and petticoat and everything ever so much."

"Really? You really like them? Why do you like them?"

"I don't know."

"I like you looking at them."

"Why?"

"I don't know but I'll show them to you again, Tommy, if you want me to. But I think I had better put my skirt down now because somebody's coming upstairs."

Chapter 2

Playing with water...

As I neared my fourteenth year I began to experience pressure over what I should do to provide myself with a livelihood after I left school. I would then, of course, be expected to begin contributing to the household's income. The only significant parental guidance was that I should not go to sea, which, as it was the only thing that I wanted to do, left me at a loss over what to say. This suited my parents well and thus it was decided by default, I suppose, that of course I should follow my father into greengrocery. The only question remaining was whether this should be by simply extending my after-school duties to full-time employment. Or Ma's preference, that I should learn the methods of trading and business from somewhere more informed than my father's self-taught stool. I think, if anything, my view may have been that any course postponing my lifetime incarceration behind the veg and flowers in Mount Street was distinctly preferable; so I unresistingly went along with the arrangements made with Misselbrooks, the grocer in East Street. That was my head of those days speaking. The heart was a turmoil of thwarted despair, I can tell you.

In harbour towns like this, it is known that the call of the sea is a real thing to be reckoned with if you encounter it. A man settled for years after seafaring, confronted with some apparently minor check in his career or upset in domestic life, finds it the proverbial straw that breaks the camel's back, walks out of his house and apparently vanishes. He has, of course, gone down to a company office or to the ships themselves in the docks, got himself a berth and away he goes and that is that for six months. The ordinary fellow goes out, gets drunk and then goes home again for better or worse, as the vows have it. The seafarer knows that 'when the gangway's away, all debts are paid'. Something makes him forget the cold, bad food, hard life and furious waters, and his own ageing body. He only remembers warm days and whispering seas of yesteryear, without that much to do and being in a jolly crowd ashore with money in his pocket and liquor in his belly, looking over foreign tarts. This is the adult presentation of the same disease as grips the young, who see the spars and spires of standing rigging towering impressively overhead and have a five-minute sight of grey sails turned rose in the sunset as some old tub slips away with the ebb, and every nerve screams to go with her. Used to warm beds and hot breakfasts put on the table, they never imagine a staggering ship with green water breaking over the lee rail and the terror of crawling out up there on wet stiff rope and clawing with broken nails at straining, billowing canvas that is trying to have them off the yard. A ship from hell, like some women from hell, can still be so beautiful, and it is only the beauty you ever remember. Never being sick while you are ditching ash from the stokehold and some fluke of wind blows everything all over you. Or the Old Man's tea that you have nursed all the way from the galley, then spill when you are within a yard of him. There is a child that never quite grows up in seafarers and that child never quite stops listening for the sound of the sea. I wonder what ships it may be that your youngsters will hanker after? Moon ships? Star ships?

I had spent much of childhood's precious leisure hours, the time the daydreaming is done, loitering by the Town Quay and the Western Shore, and a diet of fruit and veg seemed intolerable. What did I need with a job forever and money for the house? For Judy? Ah yes, well, one day but not yet, for I was not fifteen years old. How mean the thought after embracing that eager, sensual little body. And yet we had spoken of it, pathetic immature young minds that we were, playing with our matches again.

Our sweet, deadly, secret vice had grown to be such a part of our lives that we hardly questioned it now. Where cousins might kiss when they meet, if we were alone she was gathering up her skirts as she came across the room to me. They were lengthening now as she grew and her petticoats, especially for high-days and holidays, were a little finer and trimmed with a little more lace. And we loved it! We really thought that we could not wait to be grown up. We would pore together over the fashion journals she brought sometimes and, as well as trying to imagine her dressed in the latest clothes from Paris, she loved to try to shame me by making me look at the drawings of ladies undergarments shown in the advertising sections. "Wouldn't you like me to wear those?" she would inquire demurely, pointing to some representation of 'unmentionables' - stays, camisoles or whatever it was - and would giggle delightedly if she could make me grow a little warm.

We had a favourite pretence at argument for a while: she would declare she could not wait to gain her first crinoline, for she said her petticoats were hot and heavy; while I would defend them, saying that they were dear friends and that I adored it when she showed them to me one by one. She would make a ritual retort that when she had her crinoline she would be able to tip it up and then I would see her form below the waist unencumbered and would I not like that? (Oh, the vision of those slim hips and slender limbs will burn me in hellfire yet.) It was my part to defend the ritual of the petticoats, saying how much I enjoyed being shown them. It had to be always the outermost first and I was allowed to finger the materials as we went, during which she sighed and whispered to herself, ostentatiously rustled her dress and fluffed up and drew back the petticoats she had shown and drew out the next for inspection. Sometimes she would pretend to plead in a little-girl voice that could she not show her pantaloons now, and I had to sternly refuse until the last petticoat had been inspected. Then when we had reached the innermost one she would look up and make her mouth and eyes round with mock horror as she slowly drew it back with a feverish giggle and let me see her legs. There might now be a cry such as "Oh, Tommy, what are you looking at?" or "Your eyes, Tommy, you bad boy, your eyes!" which was the cue to throw down her clothes, fold her hands in her lap and droop her eyelids in modest virtue. Then I was to plead that she lift her skirts again (and often I could barely speak) whilst she refused with a tiny little voice saying, "No. No, no, Tommy," and after a little while she would look up and turn those grey lamps upon me, and swishing, rustling, draw them up and reveal all again. Or better, if she had resisted a long time I would ask her if I might lift them myself. She was never known to say 'yes' but there would be an almost imperceptible nod. Then slowly, one by one, or with a rush that brought them up to her neck and with luck even revealed a little white skin above her pantaloon waistband, I would have raised her skirts and she would peep down over her petticoat hems and whisper, "Oh, Tommy, look. I'm showing so *much*," as if she were seeing the eighth wonder of the world. Occasionally, with her skirts held at arm's length above her head like a peacock's tail, and with her back to me to let me see her bottom, she would plead prettily with me to be allowed to discard the mass of petticoats and indeed her skirts altogether. She would declare that she wanted to wear men's trousers and if I brought her some to try, why, she would have to let me watch her take her dress right off and discard every petticoat to try them on, and… oh la, sir...

Oh God, how could one guess where this delicious foolery would end?

I noticed once that if she had a sash over her dress or a little belt round her waist, she would always unfasten them before getting to the business of lifting her skirts. One day I asked her why. She thought for a moment and then she told me, "When you are looking at between my legs and things, I get a feeling that I can't bear anything tight round my tummy. So I undo them first. You don't mind, do you?"

I hastily said that no, I did not mind at all. And then I said, "But, Judy, what are you going to do when you have grown up and have to wear stays?"

"Golly, I'll be a grown up lady," she responded. "Will you be looking under my skirt when I'm a grown up lady?"

I hastily replied that I was sure that I would. She thought for a moment, then said, "Well, if you are always nice to me, I *will* lift up my skirt for you when I am a grown up lady. When my skirt's up and you make me take the little step to the side and then look at between my legs, I do like it. It makes me want to lift my skirts up more. So when I'm a grown up lady I expect I'll like it just the same." Well, it was nearly so.

I hope Mrs Amelia Bloomer and her movement are quite forgotten. I would not have liked any of the ladies in my life to wear anything but their skirts and what should lie beneath. Any other would somehow demean their nature as well as diminish their allure and who would desire that?

In itself it had gone further, as worldly wisdom has doubtless anticipated. The appointed day came when her little account with me was to be settled and how she prevaricated with me. Coquette? A late (or early?) discovery of feminine modesty? Fear of the unknown? None of these really fitted Judy then. She was a colt escaped from the stable, running and kicking up her heels in our field.

I was not to be put off by a glimpse of her rosebud bosom down the top of her dress. (I had glimpsed one of the barmaids

washing, which added a new item to the excitements menu.)
I wanted to settle the mystery of how she was different from
me down there between her legs. I had no idea of how she
would contrive this. My most feverish phantasy was that she
would come clothed only in her petticoats, but I dismissed
this when as usual the pantaloon legs were visible below her
skirt and above her little black boots. At long last, when I was
cross and puzzled by her hesitation, she looked at me with
that penetrating gaze and said slowly "Do you remember?
Down on the Western Shore? I really have put on drawers
today for you, Tommy." And so she had. The legs covered
her thighs as usual but at the top there was nothing joining
them together! Still holding up her clothes she contrived to
crook her index fingers and pulled the legs of her drawers a
little more apart.

"Look, Tommy, look," she said in that hot whisper. "That
is my rude place in there. Can you see it? Can you?"

I could! I can but say that I was as delighted with what
she showed me then, as upon that first day down on the
muddy shore. How neatly she was made, with her little
white slit, and her mound and the fine black fuzz on it just
growing. When she saw my fascination and delight, she was
delighted also. All glowing smiles and breathless giggles.
We could not bear that day that she should cover herself and
her rustling petticoats had to come up again and again to the
very threshold of the room.

We must get on. It is not good for me to linger here. Our
code of rules were, in short, that if one could see one must
not touch but if one could not see, one might. That episode
was when Mr Misselbrook's was still a distant cloud. We
were together in a corner and I was pleasuring her in the
new way we had discovered with my fingers pressing into
her gusset to give her what she came to call the Exquisite
Sensations. Her little chin pressed quite sharply into my
shoulder and she lent against me more and more. She even
seemed to be loosing her hold on her clothes because I felt

them slip and I had to thrust with my spare hand under her warm skirts to keep them out of the way. Then I realised that she was whispering into my ear.

"Tommy," she said, "you will marry me and take me away from this place, won't you?"

"Oh yes, yes. Of course I will," I said. I had a passing thought that it was I who should make such a proposal, but all things with Judith were so different that the thought was merely a transient one. All was an uncharted sea.

"And I really will have a great house and servants to do all the work and many beautiful dresses and my own carriage and horses?"

"See here" said I, managing to give her waist a nudge where she was ticklish, "On Saturday afternoon I will walk with you to Above Bar to that Royal Carriage Manufactory at number eleven there, and you shall show me exactly which you like best." I do not know if she had been carried away by what we were about. Perhaps it was some wish for fulfilment of her favourite daydream.

"Do you so wish to be married?" I asked her. I felt her eyelashes flutter against my face.

"Yes," said she. "For there must be more to it than keeping house and bringing up children. There must be something more they have not told us." I took a long time to put into words a thought that had come into my mind.

"Do you think it could possibly be anything like this? Judy, where do the children come from? Not from under a gooseberry bush or brought by a stork, I am sure. Who ever saw a stork in England? Do you think it could possibly be like kittens and puppies? We saw dogs and cats doing something strange, didn't we? Or like they breed the horses, so I've been told."

She thought for a long time, and then she said, "No. Can you believe your Ma and Pa doing anything like that? Your Ma would have died of shame and so would have my

Mama. I expect they went to the doctor. I expect he arranged it for them."

"It could not be anything like we do?" I persisted.

"Oh no. I think having babies hurts. You never hurt me and I do not feel ashamed. It feels nice, as though I was about to go to a party. Oh Tommy, just there, oh please... please do it again." She giggled in my ear. "I will let you see my bottom by and by if you do it to me just there again. Oh, there..." Sometimes she would be very reluctant to lift her dress behind but not if she had let me touch her for a little while.

Perhaps at that moment she thought it might really be me. She was so young, although we did not think so. What on earth would they have done to us if we had ever been discovered? Dragged us through the streets on a hurdle? More likely the Chinese water torture by exposure to scripture, I suppose. Never fear, the debt was called in, in the end.

Do you remember how a month seems as long as a year when one is young? But then they still rolled away and there I was with a white apron almost as long as I was, with my shining boots just peeping out beneath it, standing in Mr Misselbrook's shop, no more than a step or two round the corner from home.

The novelty of it occupied the first few days. The speciality of the shop was bacon and sides, and joints of the stuff hung inside as well as outside. Collar, back, loin, streaky. *Hams: small hams are best and, on running a knife close to the bone, it should come out without any nasty smell, and should not be greasy.* Yes, Mr Misselbrook. No, Mr Misselbrook. Thank you, Mr Misselbrook. And then there was brawn...

The first week passed by as I trotted two and fro on behest, watched, listened and if nothing or nobody else beckoned, wielded my brush on floor and pavement.

The second week began with the recognition of how small a world it was that took me from Ma's scrubbed doorstep to the shop door in only a few minutes. It ended on Saturday evening at eight o'clock with a heavy promise that if I was a good and attentive boy, one day, even quite soon perhaps, I might be entrusted with a few deliveries to favoured customers nearby. I knew that I should not be so inwardly unmoved by what was obviously seen and offered as a mark of progress and nascent trust; but I was not.

On Monday morning of the third week I sat on the edge of the bed for a while through heaviness of heart, instead of getting on with washing hands and face in my washbowl, dawdled on my way and was almost late. A late evening visit to my old dreaming ground on the Town Quay provided no solace now. That had been fit for a schoolboy but not for the reality of life. I felt myself sweating and there was a sensation of constriction in the throat and an inability to take a deep breath. By the end of the week, with dread I knew I was going to have to speak to my father.

Looking back now it is easy to feel ashamed of how I felt about his attitude then. He had had a few years in a village school and wrote and reckoned laboriously, and I had been sent to the Free Grammar School. His lips moved with his pen as he made up the shop's accounts of an evening. With emotion, his voice reverted to the Wiltshire dialect of his childhood, which I despised, and the aitches soon dropped in showers. He had heard of Waterloo and the passing of Old Nops but it had made little impression on the depth of a county upbringing. He had bent his back for years and scrimped and saved and borrowed to build up his little business. It was hopeless to expect him to see more, and of course he did not have the language to express himself in a way that did not seem tyrannical and crude.

"Of course it's all for ever and ever and ever," he said. "You've got to eat every day for ever and ever and ever. Now you want to turn your back on a nice little business that'll provide victuals not only for yourself but also for a family of your own one day. I've seen lads half your age out on the land gleaning corn for the fowls and bringing in the cattle before sunup. And they're on the land for ever and ever and ever because they've got to eat and their poor old crippled mother's got to eat too and there isn't anything else. It's life. It's fate."

He seemed to have forgotten that he had escaped from the land himself. He did not apparently hear me say that I only wanted it for a year or so. (Liar as I was, for then, childishly, I wanted the sea for ever and ever and ever.) He was, I believe, too outraged that I seemed to be spurning his life's work and also forgot that you cannot put old heads on young shoulders. There is even the thought I can entertain now that I was the only one, as he had married late, when his struggles had given him a little latitude.

Ships were too often reported overdue and were never heard of again or returned with accounts of men lost to accident and foul weather. The lists of wrecks in the papers after a storm were appalling. But at that moment his business seemed no more than a cell to which I was being raised to be prisoner, and as he stood there with his red face and collarless shirt with stud a-dangling, I left him, bearing nothing but feelings of rage and despair as deep as only a youngster can harbour. There was nowhere to go for aid. What could my friends the Day girls offer? But when I could I went anyway.

I think if was the Sunday afternoon after silent meals and silent bedtimes that I went round to the Bell. I am sure Uncle Joby noticed that something was wrong, for when I went in and asked to see the girls he stopped and took the pipe out of his mouth and stared at me before jerking a thumb to indicate that that they were upstairs. I walked heavily up and opened the parlour door and they too stared. I sat in an armchair and poured out my tale. I told them how I longed for the sea, which they knew anyway. Discussing that day, long afterwards, Rachel once said that she knew how much I wanted to go to sea but until then she had thought it nothing more than one of the various dreams we all had and shared. "I thought it was like Judy's carriage and horses until then," she said.

Doubtless I became distressed as all of it poured out. Rachel came and sat on the arm of the chair and put her arm round my shoulder. "Shh, shh! Poor Tommy, don't take on so. What's to do? What's to do? We must think." Across the room, despite my trembling voice and shamefully tearful eye, I saw Judith catch my glance and just take hold of her skirt with both her hands, an action that would under normal circumstances have totally taken over my mind with the fever of pleasures to come. As it was it provoked a spasm of fear in me that Rachel might have noticed something but, blessings on her, she was too busy trying to find an answer to my plight. At least, that was how it seemed.

"You could stow away," suggested Judy, her eyes sparkling. "I want you to stow away. What an excitement that would be."

"No, I don't want that. I'll be brought back by my ear after one trip and be straight into Pa's shop if I'm lucky," I said. "I want a real job. I want to work at sea. Not for ever..." I had noticed something strange in the manner with which Judith was regarding me, "...but to see a bit of the world, make a little money of my own even, before settling down."

"Tommy, it cannot be all that difficult," said Rachel. "The pub is full of sailor men."

"I do not even know what clothes I should wear. Never mind where to get 'em," I went on hopelessly.

"Oh fiddlesticks," said Rachel. "Leave it to us. We shall ask questions just now and again and here and there. Come to tea next Sunday and see what we have discovered. And just go on serving the bacon until then and be good."

So back to Misselbrooks I dutifully went, trying to give a good impression despite a heavy heart, and in the duller moments distracting myself with fantasies of Judith. And the sea too, of course.

I could not wait until Sunday, so even if I had been on my feet for the best part of eleven hours, on Saturday evening I went to the Bell and volunteered for some potboy duty. Yawning, I helped the girls wash up and dry. Suddenly, I did not dare ask what they might have discovered but at last I sat on a stool and listened.

"We asked," said Rachel "and they seem to say that you should not just go and stow aboard some ship whose owners no one has heard of. It might be easy, but when they have got you, you might be half starved and beaten."

"I pretended it was me who wanted to go. I asked if I should wear trousers. That got them talking," said Judy.

"Shush. You must take more care of your modesty, Judy. You are not a little girl any more. I have never seen her act so artful, Tommy."

Judith pouted. "It's half true anyway. I should love to go."

"I think you must be a bad influence on her with your talk, Tommy. Anyway, they say you should try one of the big companies. P & O or the Royal Mail packets to the West Indies."

P& O. I thought about their grand office building along Canute Road and the gentlemen in silk hats and tail coats and the be-buttoned and braided officers coming and going that I had seen there, and felt over-awed by. Maybe later.

I wanted to see the ship that would change my life. I wanted to choose her, not to be told where to go by some clerk in an office. In this respect, I was already disposed as a seafarer would be towards 'The Office' and all its works The plan had several stages. Firstly, I must find a ship and find a berth. Second, Ma and Pa must be told. I was so desperate to escape that I feared any communication with them might give them time to apprehend me somehow. Regretfully, I was prepared to let them stew, but Rachel would not stomach the idea for a moment.

"Tommy," she said, "I do not care how miserable you may be, but it is never right to make others the same for your own selfish ends. For goodness sake, they are your parents. All they wish for you is that you shall be comfortably situated. You should not injure them because they cannot see further than Mount Street. They would fancy you murdered or drowned. You are their only son, remember. If you won't do something to tell them, I shall go round and tell them now what you are planning, and I don't care."

Even now - as then - I can only look shamefaced at the ground when I propose to do something wrong and dear Rachel sees it and denounces it. Judith said nothing, which, I thought, supported me - and I suppose that that is a statement of some kind as well, but there was nothing for it.

For stage two I was to write a letter to Ma and Pa. We devised it so that I would tell the girls when I should make my bid for freedom. In case it was a ship that was about to sail, it was arranged that, if they heard nothing of me for twenty-four hours, they would assume that I had gone and would take my letter to my parents. Otherwise I should come and tell them what was to be. I will say here that, later, I sat down suddenly when it came to me that other palms than mine could feel the cane and bottoms the strap if wrath was taken up by Uncle Joby. If the girls thought that at the time, they kept it from me. We were true conspirators.

Run...

It was not that difficult in those days to get past the constables on duty at the dock gates. I had accomplished it a few times before, once for a schoolboy dare but mostly to get to the surroundings where I had the sensation that I belonged. You could do it by straight concealment, loitering in Canute Road at busy periods, always tagging along with other people and watching for the moment when the constable was busy; for example, when a dray that he had waved to go in then lumbered to a halt to ask directions to some ship or other, just as a cab was trotting out and a party of dockers were making their way out of the gate as well. That was when you made your dash.

A better way was to simulate an errand and that was what I did with, I have to admit, a purloined delivery basket from Misselbrooks. I simply helped myself to it when the shop was closing and everyone else was tired, longing for supper and unobservant. I was emboldened by a terminal revulsion for bacon and a now-or-never sensation that it was time for the escape. Next morning I arranged a few vegetables in the basket, to be observable under a negligently arranged cloth, and instead of going to work, made my way to No 2 Gate. I could not believe it, I got in so easily; my basket with 'Misselbrook' so prominently on the side in black lettering, and myself attracting barely a glance. It was the kind of good fortune of which a longer acquaintance with Fate might have made me suspicious, but it appeared genuine enough at the time. And a step nearer to the reckoning.

It was a walk of two hundred yards or so to the corner of the dock with P & O steps at my left. In front was the lock to the Closed Dock. All around were sheds and warehouses. Underfoot the railway lines. The view to me was like the sighting of Jerusalem must have been to a crusader. Bustle, noise, steam, coal, engines puffing as they took up the strain, wagons clanking, stacks of goods of all sorts, sooty smoke mixed with the salty sea smell. A strange paradise perhaps but it was *my* paradise.

In the midst of all this industry the ships lay at their berths. They also towered over it all, every mast crossing spars then, steamer as well as sailing ship: up, up… so that the people in the streets could see topsail and topgallant yards rising above the dockside sheds. They seemed to me noble and as though they made polite conversation with each other, haughtily disregarding the clamour of their serving people about their feet. What toys they seem today, with their places taken by ships ten times their size and built not with wood, not with iron, but with steel; and what leviathans, my reader, do you see coming up Southampton Water?

I turned left along the dockside and passed the bowsprit of a P & O steamer, but I wanted something more than Gib and Malta and Alexandria, so I passed on. My heart was pounding and I was half scared to death. The next ship was stern on to me and her row of stern windows set in gilt gingerbread reflected the glitter of the water. She was no more than a wooden paddle steamer with her masts rigged as a barquentine, and no longer young. She was one of the original fleet of Royal Mail Steam Packets built in 1841 but, dazzled by those windows, at that moment she was my galleon bound for the Spanish Main, where I should find fame and fortune and bring home silk petticoats for Judith to put on. Reader, I dare say that you in your time may still see a boy enslaved by the charms of an older woman - and ships are always 'she'.

She was in no ways deserted, smoke from her black 'chimney', as Royal Mail would always have it in those days, was light and shimmering with heat: she was advanced in raising steam and her decks were busy preparing for departure. The seamen and company men and tradesmen seemed unreal to me as I pushed through them and felt the light buck of the gangway beneath my step. To gain the deck was to walk out onto a lighted stage and about as scaring. What should I do now?

A hand shook my shoulder and a voice said, "Boy. Boy, what's this? Are you delivering galley stores?"

I heard myself reply with an embarrassing squeak, for my voice had hardly broken then. "No. I want to come with you. I want to go to sea."

They grouped themselves around me: a small, amused crowd. "Ho, ho, that is a funny thing to want to do."

There was a comic opera put on in London a year or two ago called *HMS Pinafore*, by that fellow Gilbert, with the music of the recently knighted Arthur Sullivan. I expect it was forgotten years ago but I recall it, because it contained a song that advised one to 'stick tight to your desk and never go to sea, if you want to be the ruler of the King's Navy' or something like that, and now I was the recipient of much the same sentiments.

But then the babble stopped and the group made way for another. I knew Royal Mail officers had gold lace chevrons on their sleeves and this man had three of them, so he had to be the captain. I remember him as a clean-shaven, handsome man. Indeed I would know him at once today if Captain Moir were still alive.

"What's your name, boy?"

"Tom, sir."

"Tom who?"

"Tom… White, sir." It was the only part of the plan begun as yet.

"Hmm. Why do you want to go to sea, Tom White?"

"I've always wanted to go to sea, sir."

"Then why are you doing it like this?"

I found I was becoming upset. I held out the basket. "Because they have put me to this, sir."

He bent down with his hands on his knees, so that he could look me in the eye.

"Now, Tom, answer me truthfully. Have you done anything wrong that you are running away from? Have you been stealing?"

"Oh no, sir. Nothing like that, sir, I promise."

"Well then, show me your hands, Tom."

I held out my hands and turned them over and back as I did for Ma when she wished to examine their cleanliness.

"Not the hands of a son of toil, young man. Can you read and write?"

"Of course I can. I've only just left school, sir," I replied indignantly.

The Captain remained serious-faced as he straightened up, although I noticed a muscle in his cheek twitching.

"Well, Tom, you may discover many here do not. Some would say to be a seaman is little better than calling oneself a skilled labourer. Do you see yourself going aloft and hauling halyards for ever?" I glanced at the masts towering overhead and could think of nothing to say. "Nor do I think I see any skill at foundry or forge that might incline you towards the engineers, and I think you too small to wield a shovel in the stokehold all day."

"No, sir," I heard myself replying sadly. The dream was steadily evaporating, I could see.

"Well, Tom, I am sure you would like to go to sea, but what makes you so useful that I would want to take you?" said he.

"I don't know, sir." I heard the dismal old phrase so overused at school come floating out again. And then with the boldness of desperation I said, "But I still want to go, sir."

He sighed and looked around him and thought for a bit. "Tom, I have the need of a tiger. A steward, a servant really, to look after me. He must keep my cabins clean and tidy. Make up my berth, make sure my laundry is done and my uniforms brushed. He must serve me my meals if I wish to dine in my cabin, and bring me a cup of tea without spilling it even if the sea is rough. Some ashore might call it women's work, but we have few women serve at sea and so must do it for ourselves. The chief steward will teach you everything you need to know. Will you do it, Tom?"

I thought it was a long way from gold and gunpowder but still the only way I might go, so I said, "Yes please, sir," and there it was.

"What will you do with the grocer's basket?"

"I will take it back when I get home again. There are plenty more there and they will not miss it. It has some clothes and things I need for now."

"And are you an orphan, Tom, with no one to miss you?"

"Oh no, sir. I mean, yes sir. No, sir."

"Which is it?"

"Ma and Pa, sir. But they will have a letter."

"A letter?" Of course out everything tumbled, with the roles of Rachel and Judith in it all.

"Hmm. Should you not go home tonight and explain all that we have arranged, and come again tomorrow before we sail?"

"Oh no, sir. They will lock me in my bedroom and I shall be beaten. Please do not make me do that."

He thought some more and then I saw him make up his mind and I was handed over to the chief steward to be fitted out with trousers and white tunics from the slop chest and found a bunk where I might sleep.

It was when I got home again from sea, a very different lad, that I discovered bit by bit that of course someone had been sent to Misselbrooks and my address discovered and Ma and Pa, indignant but reassured, informed of my whereabouts, but too late to do anything before the ship sailed.

My ship, my first ship, was the SS Trent and I was put on the ship's books as 'Boy'.

Chapter 3

A-roving, a-roving...

A while ago, feeling jaded, I took my family on holiday to Bournemouth. It is always pleasant to feel it is someone else who has to worry about washing up and clean sheets. Also, one can observe how that someone else goes about things, with a view to improvements back home when the holiday is over.

One afternoon, after a careful examination of wind, sea and sky with a suspicious eye, especially for my wife's sake, we went on board the little steamer *Lord Elgin* for a coastal excursion. It is only thus in these days that I can re-visit the old times, for myself and for you, for the last paddle ship has quite recently been withdrawn from the Atlantic.

The sound is a wham-bam-bam-bam, wham-bam-bam-bam with an infinitesimal pause between, which I suppose is due to some minute hesitation when the gleaming pistons down below finish their cycle. When she rolls a little, which a narrow-gutted paddle steamer with her heavy driving shaft high in the hull always will, the floats (the blades in the paddle wheel) beating the water deepen their note on the lower side, as those on the upper side become shriller, and more splashing spray flies. If the sound seems to be everywhere, I can tell you that after nineteen days to Barbados you hear it no more, although you will wake from the deepest sleep if there is the least variation in that rhythm. What am I saying? Like the Dodo, will not the paddle steamer have passed away long ago?

If in my today you look at Royal Mail ships like the Tagus or Moselle and think of the Western Ocean, you would wonder how we dared to do it. Not for nothing is the popular description of Atlantic weather as fifty weeks storm and two weeks of fog. The green grey swells are so big that they seem hardly to move, while the wind tears the spindrift from their crests and drives it away like smoke. And we presumed to set off across this at nine knots in an ageing wooden paddler of what, 1850 tons and two hundred and fifty feet long? Oh, and helped along by a barquentine's suit of sails. Well, we knew no better, and when she came out in 1841, she and her sisters were thought of as a miracle compared with what had gone before - and so it was. This ship did not steam out of port to disappear for weeks or months. It might be a few hours more; you might be a few hours early; but it was now nineteen days to Barbados and this was unprecedented. She was a veteran of the Crimea and already getting out of date, but we were all fond of our creaky old ship as, complaining and groaning, she ascended and descended moving mountain after moving mountain, day after day, night after night, all nineteen days of it to Barbados. Those twin-churned wakes so impressively laid down in the Solent were no more than pathetic traces in all that roaring immensity. Perhaps we comforted ourselves with the old sailor-man's saw: 'if she creaks she swims'.

And that is the end of what I describe as the yo-ho-ho type of yarn. Nor do I intend to give you an island-by-island description of the West Indies. You might do worse than reading Tom Cringle's Log or Mr Kingsley's writings for that. Generally, some of the islands are flat, with white coral sand that blazes at the eye in the sunlight, and are inhabited by only a few sparse palms because there is no water. Others are mountainous or even volcanic, hot and wet with dense green forest that comes down and hangs over the deep blue sea itself. And it is deep and it is blue, yet it amazed me how clearly you could see rocks and weed many fathoms below, especially if you looked downward from a little height. All rather different from Southampton Water or Bournemouth Bay.

Some of these islands are British, some are French, Spanish, Dutch or Danish. I never saw a native South American Indian, even in Guiana; all long gone. I saw the odd indentured Indian labourer from India itself. Mostly I saw blacks - one-time slaves from Africa, survivors of the manacles of the slave decks in ships hailing from Liverpool and Bristol (and even Lyme Regis), and of the crossing itself, the infamous Middle Passage. I was told that you might retch at the stink from a slaver, miles downwind of her. It was only a quarter of a century or so before I first went that slaves had been freed, but I was merely a lad and I gave it little thought. To me, it was history.

I became adept at producing a mirror finish while cleaning shoes, and learned how to starch and press a dress shirt and which glasses are for drinking claret and which Chablis. Indeed what claret and Chablis taste like and how warm or how cool they should be served. Nothing of knots, canvas and terrors aloft from a hurricane passing near, nor lying on your back in the bilge with massive machinery inches from your face, trying with a sledge hammer to move on an engine which has stopped at dead centre. These stirring events were happening to my shipmates. In this apprenticeship I had chosen, I learned the more mundane skills supporting genteel living, and these I still use today, so long after.

All the yo-ho-ho was there, of course. Driven on deck for a minute by the thick air and animal smells below, the wind drew tears from my eyes and tried to tear my hair off as well as anybody else. Or that oily, eerie calm in the Sargasso with clumps of yellow-brown seaweed as far as the eye could see; yes I leaned on the bulwark with the others, staring. But this is not what I am about. I am about Rachel, Judith, and myself. And confessing like a papist.

I will digress to tell you that on that first ever trip I made a friend, a young engineering apprentice aboard: a Scot, name of Roderick McKay, a big, big gentle youngster with a mop of black hair. He would tend some maddeningly recalcitrant piece of machinery with his huge slow hands, for all the world as if it was a sick animal, and as often as not seemed to coax it back into function by sheer affection. Now, he has his own forge and engineering works a mile or two out of the town, in the village of Shirley. As well as being my old friend, his improvement of himself is a part of this story. Then, all he had was the bottom berth and all I had was the upper one.

So it was, that first trip, I began slowly to learn my trade from the chief steward and the rest of them - even from the Old Man, who patiently explained what was wanted and never forgot to praise or encourage along the way. I surprised myself, for I might well have called it women's' work - although at first I did not care what it was, so pleased was I to be there. I take pride now that I can teach a new chambermaid to make a bed as well as a hospital nurse and, although naturally I keep my opinion to myself, better than even my doughty hotel housekeeper herself.

I was also fortunate in that I was naturally a good sailor. I discovered I had good sea legs and, although I might go green and would die rather than eat, I can only remember twice that I was sick at sea from *mal de mer*, and one of those occasions was probably due to an attempt to acquire the manly habit of smoking a pipe. Smoked or sniffed or chewed and spat, tobacco is not for me, even from the West Indies. Rum is - however, as with all liquor, it is a good friend but a bad master. I do not think in that first trip I had even a taste of it. There was enough of that and to spare when it came later.

Did I miss home and family? That first trip was a torrent of new experiences and I was greedy for more. Eating exotic foods and drinks; that first taste of fresh cocoanut milk; feeling like a real man; glancing at the bold eyed, laughing black girls in their bright thin clothes and headgear and hurrying on, feeling like a boy. Yet as the weeks turned to months and we ploughed from island to island, port to port - Bridgetown, Georgetown, Kingston and the rest - when I knew that we had gone as far as we were going and now were heading back, my thoughts turned to home and all that were there. Judith's image had come voyaging too. In our last private time together, a few days before the great escape, she had been of uncertain mood.

"I don't care. Go away for months and leave me on my own here and see if I care," she had said, tossing her head and flouncing herself down on the couch. She threw her skirts up over her knees and sprawled there like a sulky boy, even putting one foot up on the couch so that her legs were spread apart. The delicious scandalous game still went on and the recollection of it still makes me sweat, despite all. Hell fire remembered... On. On.

"It is my fourteenth birthday next month, as you very well know," she had said. "There is to be a party and you will not be there, so who shall I dance with? I shall be almost a young lady and my skirts will go down to my ankles soon, so that no man may guess at my legs or my form underneath that you enjoy so well, Tom. Perhaps this is the last time I should let you look at my things and my female private places? Perhaps I should be a real lady now?"

I did not know what to do then, for I was unsure of her temper and in an agony of apprehension lest she carry out this threat, despite the forbidden feast for my gluttonous eyes that at that moment she was spreading before me. My head throbbed and urged me to go and lay my hand upon her, but I felt a little in the wrong and did not dare. As for her, she continued to scowl at the ceiling. Then I saw her glance down at herself and, discovering a fold of her innermost petticoat, the plainest (I always thought it should be the richest), drooping down a little between her thighs, she drew it out of the way so that her crotch, drawn tight in the white pantaloons, was clear before me. And she glanced at me and smiled the old secret smile that told she was as thrilled as ever to be performing the forbidden. "Is it alright? Can you see all you want of me? Me and my pretty pantaloons?" she whispered in that strangled way of hers.

"Oh, yes. Oh, yes," I responded and went towards her, but she slammed her knees together, frowned again and threw down her clothes.

"You're a bad boy, Tommy Musselwhite," she said, "and I am not sure if I like you any more. Go away and sit over there."

But by the time I had reached my seat and looked at her again, she was on the couch facing me with her skirts above her knees once more, her knees up under her chin and she had not tucked round her petticoats either. Oh God... "Well, shall you miss me, Tommy, out there in your wild, cold sea? Leaving poor Judy with nothing but drawing pints and washing horrid pots? Why cannot girls go to sea?"

"Oh Judy..." I choked out and went towards her again but it was "No!" again and again she put down her legs and swept her skirts down. I was thinking that this was a miserable start to a voyage and so excited by her person that I found myself even considering abandoning the project.

"I do love you, Judy" I heard myself stammering out, and I was covered with confusion because I had never said such a thing before and knew now that it was true, but knew not what to do. "I shall miss you terribly."

"Do you? Will you?" she said, more a statement than a question. "Well, I think you really may." Then she came close and, unbelievably, she seized my wrist and drew my hand up under her skirts until I could fondle her. Oh God, I can hear the rustle of her clothes and feel their drag on my wrist today. She was right; her skirts were heavy and I could well believe hot. I stood up, put an arm round her waist and drew her to me and gave her a clumsy kiss, although I continued my intimate caress. She stayed a long moment and began to lean more and more on me, and I knew her knees were beginning to sag for I felt her crotch press down and her pantaloons felt hot and damp between, but she suddenly twisted away.

"That's enough," she said quite sharply, but she was flushed as though in fever and her eyes were closed.

"Oh Judy," I pleaded. "Will you not please show yourself to me just once again before I go?"

Still with her eyes closed, she began to gather up her skirts, but when they were just above her knees she opened her eyes and dropped them.

"No, Tommy," she murmured. "I'll make you come back quick because I won't do it again until you do. Off you go now and bring me back lots of your pirate gold. For my carriage and horses."

So worked up was I by then that I was of a mind to drag up her skirt myself, but I caught a glint in those pale eyes that seemed to speak of screaming and fainting like any ordinary girl, and I dared not. Despite that, my heart swelled with gratitude for this girl in my life who gave me these precious, unheard-of liberties with her person. And what was lust and what was love? For now I was not sure.

"And you will lift your skirt again for me when I come back, even if you are a young lady? You will? You promise?"

She gave me a peck on the cheek and I felt her lashes flutter against it. She sighed an ostentatious sigh.

"You are a bad boy, Tommy. Last time you said it might be a sin and I did not like that. (I had had an agony of conscience.) But when you get home, I promise faithfully I will lift up my skirt and all my petticoats one by one the way you like, even if it is a bore when I want you to admire *me*. And if you bring me a nice late birthday present, I'll let you look at my bum."

"Judy, you should not say that word if you are going to be a lady," I said. I was addicted to her behaving immodestly, yet shocked if she used vulgar words. It was, I suppose, a variant of what the foreigners say about us: that an Englishman requires a virgin with the manners of a trollop. When I consider, that was what I had in Judith.

Her face went red and her eyes opened wide. I thought she was trying to hold back a sneeze but then saw it was laughter. She arose and began to jig and dance around me. "Titties, titties, titties," she sang. " You like to see my titties. May I not call them my titties then, Tommy?"

I was terrified. Here we were, deep in my conspiracy to escape from kind Mr Misselbrook and the last thing I wanted was to attract attention. "Shh," said I, immediately aware that I had said it too noisily.

"Titties, titties, titties" she continued in a loud whisper, still dancing around. "Oh, Tommy, don't you want to look at my titties? Down my dress? I'm sure you do."

I was steeling myself for a shout of inquiry or even somebody in the bar knocking on the ceiling with a broom, but to my relief she collapsed once more onto the couch. When she had regained her composure as well as her breath she looked at me sideways. "Tommy, you don't know how lucky you are. I do not have to be a young lady quite yet, I think."

So Judith was there on the SS Trent, in a series of what the Reverend Edmunds over at St Michael's would have called "impure thoughts", which awoke and tormented me through the middle watch. Of course she was there. Something told me, even in such youth, that that extraordinary pleasure I experienced when Judith first innocently uncovered herself all that time ago on the beach at the Western Shore was forbidden in some way. Later, I took it into my head that it might be fornication, but when I looked up that sin in the Imperial Dictionary in the school library, all it spoke of was 'incontinence' or 'lewdness' of unmarried persons. We were certainly not married, although when we were small we had played let's-pretend games and sometimes I thought how very nice it would be to marry Judy. 'Want of restraint of the appetites or passions'? What had appetites to do with it? Or passions? We did not often quarrel. Lewd and lust? Carnal knowledge? Sexual intercourse? We were different sexes, we knew. Intercourse? Was that me calling Judith's rude place her 'fanny', and she my 'dick' when she said it was my turn and made me undo my trousers? It seemed to go round and round.

Judy was very quickly bored by it all. "Are not we going to do it now?" she would inquire crossly, and when I had stifled my not very deep and infrequent doubts, she would gleefully go about the ritual. I asked her sometimes why she liked doing it but all she could say was that she did not know, or that if I fondled her it was 'nice and exciting and I like it'. It did not seem as if it could be a sin like stealing or lying. It simply seemed too pleasurable sometimes, like eating jam with a spoon out of the jar. Without the bread and butter.

But to return to this, the first of my travels. I think I saw real sin: I saw a gang of slaves and I shall never forget it.

We were often coaled by black women. They came in a never-ending procession, swaying and often singing, up one gangway with a basket full of coals on their heads and down another with it empty. What I saw was not on a British island of course. It was Havana. I had no idea of what I was looking at, at first. I stared idly at the coaling and perhaps had noticed that these women were dressed in poorer raiment and they did not sing. Also that they moved slower than usual.

"Now then, young Tom," said a voice in my ear - and, my goodness, it was 'Mr Pickwick', the Chief Steward. "Do you know what it is you are looking at?"

Of course he was not really Pickwick, out of Mr Dickens's story, although he looked rather like that. I suppose I frowned and shook my head.

"Them's slaves. Real live slaves," he said. "You'll see a lot of that if you ever get to America, to them slave states down in the south, Alabama, Mississippi and that. Do you see that fellow over there? What do you make of him?" I had not made anything of him. He was just another black man in a straw hat sitting in a bit of shade. Maybe not as black as some.

"What do you make of that alongside him, down on the ground?" I strained my eyes against the bright sunlight and then suddenly I saw what he meant. It was a whip!

"That's the slave driver, Tom. D'you see? Probably a son of the owner from the wrong side of the blanket. Given his freedom and given a living, see?"

I was shocked to the core. The thing was before me for the first time. It took me back to a book. Ages ago Judy and I had come noisily, boisterously running upstairs, only to discover Rachel, her eyes red from weeping. She had been making herself miserable with a book. Books are for fairy stories. Or fabulous adventures. Books are not of real things. I took that book from Rachel and looked at it. It was called *Uncle Tom's Cabin*. She let me read it later. Now before me were real slaves and the real slave-driver. Not a boy's world any more. There was real wickedness in it.

Now I know it is not literally true that slaves do not sing, for I have heard different with my own ears. In the old days they were marvellous clever at making up songs that ridiculed their owners within an inch of retribution. Also, although on the British islands they speak English, it is with strong strange accents and many words of their own that are hard to catch, especially when sung. But I guess they were sung softly then, not loudly and cheerfully as now.

I was sorry for these slave women. I do not remember thinking much about it at the time I read Mrs Beecher Stowe's book. I suppose I was sorry for the slaves in the story, but I forgot. But I have never forgotten my first real slave women.

In those days, Africa was indeed the Dark Continent and the interior really unknown. Doctor Livingstone's reports of his journeying were as fascinating as though they had come from the moon. But they had left me with a vague impression of ignorance and superstition and cruelty. The natives seemed to behave like black, lazy, evil, naked children, ignorant of everything that supported society and civilisation. Their own enemies put them up for sale and it was not so surprising that white men bought them. But for white men to treat them as cattle to be driven away to labour from dawn to dusk for our sugar and cotton and tobacco was Bad. For Great Britain to have freed our slaves at home and in the Colonies, and set the Royal Navy to sail against the slavers, was Good, even if Rachel had spoken of it *ad nauseam*. As for black Africa, it ought to be left alone. There was little knowledge of gold and diamonds then.

So the months positively flew away and suddenly - wham-bam-bam-bam, wham-bam-bam-bam - with a sudden white spray over the bow, Barbados was astern of us and we were going home. As day followed day, my attempts to look after my captain were not sufficient to keep my mind off what I had done in that other life and to wonder what sort of a homecoming there might be in store. In blacker moments I imagined that I was cast out of doors and my sweaty narrow bunk was all the home I had. And there were such men aboard, I knew. There would be nobody on the dockside to greet me unless the girls (well, in truth, Judy) had received my few letters. So it was with mixed feelings I saw the muddy old salt pans again and watched them slowly, slowly turn the old *Trent* across the Itchen until she was pointing at the dock entrance, and with all of us on deck coughing and choking in a thick cloud of green coal smoke from one of the attending tug boats, there dimly spread before us was home. There was St Michael's spire in the distance... wham-bam-bam-bam... very slowly creeping in... past the big sheerlegs to starboard and the chimney of the dry dock pump house to port... the faces of people on the dockside growing from pale blobs to features and, bless me, there they all were. Ma and Pa, Uncle Joby, dear Rachel, a little taller and waving, waving. And Judith, smaller, watching. She was still; alert like a cat and, like a cat, not looking at what you wanted her to. In fact, she reminded me of a cat that used to come round from next door sometimes. A pale tabby. Thin legs and a stripe from the inner corners of its eyes, slightly slanting eyes. Eyes that you would look up to find watching you. When I remember Judith standing on the quay I often remember that cat also.

I had a few chores to do for Captain Moir, but they didn't take much above half an hour. Then - after I had queued up with the other hands who did not want a new ship, and signed on for the next trip - we all went home to Mount Street.

I did not entirely trust my parents with my future. And I was extremely glad that, because Uncle Job and the girls were present, they were unable to give me their undivided attention. The tea was scrumptious but the partakers were silent at first. Falteringly, then with a confidence that grew when I began to see all eyes and ears were upon me, I gave an account of my youthful adventures. To my amazement, at the end of it, they started clapping and Pa actually got out his famous bottle of sweet sherry, so all could drink my health. Heady stuff for the ship's 'boy'.

Chapter 4

Oh when I sailed across the sea, my girl said she'd be true to me...

Those five youthful years aboard the old *Trent* were like the prelude of an opera. The stage before the curtains was shallow, and we the characters were shallow, because the plot had not yet introduced full depth to our lives.

Because my brains and education were more than the task required, I rose quickly through the ranks: table steward (the pleasure of seeing a well laid table with sparkling glass, starched napkins and bright cutlery has never left me), bedroom steward, wine steward, and all whilst still very young. Of course I did not consider the matter much then, but for anyone contemplating a career in the hotel business one could do a lot worse than a spell at sea in a passenger ship. Swiss hoteliers frequently send their sons to sea in British ships. It would likely have not been so if I had signed on as a seaman, which was my earliest, boyish dream. Since I was literate, numerate and articulate, I was often entrusted with messages ashore, and by nineteen I was assistant yeoman of the wine and spirits store. Life seemed good and I was pleased with myself.

Behind the curtains, if we had paid them much attention, were the noises off of the scene being set for the act to come. This was to be a tragic opera: the American Civil War. In those days it was news that was weeks or months stale, and for us at sea found in the inside pages of old newspapers. The Americans had decided to go their own way by force of arms in the last century and had fought a war against us in the twelfth and thirteenth year of this one. If this arrogant, youthfully uncouth United States now did not seem so united after all, Great Britain could surely watch their difficulties with a touch of sour pleasure. Our eyes, reading the cramped, blurred print, glazed over at their conventions and presidential candidates, their addresses to the nation; their senators, representatives, Democrats, Whigs and Republicans were mere names. We quickly searched the newspapers for something more interesting. Slavery and the slave trade had been gone from Albion for many a year and good riddance, considering the canker of it over there. And good luck to the Royal Navy amongst the fevers of the Bight of Benin, stamping out what was left of the trade. The unblushing hypocrisy of it was that many of those slave ships were Yankee. Not from Charleston or Savannah, as one might have expected, but Boston and New York.

One got used to being out of touch during months at sea and the little world of the ship seemed world enough. Leave was for rest and recuperation and catching up and the capacity of the young for sleeping late in bed. It was for taking up relationships again. It was for making New Year resolutions with Judy to kiss and cuddle a little more first, like other couples, before we dragged her clothes up and her hard little fingers were unbuttoning my trousers. Kissing and cuddling were for those occasions when she was especially pleased to see me, and I was aware of how petite she was and how she seemed to glow and how there was love that seemed to be growing beyond the family love that had always been there. The other thing, this illicit excitement with each other's bodies, was too urgent for the courtesies. What a terrible preparation it was for real life with real ladies. Yet it was our life and all might have been well. We were happy together, one minute playing the embarrassed childhood sweethearts whilst the friends and families cooed; then a quarter of an hour later, somewhere still within earshot of the ballads being sung round Ma's piano, this miss of our respectable Victorian times might well be giving her rapt and delighted attention to making me have a stand.

I can see now that the cusp of the whole affair was my seventeenth birthday. Before that I did not know. After it I did. There should have been something better for us than ignorance and prudish silence. But it is still so and, speaking as a father, very hard.

Nearing sixteen, everything remained confusing.

"Why does it do that, Tommy? When I spread my legs? You like it when my skirts are up and I spread my legs, don't you, Tommy? Although I am sure a lady never, never, never should. But why does it make your dickie do that?" As far as her skirts were concerned they were all up in her lap because she had tired herself out twirling about in a pair of my trousers and now sprawled like a hoyden on a sofa because she said she was hot.

I could tell her that even the memory of her spreading her legs did it, or hearing her footsteps coming, or even the thought that she would soon be here. But I could not tell her why. I did not know; but I did know it put me almost in pain. And it became slowly worse and dark desire began to rise like a great fish rising in the shadowy water underneath a tree. Came a day and I could hardly recognise my own voice, so hoarse it was. I said, "Judy, I want to touch you."

"Oh yes, I'd like that too," she replied, "for the feelings that I have when you push your fingers in there, are...well, exquisite. And I am in pantaloons today, as you can very well see, can't you? So it is allowed."

"No, Judy," I got out somehow. "I want to touch you with this. I want to touch you with my dick." And she was afeared. Bold Judy was afraid and I could see it in her face.

"Why? Why do you want to touch me with... with that?"

"I do not know," said I, and I did not. "Oh but I want it very bad, Judy. Please?"

"But where do you want to touch me. Tommy?" And I told her the truth.

"No! No, no, no, no, no!" She jumped to her feet and ran behind the table to keep it between us.

"But why not, Judy? What harm could there be? And you said yourself that you have your pantaloons on," said I as though I were half-strangled. So I caught her and persuaded her back to the sofa and kneeling at her feet gathered her skirts back over her knees again. There was a new queer excitement in disarranging her clothes myself.

"No. *No*!" And to my despair she flung down her clothes. I found myself with my face buried in her lap, pleading, and also surreptitiously trying to get her skirts up again, but she would not have them further than barely at her knees. She also tucked her clothes in behind her legs at the sides, which was the sort of maternally approved act of modesty she usually had most pleasure in discarding. I was aggrieved that she cut me off now from what we had both wanted before. However, I was able to stroke and tickle her legs just a little above her knees and a little way under her skirt, which she did not try to prevent.

"Why do you want to do such a thing?" she asked. I did not know but that was little help. "Why must you spoil everything? What is wrong with looking at me in my drawers and touching me when I am in pantaloons? With your hand. I like you to touch me with your hand."

It would be wearisome to detail the length of my pleading. After many hours and many days I changed tack, and asked if it could be her bottom. It was a desperate move because quite frequently she would refuse to let me see her bottom. She resisted long, but sufficient to say in the end she was persuaded, cajoled, I know not what, and reluctantly she agreed. At last I persuaded her to her feet and got her to turn her back with her pretty hair all loose down it, complaining and with piteous looks over her shoulder all the while. So piteous she seemed that she would crack a heart of stone, but I recalled brazen Judy with busy fingers, shifting her drawers asunder with feverish whispering. "See. Look at me. Can you see it? Do you like it? Oh you do like it, don't you?" and I made my heart like adamant. Besides, if she was really a little afraid, I found it seasoning to my desire.

I ordered her to lift her skirts and despite the protests she reluctantly raised her dress at the back but she would not get up her petticoats. I got them up in handfuls myself while she moaned and pleaded, "No, no, no," and even reached behind her a couple of times, took the stuff out of my hands and let them fall again. However, I had noted she did not run away and she had not thrown down her dress, which hung like an apron only over her front. Ah, the skirt, that impregnable city wall of women, but if it be raised, all the petticoats in the world will not keep the gate. At length with another armful, which I tucked into her reluctant hands and which she accepted at last, there she was with her bottom exposed; well, inside her nice white maidenly lawn of course.

Very slowly, very gently I held her by her waist and felt her shiver. I brought my body near to hers and let my member just touch her. I could see her face in a mirror; her eyes sprang open wide and she froze as still as stone. I could not help it, I could not hold back and I thrust twice deep between her cheeks. And she sprang from me like a deer, whirling round, crouching and holding down her skirts with both hands while she glared at me as though she really were at bay. Just as well that first time, because we heard a step on the stair. Now, I fancy that that hoary ancient deity that dwells above the Norman arches in St. Michael's tower heard something, turned his bony eye sockets in the direction of the Bell, and his bony hand began to grope towards us.

"Why, what have you two been doing?" I recall Rachel asking. "Oh, I see." (But, my dear, I think - I *think* - you did not.) Judy blushed, drooped her lashes and hung her head like a daisy at evening - well why not, indeed? I was still trying to think of something credible in my humming head.

"Oh, I think perhaps you two should come down again now, for tea is almost ready."

As we went downstairs Judy pinched me and I could see and feel her silent giggling. What an actress she would have made. And where was the outraged maiden now? Yet I was sorry we had misled Rachel, although what else we could have done I do not know.

At our next tryst I wanted to do it again. Again there was much argument and much deployment of that difficult question, "*Why* do you want to do it?" and I did not really know. There were more murmured protests along the lines of, "Oh no. I don't like this. Why do we have to do this? Oh dear, I don't want to, really I don't," but it was more as if she was quietly talking to herself rather than me. Also, I noticed that unlike the first time, she turned her back on me and lifted all her clothes up as one. She shivered again when I took her by the waist, and I tried to be as gentle as I could manage. It seemed to me I managed four or five thrusts before she sprang away, holding down her skirts again. But she was less upset, I was sure. Instead of glaring at me as though I was a fiend, she seemed to look me over thoughtfully. Then she said quite composedly, "I think that is enough for today, Tommy Musselwhite. I think we ought to go down."

I thought to dumbly follow her, but with her hand on the big brass doorknob she suddenly turned round with the expression of a disappointed child. Back she strode across the carpet, gathering up her skirts as she came. She stopped, looked up at my face, and then gave an extra heave that bunched all of them onto her hips so she was really there in her long white pants. "Can't I have my Exquisite Sensations now?" she said.

By the end of my leave she would stand there quite quietly while I pleasured myself. Provided the Exquisite Sensations followed after. Then hot desire, the impatience of youth, and the imminence of sailing day, caused me foolishly to ask again if we could perform it face to face. And I got "*No!*" a slapped cheek - not very hard, I must admit - and three months wondering if she would be as adamantine when I arrived home again. And yet neither of us knew what drove me to ask, or why she was so fearful.

I can report that when I did return, after several days of manoeuvring so that she was not left alone with me, I had the elementary sense, or even good fortune more likely, to ask again, after she had been having Exquisite Sensations for some little time. She pushed her face against my chest and I heard her murmur, "Oh, if you must, I suppose." She sprang away at first touch again, but after a few days said she thought that it gave her the Exquisite Sensations in another way. Yes, it was quite nice. And one day towards the end of leave she came running. I would lift up her skirts or support them if she had done so already, while she giggled and fumbled to get my trouser flies undone.

I shall never forget the day when she was so engaged and yet reproved me. "You are bad to me, Tommy," she said. "Why must my skirts be so high while I do this? If you treated me like a young lady, you would wait until I have got you ready." Now, I wonder if it was the first leaf of autumn.

So I think we would have found the way in the end, from our animal natures so interestingly described by Mr Darwin. And Satan knows I was hungry for her in this immature, fumbling relationship; this piquant situation where I had known Judith all my life and was acquainted with the intimate secrets of her body in a way that many a married man never knew his wife's. And I truly loved them both - the demure Judith, and this wonderful trollop Judy.

But come my seventeenth birthday, whilst I was away, everything changed.

I do not know exactly how the other members of the *Trent's* forward crowd found out, although I can guess we were overheard, probably when I was talking to my friend

Roderick, the engineering apprentice I mentioned earlier. Everyone knows everyone else's business in a ship. Putting up with it and tolerating each other is what turns men into shipmates, and that can last a lifetime.

Birthdays are still important to people standing on the threshold between childhood and adult life and possessing little more than the clothes they stand up in. Even if one is a little shamefaced about it, the eye still brightens at the prospect of some celebration. Presents maybe, a trip somewhere, or a treat, a special meal, and voices may be incautiously loud. After three years I was long past being sent on errands of the left-handed screwdriver variety, but not beyond the occasional surprise practical joke - and on this occasion it was an echo of something much older and darker and masculine. Maybe they thought me a little too well pleased with myself.

Roderick, myself and another pair of the younger crew members had promised ourselves a run ashore with a blow-out meal in our favourite eating place, followed by a bit of a pub crawl. Because it was my birthday, I was to have my drinks bought for me, and we planned to entertain ourselves with anything of interest we came across, which, as we were in Kingston, Jamaica, we expected would be plenty.

Of course, nothing ever quite goes as one expects. We were lying at that stumpy little pier at Kingston and, quite late in the afternoon, while I was still at work below between the cabins and the tables, trying to get some pitch off a carpet, I heard shouting. I looked through a stern window and there was the schooner *Liffey* tying up. She was Royal Mail too. There were three of them. They collected and delivered mail for the smaller islands and cays.

After dinner was served and cleared away, work for the day over and feet hastening down the crew gangway into the hot dark early Jamaican night, we heard more feet similarly rattling down the *Liffey's* gangway. Some of her people were also intent on a night ashore. Seeing each other, there was a cheerful shout and forces were affably combined. So it was a larger group than we had envisaged and an older one. Drinking was harder. Roderick and myself tried to stay with beer, with which we had a little experience, rather than rum, of which we had a lot less but rounds went down quicker than expected. In the end the beer bloated one up so that to partake of a tot of rum was easier. I know we had pepperpot to eat, of which I was very fond because of the outrageous number of its ingredients - from lobster to banana by way of diced lamb and bacon, and even monkey sometimes - and there were mangoes amongst the fruit, but the meal made pouring down the beer even more irksome, and under the influence of what had gone before we gave in to the rum. Sound became a blare and sight a glare. Possibly the evening would have followed the time-honoured routine of the men getting the boys roaring drunk, carrying them back aboard and teasing hell out of them in the morning. But there were others about with other plans. At that state of happy befuddlement one accepts what would otherwise be significant events as though they were routine. Suddenly, there was Mr Pickwick the chief steward, and the second steward as well.

"Oh, hello, Mr Sewell. W'a you doin' 'ere?"

"Hello, young Tommy. Happy birthday to you. Are you enjoying yourself? Are you ready for your present?"

I noticed it was a little strange but one of those huge black women in a great coloured turban seemed in some way to have joined the party.

"W'a present's that, Mr Sewell sir?"

The woman appeared to be accompanied by two girls, one tall and fine featured such as may be found in East Africa and with an almost haughty eye as she looked at us. The other was little and jolly and very, very black with cropped frizzy hair under her kerchief and big brown eyes that caught one's own and made her giggle and look away. It is hard to tell how old black girls are because they blossom so young. These two then appeared to be much of an age with me and Roderick. Suddenly they were quite close to us.

"'Hullo," says I to the little one. "Wa's your name?"

"That's Polly. Do you like her then?" said the chief steward.

"'Course I do. She's Pretty Polly and all. 'Course I like her."

"Ah well, that's settled that. The Birthday Boy has spoken," I seemed to hear *sotto voce*, and then suddenly we were on the move.

"Whe're we goin'," I remember asking, but discovering I was somehow now hand in hand with Pretty Polly it did not seem to matter much.

What else? Potholes underfoot. Sweating black faces in lighted doorways. Singing and banjo music. High pitched laughter. A house with white peeling paint. Lamp- and candle-light hurting my eyes after the dark street. Hustled past a bar. Curious white and black faces staring at us. Good God, half undressed girls, but only black girls. Upstairs. A giggling drunken outrage of having my clothes pulled off me and discovering Pretty Polly lying on a little towel on a bed with only a bottom sheet and a pillow, naked except for her spotted kerchief still round her head. It is formidable to see a nude girl, any nude girl when you are seventeen, but of course in Africa she would be running round in just a loin cloth or leaves or grass as you see in the engravings, and it is not quite the same, is it? Not the same as Judy would have been naked. But Judy was far away.

It's like a football game now, with shouted encouragement. All these people! Somebody (I know, it's the fat old black lady) whispering in Pretty Polly's ear. She looks at her, then at me, and then opens her thin black legs and puts a finger in her mouth, watching me. Her big brown eyes look frightened. She rolls onto her side away from me but they turn her back and she has to open her legs again. That was twice she's done it now. She's naked, black. Judy's covered from waist to ankle when she does that, except when she's put on drawers and then I mustn't touch. Polly's muff is black and curly but she's just as neat.

I've got to get onto Polly. She's got little wobbly breasts like Judy's and her stomach skin's warm against mine. God, I wonder how old she is. Not as old as me, I think now.

"Get your leg over."

"All right."

"Go on! And the other one, Tommy lad! - 'ow much 'as 'e 'ad to drink?"

"All right, all right!" Oh, I wish I was getting on top of Judy like this. As if she would ever let me!

"Go on, shove it in. You haven't got all night. Only half an hour, you know. We aren't made o' money."

In where? In there? That's right, that's what I've wanted to do. I see it now. It's dry and hot and now it's wet and hot and oh, muscles tightening in my back and bottom. Again and again and again...and I've had her. I've really had her! Why's there a tear? I didn't hurt you, did I? Oh, so sorry, Polly.

And now all the girls in England can shriek and pull up their skirts and I would not care. I'm free of them all. No sir, I don't care a tinker's damn for any of them. For now...

So was this fornication? There, there at home were the works of a misery of a Deity who kept His place by keeping His creation even more miserable than He. Sundays with no playing. Bed with no supper. Men in white collars and black gowns with Judy's best birthday petticoat over their shoulders reciting meaningless old words in silly voices three times a day on Sundays. Away with you. Not here in the hot night and the laughter. There's no God here. Surely this was not fornication. Only the follies of youth and it's immortality...

I have written down here something of the memories that come if I remember Pretty Polly, and I do. I asked someone where I might find her again but was told she had gone back to her mistress. My head was aching and I thought no more of it at the time. But her mistress? Is not this a British Colony? There can be no more masters, mistresses and slaves here. In later years, I realised the law may propose and others dispose in the lands of the Caribbean Sea. I hope Polly is still alive, well and happy somewhere in Jamaica and that she remembers me kindly, as I do her. I'm old and sad enough now to know she probably isn't and probably wouldn't.

Rod took to disappearing ashore whenever we were in Kingston. I believe - no, I know - he was searching for Hope, the tall girl. I do not know if he ever found her and what came of it. He never said.

The thing was that now I knew. Judy and I, our secret society for two, where breeches were unbuttoned and skirts lifted for a thrill, was gone, blown away to leeward forever. She did not know. But I did. Judith was a virgin and had to remain so until marriage! I suppose one could truthfully call it the fruit of the tree of knowledge of good and evil. And if it was the apple, by God it was sharp to taste and a bellyful of pain to follow. Green apples, d'you suppose?

Chapter 5

Distant thunder...

Those years of the American Civil War, 1861 until 1865, of course they remain in my mind. You might think that for an Englishman, even one steaming regularly across the Atlantic and round and about the Caribbean, it would be but distant thunder. But it was not. The shock from the myriad deaths and casual wholesale destruction, as of some catastrophic force like an earthquake or eruption, came without warning into the very living room of our lives. These memories are, of course diminished by time. They have become miniatures, their vivid colours painted as if with ground up jewels, but the details drawn in fine line are meticulously preserved for close inspection. The years before have the downy imprecision of youth. Those that came after are a long road over barren country, away from the darkness and chaos. And 1861 began, and indeed continued, in such an ordinary way right up until November.

In the spring Judith and I had words. Still well wrapped up against the cold that I felt all the more after the warmth of the West Indies, we set off to walk as far as Thorner's Charity and East Park, which of course took us past that damned carriage builder in Above Bar. For some reason that day I could not feign interest. For a moment I could see myself stepping out of one, donning my topper and holding my cane and running a glittering eye over the world, but it faded. However, the place jogged Judy's thoughts and they were in the usual vein. The big house with broad lawns and

Virginia creeper ascending the walls. No more Bell Inn, with what she saw as the menial tasks she had to perform. The servants that there would be. The dinners and dancing she would preside over there. I should have let her dream as I usually did, with all the superiority of gender and a year's seniority of age. Or pretended and joined her at play on those ever sunny lawns or in the glittering salons. But although the store of golden guineas grew in the bank and was indeed quite respectable for a young chap such as I was, and I knew I could give her a comfortable little home in Bevois Mount, or even as far as Portswood, with a daily to do the heavy cleaning and perhaps a maid of all work to live in. But not these dreams of, oh, Banister's Court or Portswood Lodge. And I said as much, which was not wise. I was already feeling the low spirits of sailing day coming on apace, for there were but three days to go. Oh yes, I was a seasoned seafarer now.

She was quiet for a moment and then demanded to know just how many guineas I had. This offended because I had somewhere acquired the notion that money was man's business and not for women to poke their noses into. She reminded me that it had not been formally agreed that we were to be engaged, and I said that when she was too grown up for fairy stories perhaps then we might be. And she said and I said et cetera and so on and so on. You will know how it is when a word is but half spoken and you regret it. The centuries do not change that much, I am certain. We went back and she hurried on always a step before me, trembling with indignation, and would not take my hand or my arm.

I followed her in to all the warmth and cheerfulness of the Bell and we both dissembled that all was well and how bracing had been the weather and our walk. In the parlour upstairs, after we all had taken tea together, we found ourselves alone for a moment and like a fool, a complete fool, I asked her to lift her skirts and she would not.

I felt frustrated desire. I felt injured that my fellow adventurer suddenly refused to take to the road. I did not dare say so but I threatened her within my mind that, if she declined, there were girls aplenty where I was soon to go. I called myself a fool not to have taken my pick of these and for telling myself, nay for believing, that a romp with Judy was better than a riot with such as those. I hated her and wanted to bellow it out at her but in view of the fact that I had just asked her to do something utterly disgraceful and she had politely declined instead of screaming the house down, I felt I could not. So I bottled it up. I was hurt that a chasm had opened between pretty Judith and myself. I felt lonely. I left in a temper. Sailing day was now the day after tomorrow.

And what was I to do? Of course I had never told her about Pretty Polly and that I knew now which was key and which was lock, and she did not.

Our spat did not last, but there were busy times as sailing day approached and there was no opportunity for us to be alone. I was seen off by Pa and Judy. On the dockside, as she turned to me for a final embrace, I saw her take hold of a fold of her dress in each hand and, expressionless, she looked me straight in the eye. Nobody else would have thought that the glimpse of her petticoat hem was anything else but a pretty accident. However, this was our sign: to say in public what we wished we were doing in private. So I was happy enough as I trotted up once more into that whiff of hot oil and cigar smoke and the quiet trembling from the machinery beneath my feet.

But across the Western Ocean, while plates were filled from the slopping tureen and boots were polished at dawn, I debated the question with myself. Judy was a virgin. Of course she was a virgin. Did it matter? We had an understanding. Did I want to see her come up St. Michael's aisle with Uncle Joby, in the knowledge that even if I knew far more than usual about what was under the fine white dress, she was still as she should ideally be? I thought, in spite of all, I might be still more proud that she was so. Only the best for Judith would do.

Why to God do people build these barriers for themselves? Do we put the first word or the first step on a pedestal to worship like this? Aye, down to God it is. The God who repented Himself that He had created this riotous world of warmth, life and fecundity and could find nothing better to do then, than to demand that we give it all up. For Him. And if not, suffer His wrath. But that inner diatribe changed nothing. The barrier was there. How high was it?

I must confess that well before then I had persuaded Judy to let me put my member between her legs from the front. The course of this conquest was much the same as that which went before. The pleading, the submission, the acceptance and then the appetite. It was pleasing. Now she would hurry across a room to me gathering up her clothes as she came and go on tiptoe to almost impale herself upon me, which was a pleasure like neat rum in the throat. So it was no higher than the thickness of a fine cloth gusset - I knew now what it was about, and Judy did not. I suppose she did not.

I would be so hot and bothered in those days that I must take a long walk before going to my home. Of course, as she was female she would not be subject to such raging feelings. Women were not like men, I knew, although sometimes it seemed to me that Judy almost craved her Exquisite Sensations, and I recall, rather to my surprise and even a little distaste, that she told me once she could not sleep after we had been alone together rather late one evening. At that time, it never occurred to me for a moment that she had no mother she might ask. I suppose I would have been horrified if I thought she had done, and she could hardly have asked Ma about this. I could never have asked Ma for information on the subject. Nor dared I talk to Pa, who would of course suppose the worst and then, like a loose cannon, roll who knew where. Nor did I discuss it even with Roderick, my mate aboard, because I thought he might think me a poor sort of fellow to have gone so near but not to have accomplished the act.

So again to the round of the islands where, instead of wondering at how the milky green of the light on the lagoons transformed by reflection the white breasts of the gulls overhead, I wrestled with plans of seduction for my cousin, my friend, my love. A rich adventure was neglected for feverish contemplation of how to lure Judith into taking off her nether garments and how to break our golden rule and put us both out of out of misery: as I see it now, not then. Poor, silly, over-read steward. Poor, silly, little innkeeper's daughter. The world is truly wasted on the young. But for every course charted, there was always the same rock. Higher than the Mountains of the Moon. She was still Judith and she was still a virgin. As was the Queen of Heaven, so the Romans said.

The road to Hell…

I have said, 'When the gangway's away all debts are paid'. Perhaps for some Jolly Jack Tars. For myself, I have found that to take a problem to sea is the worst place for it. With nothing to do but look at the sky or the deckhead over your berth, round and round and fruitless round in your head goes the difficulty, as annoying and maddening as being anchored in fog and subjected to the irregular clang of a nearby bell buoy.

As we made our way from harbour to now familiar harbour, delivering and taking on board the mailbags and the passengers, like a rock slowly being exposed by the tide my decision became plain. I must marry Judith. Once I had said it to myself, the great problem was gone. There were numerous reasons against this, of course. We were rather young. There was money; a little. Money enough for a young bachelor to indulge himself with a rather expensive watch and chain without then having to dine on bread and water for ever. Not enough for the house I had always fancied myself buying. We should have to rent somewhere for a while. I would have to continue at sea to keep adequate money flowing. I might have been young but I was experienced enough to know that it was often hard and lonely for the womenfolk left behind for months with the worries; the great ones of 'rock and tempest, fire and foe', if you will pardon me. The list of our old girl's sisters that were no longer with us - the *Amazon*, terribly by fire; the *Forth*, *Isis*, *Medina* and *S.S. Uncle Tom Cobbleigh* and all - you did not rehearse these in front of your ladies if you were kind. Enough the lesser worries of slates from the roof, unexpected expenses and childish ill health.

Children! What if we had children? The cost of bringing up children would keep me at sea for ever, like the Flying Dutchman. We must not have children yet, but I recognised that the fire my Judy had between her legs might be irresistible, and even if I was not sure of the ultimate facts of life, I had a shrewd suspicion of what might follow. She was not as other women, I decided, and I dreamed of Judy stripping and stripped and waiting like Polly. The conceit of the puppy!

And the island schooners went by and our smoke blew across the bright Caribee sky, and all was as usual until the bells and smells and fortifications of Havana in Cuba were sliding past again.

Beyond avarice...

It was late. Not much left of the fourth of November. The Spanish early evening begins at about nine o' clock, when it is not only dark but the walls and the streets have lost some of the rays of heat that earlier ascend unpleasantly to keep you still in perspiration. We had found a nice little bar, all tiled floor and white arches, a dried up little old waiter in a corner and nobody else at all to begin with. It had been too hot to wade into English food on board, but we were old enough sea dogs now to know that there were other things in the world to eat than meat and two veg. This place had a wonderful collection of dishes of small eatables upon the bar, some kept warm over little copper heaters and some cold, soaking in sauces. The charges must have been included with the wine or the beer because nobody seemed to care how much we ate. In fact some fat old granny would appear from time to time cackling in Spanish and grinning and indicating in mime what had been the ingredients before it reached the dish and exhorting us to try something else.

The hours wore on and the place filled up and the wine soaked in. The tables became occupied, many by families with kids who prattled away in their high voices amongst the rattle of Spanish from their elders. No early to bed here. Children slept their siesta in the afternoon and were noisily playing long after midnight in the cooling streets.

I had just turned to Roderick to observe that at home it would be Guy Fawkes night tomorrow, when a young female came in and began to make her way from table to table. Her clothes were worn and shabby. Her skirt frayed a little at the hem. She had a leather satchel hung from her left shoulder and was selling something, but what? At length she came to us and said something in what seemed to be polite Spanish. Before we could say or do anything I noticed firstly that she was tapping her way with a stick, and then she turned her face to me and I realised from the way her gaze was directed a little past me that she was blind. Of course the face was different, the olive skin finely drawn over different bones, but the eyes were the same. Great grey orbs between sooty lashes that seemed to look through me and it was almost a pain to know that she saw nothing. But what did she want?

The stubble chinned fellow next to me suddenly turned round. Gesturing and nodding, he explained to us in fragmentary English that it was the lottery and she was selling tickets. We looked at each other, full of wine and full of the beautiful blind girl for whom at that moment we would have gone to the ends of the earth. Or I would have done, anyway. That's right, my friend. Full of maudlin sentiment.

"How much?"

There was a chorus of explanation that meant nothing to us. We put our hands in our pockets and drew out what we had and dropped it jingling on the bar. Spanish, American, British; any of it buys in Cuba. Hands reached out selecting from the money until there was not much left. Our blue-jawed acquaintance was forced again to draw on his little store of English. They wanted to know whose name to put on the ticket. We looked at each other. Heaven alone knew who had paid for what. "Both of us!" Cheers.

"And where you live? Where your casa? 'Ouse?"

We explained. Ship *Trent*. "T-R-E-N-T". Much sage nodding and backslapping. I realise now what a joke they probably thought it. Two sailor boys relieved of their money and too drunk to remember anything in the morning and probably leagues out to sea anyway. More money for them with the rollover of unclaimed prizes to the next draw. It was a good joke and worth somebody refilling our glasses.

On the way back to the ship, Roderick recovered first and I was soundly berated along traditional Scottish lines for my unsound investment of our cash, no less!

Long afterwards, someone who knew Old Spain told me that there they called those with such grey eyes 'Vandal Eyes' and associated them with the first tribe that overran

Roman Iberia. It is not surprising that I have a vivid memory of Vandal Eyes despite all the vino.

Next morning was just next morning alongside. You get woken by what to everyone else are commonplace sounds: wagon wheels grinding over cobbles; loud conversations in Spanish, instead of the paddles beating; slow footsteps getting fainter and fainter and then louder and louder, and when in exasperation you screw your head round and try to see who it is, the porthole is just below the level of the dockside and you cannot. Why do I waste my time and yours? We both know what happened. The world began to go mad.

I suppose they must have had the draw about midday. I was thinking of taking a nap once lunch was over and I was just about to lock up the saloon bar, having replenished it, when the breathless captain's tiger came tearing in and said I was required at once in the captain's cabin. The captain's cabin? I hurried up there after the lad and, oh dear, there was the Old Man and the chief steward. *And* the chief engineer. And a couple of locals wearing sashes. And Roderick talking nineteen to the dozen and waving his arms about. I just stood there with my mouth open.

There was something about Captain Moir's expression that immediately suggested to me that he was trying to keep a straight face. Then he sighed and, sounding exactly like he did when I had been his tiger, he said, "Musselwhite, what on earth have you been doing now?"

There was a box about the size of a child's coffin on the deck at his feet, with the same sort of rough boarding you see at a pauper's burial. This however was gaudy, with red and yellow ribbons. I could not imagine what it was, except that somehow its funereal aspect made me feel anxious.

"Open it, Tom," the captain commanded. Squatting down, I picked up one end with the idea of stripping off the bunting. By heavens, it was heavy and that at least drove off the notion that it contained a dead baby. The lid was also a coarsely made thing, but it came off in one, and what I saw made me topple backwards onto my backside. The box was full of money!

Money? I recognised British sovereigns and half sovereigns, but there were gold and silver United States and Mexican dollars, francs, pesetas and a scattering of I knew not what from the foreign Windy Indies and the Central American republics. There were no gold cups or stolen strings of pearls, but otherwise it was a child's dream of pirate's treasure. I gaped up at the faces around me and the only thing that occurred to me was that it had been stolen and it had somehow been planted on board to incriminate me.

"I didn't do it," I gabbled. "It wasn't me. Who says it was me? I've never seen it before in my life. Whose is it?"

It was then the turn of the others to gape. Then they all roared with laughter. Even the local persons, a little after everyone else.

Roderick began to speak. "Tom, Tommy..." he got out. "It's all right, mon. It isn't pinched. It's ours!"

"Ours?" I said stupidly.

"Yours," said Captain Moir. "It's yours. Don't you recall buying a lottery ticket last night? You have got it, haven't you?"

I groped about in my memory and suddenly the vision of Vandal Eyes floated before me. "Well yes, sir," I said. "But I never win anything like that. It's a well-known fact. I was just a bit sorry for her because she was blind, that's all. She reminded me a bit... she reminded me a bit... Oh, just of someone back home." I was feeling in my pockets like a fool, because I had not been wearing these clothes last night and suddenly felt panic gripping me because the ticket was not there. But Roderick had it, - oh thank God - and my knees stopped buckling.

"Well now," said Mr Sewell. "That must have been Lady Luck herself. She's blind, ain't she?"

"I think that might have been Justice," said Captain Moir. "Is not Lady Luck the fickle one? But never mind. She seems to have fancied one of you, or both of you, last night. Well, young Mister McKay and Tom Musselwhite, I hope you are ready for a change, because I don't think your lives are ever going to be the same again."

So there was Judith's pirate gold, at least a portion of it from the Spanish Main. It seemed to me almost too good to be true.

Chapter 6

The Saucy Jack...

That first day after the lottery win, Roderick and I were stunned. It was like being on a day-and-night binge. Time passed as a bright blur. We had no idea how much we had won because we didn't know how to count it. The sovereigns, of course, were all right but our familiarity with exchange rates was sorely lacking for much of the others. We didn't even know where to put it. At first we implored the purser to lock it up for us but his safe was already loaded with passengers' valuables and there was simply not enough room. Captain Moirs' safe was smaller still. I suppose we could have asked to put it in the Mail Room but we did not feel it was sufficiently secure against a determined thief, although we refrained from mentioning this to Commander Williams. In those days the mail packets had to carry a mail agent, a retired naval officer. Commander Richard Williams, Royal Navy (Rtd.) was a plump little man who was going bald on top and seemed to be trying to make up for it by letting it grow rather long round the back and sides. Never mind; handsome is as handsome does - although this is not always accepted by ladies, I find.

A little time passed and through our euphoria we began to see genuine concern on the officers' faces. All this loose change as it were, could behave like a keg of gunpowder. If its presence became generally known on board - and what secret lasts more than five minutes in a ship? - it could become an irresistible temptation to crew members and criminals ashore alike.

In the end the following solution was hammered out. We had by no means a full passenger list for the coming transatlantic trip. November was definitely included in the Atlantic's fifty weeks of storm. The bedroom stewards would be far from overworked and Roderick would not be sorely missed from amongst a number of assistant engineers. We were therefore formally discharged from the ship's books with effect from Havana, transferred to the passenger list, and given our own double cabin on the starboard side. Quite a change from our previous quarters and the manly odour of sweat and hot socks!

Into this cabin we removed the treasure chest. I locked myself within while Roderick, who had had an interest in firearms, went ashore to a gunsmith's and returned with a box containing gunpowder and bullets and caps, and one of those American Colt revolving pistols - a great heavy thing it was. I found it difficult to aim it steadily for more than a matter of seconds because of its weight. Fortunately we never had to fire it, which was just as well, because I had great difficulty remembering how to load it. It adorns Roderick's parlour wall these days.

We paid off our shipmates who were to be doing our work with as handsome a financial recompense as we could calculate, and there and then settled down to a routine, which we proposed to maintain until we were once again tied up in the Tidal Dock, safe home in Southampton. That is to say, one of us sat on the chest with the loaded pistol while the other slept, ate, took a little exercise on deck, or whatever. We set out intending to do this watch and watch about - four hours on and four hours off - although even on that first day it was clear that boredom in the extreme was to be our worst enemy in that hot little cabin alongside a Havana wharf, despite its window and relative luxury. That window was tantalising. Closed, we sweated. Open, the infamous harbour stench. We preferred to sweat. We found ways in which we could slightly liberalise our self-imposed sentence as the voyage wore on, but on that first day we dared not even indulge ourselves with a bottle of rum, let alone a raucous celebration ashore. Only beer, a few bottles of beer, we allowed ourselves.

So the hours began crawling away towards St Thomas and the nineteen days of the crossing. Next day the thumps and bangs and muffled conversation of other passengers moving into the cabin next door became a prime source of interest to us. We were reasonably familiar by now with the accents of American English. Enough to know, we thought, that our neighbours came from the southern States but we could place them no nearer than that.

I remember distinctly leaving our cabin and noticing a piece of luggage still left outside their door. It had a label attached for a ship called the *Theodora*, of which I had never heard (and if that sounds arrogant I had been around these waters for a few years now and had at least a nodding acquaintance with ships regularly plying there). The family name of our neighbours was Slidell: man and wife and three daughters, who had the next cabin aft. The father was a man well into middle age and tending to run to fat, with hair that was almost white. His wife retained some remnants of a dark Creole beauty. Beyond the cabin bulkhead they seemed to converse in French as well as English and with such aptitude that frequently one would be speaking one language and one would reply in the other with no apparent difficulty.

They had a kind of partnership with another Southern man who had a cabin on the other side of the saloon. This was a Mr James Mason. I did not care for the fellow, who was old and nearly bald and was one of those people who scrape what little hair there is over the scalp and pomade it down and at the same time cultivate excessively that thickening of the eyebrows that accompanies ageing. He reminded me a little of a bust of Beethoven that Ma kept on the piano at home, except that the bust had a lot more hair. He also had a prominent red nose and a booming tone of voice he used particularly on the bedroom stewards, which I instinctively still resented. It seemed to me that, rather than that of a true Southern Gentleman, his manner was more like those Yankees who behave as if their passage money had bought the entire ship. Forgive me, reader, please, for this demonstration of the hasty intolerance of youth.

With secretaries for each, Messrs Macfarland and Eustis, as I recall, it appears they constituted a sort of ambassadorship from the Confederacy to the governments of France and Great Britain respectively. Obviously they were important persons, although not as important as they would have been if they were representatives of the British Empire, of course. The Slidell daughters, appraised as young females usually are by young men, were presentable, nothing more. And out of reach.

Eventually we sailed and I watched Morrow Castle slide by and wondered if I should ever see it again. We opted to take our meals in our cabin, for we felt too bashful to take our seats with the other passengers. The meals were served by our ex-colleagues, with broad grins and many whispered witticisms, to which we replied with vigorously mimed abuse. That evening of our first day, our cabin lamp was extinguished with all the other lamps at eleven o'clock, and the night watches began.

We were, as usual, steaming down the Old Bahama Channel and not far from the lighthouse on Paredon del Grande. Late next morning, with both of us below and, inactive though we were, young appetites beginning to remind us of luncheon, we were drowsily aware of some stir on the deck above us. We heard the officer of the watch hailing the forward lookout, although the reply was too faint to be intelligible.

Silence. Except for the steady beat of the paddles and the passing swash of the sea.

BANG.

'Bang' is the only way I can convey it. It was like a truncated clap of thunder. We stared at each other open-mouthed and simultaneously we spoke.

"What the fuck was that?" was regrettably how we greeted the onset of history. Pardon the casual profanity of the seafarer. I do but try to give you the true flavour of the moment. We sat as rigid as statues. Nothing happened. The paddles steadily beat on.

Then it came again; a bang with a reverberatory after-sound, a kind of howl and another muffled explosion with irregular splashing, not far off. I sprang up at the window and could see nothing except the blue-glass sea passing by.

Pandemonium on deck above us. Telegraphs clanging. Feet running. The paddle beat slowing, with that damnable squeak becoming audible, then stopping, then churning astern and we could feel the way coming off the ship. We collided with each other in the cabin door.

"What about the box?"

"Fuck the box! Och, unlock the bloody door!"

I was all fingers and thumbs with the key and the lock.

"Suppose it's pirates?"

"Oh, for Lordy's sake, grow up, mon! How long have you been at sea? This is eighteen sixty-one, isn't it? Not seventeen sixty-one."

I suppose the greatest piece of luck was that in the excitement we left the revolver in the cabin. Clattering up the companionway to the deck, our boots suddenly sounded like the last sound left in the world. Looking round, for a moment I got the impression of stumbling in upon that children's party game of 'statues'. Deck officers, ladies in

73

crinolines, men in top hats, crew with lines in their hands, all silent, all motionless. The sails were thundering overhead as the wind spilled out of them and she was hove to. I suppose there must have been sixty people up there, passengers and crew. All spell-bound. All looking the same way.

Out on the starboard beam, about two hundred yards off, I should think, lay another ship.

I still find that at first sight warships look smaller than they ought to be. And these United States Navy ships seem painted unnecessarily dark. Out on the bright blue Caribbean water, where it is so clear you can see rocks on the bottom ten fathoms down, all I could make out of her seemed black. Black hull, black masts and rigging, black funnel. Except, as the eyes accustomed themselves to the sunlight, that gaudy ensign of theirs, flapping from the gaff now and then, and an occasional glint of brass.

Then I saw that there were rust streaks from her anchor cable and hawsehole, and her chain plates. She looked to me as if she had been long at sea.

They were sending over a boat. Someone was shouting through a megaphone at us: "Prepare to receive a boarding party." I remember how the sparkling water made a black paper cutout of each oar as they dipped and light shone and outlined the very keel. You have no idea of it, if you know only the grey-green sea of home.

Then they were out of sight under the ship's side but we heard the order, "Toss in your oars," with a Yankee twang and the wooden clatter that followed. A pause like a century, then a man appeared in the bulwarks gangway and stepped briskly aboard. He was dressed in a blue frock coat with a stripe of gold lace and a star on the cuff - a tall bony sort of man with a look of vinegar about him. From my view of the world, he was the type of officer of whom to steer clear, if you can. He swept a sharp eye over us with an unsmiling face, saw Captain Moir's chevrons on his sleeve, walked over to him at once and gave him a sketchy salute and a brief - a very brief - smile. One was in no doubt as to who was Navy and who was merchant marine.

"The name's Fairfax," he drawled. "I am the executive officer of the United States Ship *San Jacinto* over there. Who have I the pleasure of addressing?"

Our captain was pale with a brick-red spot of anger on his cheek and was rigid with rage. When he spoke his voice was low with the effort of keeping control.

"Captain James Moir, Royal Mail Steam Packet Company," he said. "What the hell do you think you're doing, mister? What the devil do you want?"

The people on deck began to gather round the protagonists. You could see this made Fairfax nervous. The man was not used to a deckful of people that were not bound by service discipline.

"Well, sir," he began, "we have been informed... my commanding officer has been informed... that two enemies of the United States... that is to say, two men called Mason and Slidell are on board..."

"What's that to you? What if they are?" snapped Captain Moir. "We are neutral in such a matter. A neutral ship travelling from a neutral port to a neutral port. Havana to St. Thomas to Southampton."

"And I would like, sir, to examine your passenger list."

I saw Commander Williams pop up almost from under Captain Moir's elbow. Captain Moir was clearly on the edge of losing his temper.

"You damned impertinent puppy!" he exploded. "You go back to your ship, young man, and tell your skipper that ye couldn't accomplish your mission because we wouldn't let ye..." Old Jimmy Moir's Scots accent, usually minimal, was getting broader. "Do you understand that? Do you *understand* that? I deny your right of search on my ship."

As he said this there was a growl of approval from the spectators, succeeded by a storm of hand clapping. Then I saw Mr Slidell walk out of the crowd towards Lieutenant Fairfax and introduce himself. He was quickly followed by Mr Mason and the two secretaries. I suppose at this distance of time I can feel a certain sympathy for Lieutenant Fairfax alone on the deck of a foreign ship in the face of an increasingly hostile crowd. I saw him take out his handkerchief and briefly remove his cap to mop his brow. It also bought him a second or two to review his orders in the face of the situation, before his next move.

"Well, in that case," he began, "I regret that I have orders to arrest Mr. Mason and Mr. Slidell and their secretaries, and take them as prisoners on board this United States warship that you see there."

There was another more ferocious growl from the crowd, which moved in closer. "Throw the damned Yankee overboard," someone shouted. You will have gathered by now that there were many other Southerners on board.

Fairfax backed towards the gangway. He gestured in the direction of the *San Jacinto*. "I must warn you," he shouted above the din, "that everything that is happening here is being closely watched by telescope and if any of us get hurt the guns are loaded and it might lead on to dreadful circumstances."

Commander Richards's eyes looked as if they were going to pop out of his head. He drew himself up to his not very considerable height. "You do know that this is a British ship, don't you? A *British* ship."

"Who are you?" said Lieutenant Fairfax. Richards seemed to swell up. I thought he was going to go off bang and then I thought he might go up in the air like a balloon because, in his passion, he went up on the tips of his toes, as small men sometimes will.

"I am Commander Richards, Royal Navy. I am the mail agent in this ship and *you will call me sir*. I represent the Admiral Superintendent of Mail and the British Government and…"

Captain Moir had turned his back and was placating the crowd of passengers. The noise was just dying down when another roar erupted, accompanied by pointing arms, which made him spin round. There was another American officer arriving on the deck, closely followed by half a dozen or more sailors carrying muskets with fixed bayonets. The boat's crew. They must have heard the confrontation and decided Fairfax needed support. Captain Moir advanced, shaking his arms at them as though they were chickens that had escaped from their pen. "Off. Off. Off. Get off my ship!" he was saying.

The sailors bunched uncertainly in the entry port, looking to their officer for guidance. I could see Commander Richards was by now hanging on to Fairfax's sleeve.

"I represent Her Britannic Majesty's Government in this ship," he was bawling. "This is an illegal act. This is a violation of international law. I protest! You would not dare to attack a ship capable of resisting your aggression. It's piracy. I warn you, you'll start a war. You'll be blockaded…"

I was close enough to hear our Old Man whisper to him, "Take it easy, Dick. We don't want to start the war now."

Fairfax had one of those long noses that always look a little red and damp at the tip. He peered down it at old Richards now and I heard him saying, "Well, Commander, sir, as a British Navy Officer I have no doubt you are more experienced than I am in stop and search procedures in neutral vessels. Although the thought does occur to me that sauce for the goose is sauce for the gander. Sir."

Of course he was right. If you are a British captain in by far the biggest navy in the world you do not bother yourself with the legal niceties overmuch. But after a while it all looked as if it was going to end peaceably. Fairfax managed to detach himself from the Commander, although that personage trotted after him demanding loudly that all matters be referred to him for a decision. I saw a spasm of irritation cross Captain Moir's face as he watched the mail agent determinedly complicating matters. Fairfax ordered the boarding party back into their boat. The two Southern diplomats were giving instructions about packing.

"Come on," I said to Roderick. "We've been away quite long enough. Let's get back down to the cabin. It's nearly all over. " I was wrong.

We found ourselves going down the companionway just behind Lieutenant Fairfax, Messrs Mason and Slidell and several bedroom stewards. We ducked past them when we reached the deck below, arrived at our cabin and locked ourselves in. All was well and as we left it.

Almost at once sounds of strife began outside in the saloon. From the trampling on the companionway many people had followed the American officer and his intended captives. Quite what Slidell and Mason intended was never clear to me but they resisted going any further. There was struggling, irregular sounds of feet on and off the carpet, heavy breathing, panting and monosyllabic speech through clenched teeth. It was exactly like listening to the sounds made when Uncle Joby ejected undesirable clients late at night from the Bell.   What was new was the increasing volume of females screaming - and I mean real full-throated screaming, where they really put their backs into it, if you know what I mean. Our frantic attempts to see what was going on through the jalousie and keyhole in the door were worse than useless.

I heard Fairfax's voice suddenly say, "OK, Mister, you've asked for it and now you git it." And then the immediate command: "Petty officer, go and get Lieutenant Gee and the marines, at the double. *Go!*" A second boat must have come over.

Intriguingly, I heard Mrs Slidell say to her husband, "You do know it is Charles' ship, the *San Jacinto*, don't you?" And Slidell say, "Charles Wilkes? Do you really mean that? Charles Wilkes is Captain of the *San Jacinto* now? Oh, for God's sake..."

"I thought he was on anti-slavery patrol off the African coast," said she.

"Oh, you still keep an eye on his career, do you?"

"John, I was going to marry him, remember."

"Oh, I remember all right and I reckon he does too. Poetic justice in a way for him. And no doubt he'll be carrying out his duties with that little extra zeal. Well, there's no time to worry about all that now. Look, here's the tin box. What I want you to do, without fail, is to sit by that cabin window and if anyone comes a-foraging for papers and such in here, you throw it into the sea."

Of course, it was foolhardy. Of course, we should have lain low in our cabin, but excitement and curiosity must have driven us half crazy, for we unlocked and opened our door a crack to see what was happening. What was happening was that Fairfax was coming back down the stairs, followed closely by eight men in blue uniforms and white cross-belts, wearing those Frog-style kepi's of theirs, clattering after him. They had fixed bayonets! The sight of this proved too much for the eldest Slidell girl - Matilda, I think it was. She threw herself across the saloon, grabbed the doorframes with both hands, shrieking that nobody was going to take her daddy away, with much more of the same and accompanying screams and tears. I do not remember - I do not remember, and I say that with care - if someone ordered the marines to force an entrance at bayonet point. I think probably not. It was merely an individual's oafish zeal. At any event one of them appeared to charge at the doorway and Miss Slidell with his bayonet levelled. And the ship lurched.

She had been drifting all this time, lying-to peaceably, but the breeze had increased somewhat and stirred up small waves enough to provoke an unexpected movement. Old Commander Williams dined out for years on his version of events, which were that he threw his body between lady and bayonet. He was there all right because when we poked our heads out of our cabin door I found myself staring into his eyes almost inches away, but their expression was not the gimlet glare of impending action. It was the pop-eyed, open-mouthed face of someone taken by surprise. I am sure that he overbalanced from the unexpected movement. Never mind; he in turn unbalanced the marine who staggered a couple of steps in our direction.

Now I have also seen stories in the newspapers that the gallant Commander struck the marine down. This I know to be untrue because it was Roderick that did it. As the fellow lurched in his turn, Roderick raised his two great, indelibly grimed, engineer's fists and brought then down on the marine's head, neck, shoulder - I know not what. The man fell over and the good fortune of it was that nobody was accidentally impaled on the bayonet. All this was not followed by a concerted charge from his fellow marines and indeed there was a loud command that they stand firm, which makes me believe that the fallen one had exceeded what had been intended. Indeed, it may even have been Miss Matilda who made the final contribution, because as she collapsed in hysterics, sobbing and screaming across the threshold with her heels drumming on the deck, her skirts became disarranged quite to her knees showing her black stockings. I have an interest in such things but, for a precious moment, this was quite enough to inhibit every single male in that saloon who could see them from action. Sin also sleepily awakened inside me at the vision and asked if we were homeward bound as yet...

All this takes much longer to write than to experience but if it were not enough, at the same moment we heard a crash of broken glass from behind us and whirling round observed Mr Slidell falling, jumping; at any rate coming inboard through our cabin window. Some instinct to escape had led him to climb out through his own window and it was only the instant that he got out there, clinging onto the 'gingerbread', that he perceived there was nowhere to go. We were brushed aside, perhaps shoved aside would be better, and he was seized and arrested by Lieutenant Fairfax. Thankfully, I had hidden the handgun by pushing it under the bedclothes on my berth, so that probably fatal item of temptation for Slidell was not presented to him.

The US Marines were sufficient now to quell the crowd, which to a degree was still fired up with Southern anger and British outrage. They forced a passage to the gangway and our unlucky passengers were taken away to the Federal warship. We heard Mr Slidell call out to his wife as he went down the ships side something like, "Don't worry, my dear. We shall meet in Paris in sixty days."

We could but watch as boatloads of their baggage were rowed away after them. We could but stare when another boat pulled across from the 'Saucy Jack', as we had learned her people liked to call her, with a paymaster's clerk to buy extra sherry from our purser and several water jugs and washbasins to alleviate accommodation too spartan for unwilling guests. We looked on as, at the last, Lieutenant Fairfax came back on board to take leave of Captain Moir and tell him he could resume his voyage. All ended with great courtesy. Even Commander Williams complimented Fairfax on the way he had handled "such an embarrassing and perplexing duty." I would bet that this cordiality arose from the inward conviction of all parties that it might have been far worse than one marine nursing a sore head. Black smoke was soon pouring from the *San Jacinto's* funnel as she got under way turning north, and much the same began from ours to the distant sounds of shovelling. She was not a big ship, our old *Trent*. After which there seemed nothing else to do but to go on going home.

Chapter 7

The third wave, dear reader, seemed but a ripple at first.

Particularly after such an upheaval as the *San Jacinto* Incident, as it was called at that time.

The atmosphere changes in a ship that has been away for a long time and is approaching home. No matter what the time of day, the ship's routine with which crew and passengers have comfortably conformed is inconsiderately swept away. There is unseemly noise; loud conversations are heard, with no thought given to those still trying to sleep, and indeed may serve notice on passengers to rise so that cabins may be stripped of their bed linen for the shore-side laundry. There are noises of heavy objects such as cabin trunks and coils of mooring ropes being dragged along. There are inexplicable, startling sharp knocks on the deck above one's head, almost as if they were done on purpose, as chambermaids are noisy when late sleepers prevent them completing their duties. People appear in the saloon in search of tea, only to find it unlit and unwelcoming. There is a new distancing of crew from passengers, rather after the fashion of the unsmiling face of the shop girl when you meet her in the street and it is no longer required of her to be amicable. It gives a slightly unpleasant shock, particularly if one has tipped what one thought was handsomely.

And this was the ripple. Roderick had the last of our private watches in the cabin and I had gone on deck for a blow and to watch the last miles from Hurst Castle and the

Needles, past Calshot and then up the low wooded shores of Southampton Water and home. It was not an experience of which I had had much as a working crewmember, and I savoured it in case it did not come again, now that the world was changed. The ship and the sea were still mine for a little while more, you understand, but nouveau riche young men (for that is what we now were, oh yes) are not usually employed as stewards and engineers at sea. It was thus with a change to melancholy that I watched the bosun laying out his mooring lines and teaching a couple of youngsters to kick them straight with their heels until they were as neat as the lines in a book, wondering when I should see that sight again.

It was a cold, calm, grey day that made sail useless and the crew were already aloft doing an early harbour stow. Anything to get away from the ship quickly.

Not long until Christmas. I had a specially made present for Judy. A little broach made of gold from the forests of Guiana with local seed pearls to tip its stamens.

There was a ship in front of us churning along at half speed up the Water just as we were and we were treading on the fading, mackerel pattern of her wake, but on the still water she was also making a wide, spreading vee-shaped ripple from her bow wave. I was not taking much notice, just watching the new military Royal Victoria Hospital at Netley with its domed chapel and long wings slide by and thinking of home. We were rich! Incredible. I could scarcely refrain from a boyish, joyous hop or two at the thought. We could have pretty well whatever our hearts desired from the town behind the grimy old walls ahead.

What news we brought, witnesses as we were to violence between nations on the high seas, and with these confounded Americans again! And what news of ourselves! What a surprise for everyone, for there was no way the news could precede us; we brought the news! The trans-Atlantic cable was not yet functioning. Indeed, how inadequate a word 'surprise' would be.

I shall tell you that, shameless as ever, I was happily contemplating giving Judith the most delectable silk petticoat that money could buy. White, of course. Then I thought that I must get something equally delightful for Rachel, in case jealousy led to questions. A petticoat? Another petticoat? How gratifying Rachel's embarrassment would be. No, that would not do for then Judith might frown. Oh, perhaps I could secretly buy Judith some delectable white silk and lace pantaloons such as a French princess might wear in my fevered imagination. But as far as I knew the sisters still shared a bedroom at the Bell and Rachel, I believed, would be appalled to think I even knew what they might have on beneath their crinolines, would she not? That is the trouble with virgins. The trouble with virgins again. Of course, it never occurred to me then that my poor little virgin might be begging, praying to lay down the burden of her white petticoat and would have been happy to put on even a scarlet one. I was a creature of my times and it was unthinkable. What prisons we build for each other. So what should I do? Here it was again, and close at hand. We must marry or go mad.

I felt the ship alter course a fraction and there was a warm and welcome eddy from our black 'chimney' in the cold air.

I had it! Petticoats for princesses for both, and the drawers for Judith somehow concealed from Rachel's attention. Hah! Then, while I was cursing myself as a fool because where would I get the courage to ever go shopping for such things in England, I felt the ship change course again and the bam-bam-bam-bam of the paddles became even slower. Also the squeak, which they claimed had driven generations of chief engineers to drink, became lower in pitch as the engines turned slower but still clearly audible on the maindeck. What on earth was going on with the ship ahead? She was nearly off Platform Point by now. She had stopped engines and was drifting slowly while a couple of launches were making for her purposefully. With the usual shattering roar, our safety valves lifted and we began to blow off steam. Ears ringing, we all of us peered ahead trying to discover what was happening. It was too bad when the itch to get ashore was more than usually urgent.

It is not easy to recognise another ship from dead astern but as the vessel ahead showed a little more of her silhouette there was something dimly familiar about her. Not to say that I knew who she was. Just a brigantine-rigged steamer with a curious upper deck, which extended from the paddle boxes to her stern. Somewhen, somehow, I felt I had seen her before, but the remembrance was quickly blown away by the relief of watching her get under way once more and two long-funnelled tugs smokily coming to fetch her in.

Now we had an unexpected and infuriating wait outside the entrance of the Tidal Dock. We carried the Royal Mail. Why was all the attention being given to this ship that had preceded us? When at last the tugs came for us and ushered us to our usual berth, all on deck looked at the other arrival with curiosity. She was in a berth on the south side, over near the gates of the dry docks, secured bows-to. Her name was clearly visible on her stern, almost as if written in fresh paint: *Nashville*. *Nashville*? It meant nothing to any of us except that it was a town in one of the Southern States. Telescopes were trained.

"There's a devil of a crowd over there. I'm sure I saw Captain Patey boarding her just now. What is going on? What is that ship?" I heard Captain Moir say from the top of the paddle box where he was standing. It was Captain Patey who represented the Admiral Superintendent of Mails in the port. The pilot spoke but his head was turned away and I missed some of it. But I did hear him say something like, "...broke out of Charleston on the twenty-sixth of October."

"You don't say so? She is a blockade runner then?"

On that still late-autumn day came one of those sudden puffs of wind that arise and die and I saw it blow out the folds in the stranger's ensign. I had never seen it before; three broad stripes of red, white and red with a big blue square in the upper quadrant with a circle of stars on it. For that was how they began. Oh yes, I remember the first time I ever saw the Stars and Bars of the Confederate States.

"No, she's not a blockade runner, it seems," the pilot was saying. "She's supposed to be a warship. Hence the agitation ashore."

"A warship? That?" Captain Moir's person radiated disbelief as he stared at the *Nashville*. "I don't believe these States in the South that are trying to secede have got a navy. They're nothing but farmers and planters."

"Well, I'm telling you that's what they say," said the pilot. "And what's more, sir, she damn well sunk something before she turned up here."

"What? Collided with something, you mean?"

"No I don't, Captain. Burned something! A square-rigged ship owned in one of the Northern States. *Harvey Birch*, she was called. It's turning into a real war all right, over there.

Sod their war, I thought. What is it to us? Let's get home.

I always remember how sharp and strong the smell of chimney smoke was in the air and of horse dung in the streets after the salty winds of the sea. And that sweetish scent of vegetables in Pa's little shop was all-enveloping. We had worked out our entrance to the Bell. Descending from the unaccustomed glory of our cab, over-tipping the driver, who continued to regard us with suspicion and ostentatiously tested our money with his teeth, we put our box on our shoulders and loudly pom-pomming the Dead March from Handel's *Saul*, made our way into the 'public'.

There were only one or two drinkers lingering over a pint at that time of day and a pair of domino players clattering their tiles on a corner table, but the familiar odour of beer and tobacco was in the air. Perched on a stool behind the bar, whiling away her 'watch' with a crumpled copy of the *Southampton Times*, was Judy.

We were not of course unexpected, the Royal Mail packets being what they are. Judy's face went from dull boredom through recognition to amazement and she slid from her stool to her feet. Under the circumstances I forgave her that she forgot our deadly secret greeting. "Pom-pompom-pompom. Pom-pompom-pompom," went Roderick and I. Then we unloaded the box from our shoulders and placed it on the bar.

"What are you doing? What is it?" she cried.

"Just a moment. Haven't you forgotten something? You know, months on the briny and all that?" said I, grinning.

"Oh..." She pushed down with her hands, lifting herself against the bar, lent over it, and I got a peck on the lips, and after a tiny hesitation Roderick got one as well on his cheek. With a spasm almost like pain I realised anew how little she was. I can remember how it felt today.

"Oh, don't torment me. What have you got in there?" she said.

"Judy, it's something pretty big. You're surely not on your own in the house?"

"Oh no. Father is upstairs having his afternoon nap and I think Rachel is doing some mending somewhere."

"I think you should bring them down. We'll keep an eye on the bar if you will unbolt the flap and let us through."

Uncle Joby and Rachel soon appeared. Rod turned the big, old-fashioned key in the lock of the box. It was not the riot of coin that it had been, because during the hours and days our treasure trove had been sorted, counted and bagged up by the courtesy of the purser. Although it was pretty obvious what it might be I seized a bag, untied its neck and cascaded sovereigns onto the bar. Some leapt and splashed into the sink below. Some bounced and fell onto the sawdust on the floor and one went clangorously into a spittoon.

Amazement was predictable but very gratifying. The bar, as I have described, was sparsely inhabited but a few free pints were distributed nevertheless. Roderick and I had rum, although in truth I did not care much for the black stuff dispensed at home and I remember promising myself that if ever I had a bar of my own I would serve some of the honey coloured liquid from Trinidad that I had grown a taste for. Well, I have at least accomplished that, although I regret the proprietor accounts for most of it. A pub bar! It only goes to show how the magnitude of our good fortune far outstripped the scope of our immature imaginings.

Of course, we became excited ourselves, telling the tale of shots across bows and boarding parties of Yankees. It is not so common for youngsters to be such a centre of interest, of open-mouthed amazement, of kindling emotions, of the stirring of patriotic rage. It was all a thunderclap, you understand. It was not for the best part of a week that the Government had news of it directly from the States.

Oh, the sweetness of seeing the Belles with big round eyes and open mouths hanging on our every word. But Uncle Joby insisted that this was no time for drinking rum and telling yarns, even if they brought such startling news. He said we had already been indiscrete by displaying our wealth in St. Michael's parish. Of course we had, but we were young. I had intended an encore performance at my parents' house but he would have none of it and out came an old porter's barrow that was far more used to casks and crates than treasure chests, and through the streets at the gallop went we to the Wilts and Dorset Bank in the High

Street. (Where else would Job and my Pa have banked?) It was long, long after three but Uncle Joby with his bowler on the back of his head used his gangling limbs to hang onto the bell handle and knock and kick the big mahogany doors and yell for the manager in a most uncharacteristic way. A police constable came into view and visibly increased his pace as he realised the disturbance was taking place in front of the bank. My first reaction was relief but, as he approached, to my horror I realised Roderick's coat had become unbuttoned and there stuck into the top of his trousers was this great cannon of ours, which must surely have condemned us all to Botany Bay as bank robbers. Fortunately, just at that moment the door opened a crack and there was the indignant, plump little figure of the manager, with a couple of clerks craning over his shoulders in support, demanding to know what we thought we were about. Joby simply pulled open the lid of the box, shouted, "Look!" at him, for there was still a sufficiency of loose coin of the realm on top, and the manager was immediately running down the steps and helping us heave it inside. No sooner was the door again closed than a second tattoo broke out on it, accompanied by shouts of In The Name of the Law. The manager thought for a moment, then with great aplomb flung the door open. Gripping the astonished constable by the front of his tunic, he dragged him into the bank, slammed the door behind him and demanded that he stand guard until our treasure was safely inside the vault. I think the poor fellow decided that he was in some dream where bank robbers committed the offence of filling banks with money, rather than taking it away, and that if he stood quietly, truncheon drawn, in a minute he would wake up safe in his own bed.

The bank manager too appeared as if he needed to pinch himself as he realised the depth of the layers of soft leather bags underneath the surface dressing of sovereigns. We might both of us have lacked our majorities that day but Mr

McKay and Mr Musselwhite we became and Mr McKay and Mr Musselwhite we have remained.

Ask a mature person how long should be allowed for the purpose of preparing a great family gathering and they are likely to reply, "A week?" We were young and said, "Tomorrow!" So we compromised and agreed on the day after tomorrow, although Ma was put out because this left no time for her to prepare her spiced beef, which was a family-wide favourite. I was sorry too. In my hotel I make sure that the cold buffet is never without it, although I get female fingers wagged at me if I am caught carving myself a surreptitious slice.

Nominally, the party was a private function but, in effect, the bar in the snug became the table for a glorious cold collation. The celebrations soon began to spill out into the public anyway and it became too tedious to try to get the regulars to pay for their drinks, so eventually it finished up as a free-for-all, in the pleasanter sense. I think we all had toe-curling qualms about the extravagance of it from time to time but it did not matter. It really did not matter anymore.

As the evening wore on we felt the need to sing. Many songs were sung, of land and sea, and other things, which, if Job considered them less than respectable, he would seize the pipe-clayed lanyard of the shining bell behind the bar and ring out a clangorous clamour that would have done credit to the approach of the fire engine and cause the girls to put their hands over their ears.

Somewhen in the evening, despite the gale of jollity, I became aware of a stranger, a real stranger, neither bar regular and certainly not family or friends of family, which was sometimes straining recognition pretty hard. This man looked like a sailor rather than just a seaman and by that I mean he was a navy man. He wore navy blue trousers and a sort of wide collared blue blouse with a white vest under it, and there was a lanyard and he had a soft round cap with a

91

prominent button in the middle of it. It was not Royal Navy rig. But it was not so much his clothes that drew my eye as the fact that he had a moustache. I might only ever have been a merchant marine steward but if there is a thing I dislike and a thing that shouts 'foreigner' it is a man in a naval sort of uniform wearing a moustache. He is supposed to be clean shaven or have a 'full set' - with a big beard - and though some may be loath to admit it, the Royal Navy sets the fashion in these things, especially when they have an actual presence aboard as in a mail packet.

Still, whoever he was, he was in no way intruding, enjoying his beer and responding affably enough to conversation addressed to him - even, as far as I could see, singing along with us all when he was familiar with the song. What was more, after a little while, he produced a banjo from a bag on the floor and what tunes he knew he accompanied, to our applause. Those he did not he endeavoured to learn, strumming gently away in our wake. I put an inquiry into the crowd, asking who he might be, which whispered from ear to ear outward bound, eventually returned with the startling news that he was a man from the *Nashville*, a sight more exotic from his circumstances than the Bell's usual visitors. I suspected his original intention had been twenty minutes or so of the time of one of the neighbouring Ladies of the Night because it was quite a long walk from the *Nashville's* berth in the Outer Dock. Someone must have given him directions or he would have sought the hospitality of a pub nearer to home.

About mid evening I got out into the yard behind the pub to get a breath of air as fresh as there was going. The windows shone with lamp-lit cheer but it was a cloudy night and the yard was very dark. Her skirts brushed my legs, as a cat will startle you in the dark with sudden, unseen entwining.

"What ho, Judy," said I. "Is that your famous first crinoline that I can feel?"

"No," said she. "It's impossible to wear such a thing behind that beastly bar. The glasses I have swept off and broken. And I was cold with winter nearly here so I went back to my petticoats. And you are home and you like my petticoats, don't you, Tommy? What a strange young man you are, to talk to a poor female about her undergarments."

"You began it," I asserted heartily but with that familiar constricted sensation in my throat as desire rose.

"Did *not!* You asked me about my crinoline," she retorted. Then her unseen hands took mine and laid them on her waist. "Do you feel? Your ma came along and insisted that we both wear stays now we are nearly grown up. Well, Rachel may need them but not I. I think my waist is little enough, don't you, Tommy? And oh, the pulling and. straining in the morning when we are getting up. Perhaps you should come to help, except that Rachel would surely die if you even looked at her ankle and I would surely kill you if you did. You would think as well that the stays themselves were indecent, for I must now wear a chemise under them and a camisole over them. Ohhh..." Which was because I could not refrain from running my hands over her body and finding the softness of her bosom above the corset.

She whispered at me through the dark. "Oh, Tommy, I have thought I should go crazy sometimes in these last weeks, waiting for you to come. Oh quick, quick, the Sensations, before we have to go back indoors."

I thought she was crazy too. I thought that there was probably no female in Europe who had desire and exposed her body like Judy. No white woman anyway. I liked it, but to be crazy was to be sick. Yet I relished her immodesty and encouraged her and thus compounded my sin.

She pressed my hands harder to her bosoms and then in a moment had swept them round her onto that often forbidden territory, her bottom. I squeezed her cheeks a little through the dress and, surprised for a moment, I thought she had pushed me away, but it was only to make a little space. I heard the rustle and became aware of pale glowing in the gloom below and knew she had impatiently already raised her dress and petticoats as one. Her elbows knocked against me and I knew, clumsy with haste, she was pinning her lifted skirts up on her hips. I laid my hand on her stomach or rather on the damned whalebone, but in a trice she seized my wrist. I felt her unsecured skirts on that side fall down over it but instantly she drew my hand into her groin and - glory! - my palm was full of her crisp, curly hair becoming hot and wet. How disgusting! How inflaming! How beautiful! After all the modesty, the gentility, the downcast eyes, the kept down skirts - how strong!

Oh, if I could have seen… because I knew from the days of the wearing and showing of drawers that this petite, dainty young girl exposed almost an aggressive shock of thick, black hair springing from a thrusting mons, dark enough to blush through the more flimsy pants she would wear under a party dress and show to me if she could get away for a moment. Her legs as well, so slender until upper thigh, there became suddenly full and strongly curved. How did the bodies of the women we love become shameful things to be covered up and fit only for the dark? I think it was driving both of us in the direction of madness.

The rule was well and truly broken that night, because she was not wearing pantaloons or even drawers at all but pantalettes as I discovered, ribboned to her thighs. All the evening, when we had found a moment to snatch a word or even exchange a smile, up there, high and hidden under her skirts, she had left herself bare. Bottom, thighs and stomach (well, lower stomach), all naked: right and ready in the hope that I would come and worship. Ah, there belike the reason for it all. When I found her cleft and felt that thing growing and pushing along my finger, she groaned aloud. My poor Judy groaned. I had never heard her groan like that, as if she were in pain, and as I felt all of it there in her crotch, swelling, moist and hot, I knew we must not go on like this. This was not like the black or brown West Indian who bared her all with that high-pitched giggling laugh they have. It was with difficulty that I gained her attention, for it seemed cruel to suddenly cease from pleasuring her, having just begun.

"Judy, Judy" I whispered urgently. She was muttering and moaning and it seemed she was torn between going back inside before we were missed or continuing her pleasure. At length she was silent and I said, "Judy, will you marry me? Please marry me, love. I'm sorry I cannot go down on one knee to you, but it's dark."

Silence, and I felt it opportune to remove myself from her body, although it was hard, hard. Then thankfully she giggled.

"If I marry you, will I ever be allowed to keep my dress on?" said she. I felt almost offended. After all, I was wealthy now and the matter was serious. I think she sensed it.

"Dear Tommy, dear Tommy" she said, very low. "Don't be annoyed with the inn keeper's daughter. I promise I will truly, truly think about it and I will tell you soon."

Think about it? Tell me soon? This was not what I expected; but her clothes had flopped down and there was no more glimmer from her petticoats. She was rustling away to the back door. There was to be no opportunity for discussing it further then. There seemed nothing to do but follow her indoors and I admit I felt rather crestfallen.

When we got inside and the buzzing in my brain had subsided somewhat, we found the bar population had embarked on a song that was becoming popular then from the music hall stage. It had a good, full-bodied tune: "John Brown's body lies a-mouldering in the grave..." Although I would have wagered no one in that bar knew really who John Brown was and why he was a-mouldering. I did not. When they had finished roaring about "Glory, Glory, Alleluia" and relative silence returned, we heard a chord - I suppose you would call it - from the sailor's banjo. Then a spiky little tune that strangely he played in strict time, so that the foot wanted to tap to it. After that he sang to it. "Well, I wish I was in the land of cotton. Old times there are not forgotten..."

I am sure that was the first time I ever heard *Dixie* and oh, damn him for it. And damn them all for their grey rags and their courtly manners. Damn them for their flapping boot soles and their rights and their slaves. And damn them, damn them for their damn war.

Chapter 8

Too much: too soon…

You go on your travels to seek adventure. You come home when you have had enough. It is much more disturbing when adventure comes knocking on the door of your place of peace, uninvited and unwelcome. Like someone from far away who suddenly turns up on the doorstep in response to some long forgotten bar room invitation.

Southampton had been quite literally a backwater for centuries. Why the trade of the medieval port deserted her I could not say. The advantages of the double tide must have been eternal. Perhaps in olden days the town was too far from anywhere, particularly London. It does not matter. A century before my time the Spa brought some genteel prosperity, but the mines and machinery and mess of the Midlands and North passed us by. No coal, I suppose, thank God for that at least, although many would not say so with their where-there's-muck-there's-money philosophy, usually accompanied, I have noticed, by an enthusiastic miming of the washing of hands.

The then Princess Victoria came and opened the Royal Pier. Then the railway reached us and the first dock was made and the inner dock grew from it, but somehow it was all happening in that distant, southeastern corner of the place and out of sight. Nothing to fill the newspapers here.

You come home with a fortune, hoping to put your feet up for a day or two at least. And now this. This intruder. This cuckoo. This worm in the apple. This ordinary passenger paddle-steamer - called suddenly by necessity above her station with a commission signed by this fellow Jefferson Davis no less, who they made their President - and with a couple of six-pounder pop guns, now the Confederate States Ship *Nashville*, Captain Pegram, CSN.

Uncle Job hired an Itchen ferryman to row us round to the docks to get a close view of this *Nashville*. Pa held the boat's gunwales with either hand and looked round cautiously. He always felt insecure on the water. There she lay quiet on the south side like any other ship in port with most of her people ashore, but we could see two sailors on watch at the top of the gangway, alert enough to occasionally pop their heads over the side to keep an eye on us, especially when we got close. The forward sponson of the portside paddle-box was partly smashed and trailing down. She must have been struck awkwardly by some great sea, which had filled the box and driven it upward and then rushed on, leaving the weakened sponson to crash down in semi-ruin. It was genuine enough damage. After that, every minute longer she spent at sea, even in moderate weather, risked compounding it.

Of course, in a tavern like the Bell, which was popular with seamen and the shipyard men, we were up-to-date with the gossip. I never saw this Captain Robert Pegram but it appears he was older than you might expect. Anyway, he was as busy as a bee visiting the shipyards up and down the Itchen and before long it was clear that he had in mind much more than the repair of his paddle-box. He wanted the whole 'hurricane deck', as an American would call it, taken off and there were rumours that he wanted the maindeck strengthened as well. It was not hard for anyone to guess that a deck satisfactory for passengers feet and even a pair of six-pounder guns was not up to bearing the weight and shocks of heavier ordnance. I do not know exactly how the powers that be get to know of things but it is easily supposed that what was going on early reached the ears of Captain Patey and thence those of the Admiral Superintendent of Mails - and from there, who knows exactly. I was not familiar with the hierarchy of the Admiralty. However, word soon came down again that spoiled the hopes of several shipyards for fat contracts, for Captain Pegram was told that he could have his storm damage repaired so that he was fit to go to sea again as he was, but these other desires infringed the neutrality rules of the United Kingdom and were not to be had here. His steamer, first of any warship of the Confederacy to appear in European waters, together with our adventure on the *Trent* with the US Navy, was causing escalating turmoil in such faraway celestial realms as the Foreign Office and Number 10, Downing Street. The ripples from all this activity were beginning to show in the newspapers.

I was spending a good deal of time in the Bell as usual. Arising from the presence and politics of the Confederate vessel, public and bar parlour discussions began on the subject of the rights and wrongs of slave ownership. For some it was an outrage on humanity. Others declared that Negroes were not fully human and they were better off fed and clothed and working in houses and fields and given the benefits of religion than running wild, superstitious and naked, in the African jungle. Oh, the wonderful wickedness of being naked.

Uncle Job kept a watchful ear and eye on such debates, in case the heat generated threatened damage. I noticed that if Rachel was doing her stint behind the bar, something about the way her eyes glittered and the compression of her lips made me nervously aware that she likely held opinions on the matter strong enough to cause a scene if voiced.

Judith? Judith was withdrawn into some inner shell away from what to her was the ignominy of being at the beck and call of the customers. She bustled mechanically about and was pleasant enough to those who spoke but at times her eyes would run over me without recognition as I sat on my corner stool with my brandy and water these days, and I knew she was somewhere far away. I doubt if she cared very much about either case. Judy was not deliberately unkind to anyone as a rule but neither would she go to war on their behalf. She would only give a little shrug.

For myself, I do not understand why men from some parts of the earth are so different from others. Particularly, why in the hot places of, say, Africa and South America there exist people who seem content to have nothing but a loincloth and a bow and arrows. People who live on what they can catch, pick and grub up. Is it that the heat enervates them and stifles thought? Or if they have discovered how to scratch in a garden with a pointed stick and plant a few crops, is it that vegetables grow so quickly in the heat that there is never need to take thought for the morrow, or the winter. And what manner of man works if he does not need to? Yet we Europeans in the rain, over and above gaining our daily bread, have found ways to cross the continents and oceans and even now are attempting to lay our hands on the oceans of the air. I do not think it right that the former with his badge of a black skin should be rounded up and shipped away to be a beast of burden, him and his children after him forever. But nor do I think he deserves the good things of life that we have found for ourselves, by the sweat of our brows and worse. Thus I thought that after all their arguments these Confederates we listened to knew in their hearts that they lied, and the war was about slavery, as President Lincoln said in the end. Nor did the ranting Abolitionists of the North beguile me either, amidst their mines and factories, for after the war they took the Negro for their brother no more readily than I, and thus they had lied also. I have no doubt that the good Father Gregory at St. Michael's would quote the parable of even the late-coming labourers being worthy of their full hire. Do not worry. I also have no doubt that God has heard me and triumphantly added another grain or two to the scale pan weighing against me.

It was about that time, in amongst my plans for the best Christmas ever for us all - one plans these grandiose events when one is young - that Judy began to pester again, about my trousers. I hated the idea because it was such an unwomanly thought. I have discovered somewhere that it was but seventy or eighty years ago that females dared to put on anything resembling men's breeches because it was forbidden in the Old Testament. It was down to the damned Froggies as usual, with the diaphanous, indecent modes from the Corsicans' court. And later nobody thought or dared to stop it. I believed, I suppose, in feverish dreaming, that my Judy's legs ought to be covered only by her hose. And for her Jade Gate between them (as a Chinese laundryman I once knew called it) she should maintain her modesty by her skill with her skirts alone, as women had, time out of mind. (Rachel once asked why we men, meaning me of course, made a religion of these things. This was very much later. I am old and shameless now. I could not have spoken of such things then, even if you threatened to pull out my tongue with red-hot tongs.)

And now, this indecent proposal... I believe I was truly angry with her, which was almost unknown, and she knew it. She neither scoffed or wheedled then but went quickly away, although I remember I seemed to recognise the look in her eye as the same one I had first seen when she was nine, after that expedition to the Western Shore. Curiosity. Then devilment. She knew I would do anything to watch her undress.

In between lounging about town, plans for Christmas were made. Ma insisted it was our turn to entertain. I was allowed to get in professional painters and decorators who, with the maximum of inconvenience, nevertheless made our little house in Mount Street shine. Ma had bustled out for something from the East Street shops, leaving Judy poring over wallpaper samples on the kitchen table. I was expected to take some interest, although at that time of my life my concern with interior decorating was small.

So things were going along, with Judy almost talking to herself or thinking aloud as she rolled out and examined the samples, while I contributed "Capital!" or "Oh my goodness!" or whatever. Then I heard her say, without raising her voice or altering her tone, "I suppose if I were to try on your trousers I should have to take off my dress."

The pressure was on.

"Judy," I tried to say in a warning tone, but of course the temptation had entered in. I had never seen her without her proper clothes except for this. For our business she disarranged her skirts and bodice. Although to see this pretty creature demurely lift her skirts for me was almost Paradise.

"Stop this at once. It's indecent." (My God, listen to me.)

She stole a sideways glance at me to assess progress and decided a little more might seal the bargain.

"And watching me undress is not? My petticoats, all my petticoats too," she continued sweetly. "You might as well untie them for me, even the most important underneath one. You know, the one that covers up my legs… I ought really to take off that one myself, did I not? In case I think you are seeing too much of me. And what if my chemise was not really long enough. So that to keep your eyes off me I had to turn to one side. Or turn my back. But then you would look at my bottom. Oh, poor me, poor me. Because you like to look at my bottom, don't you, Tommy? Even nowadays."

"Judy. Judith!" I attempted again but it sounded weak to both of us.

"Of course, I could take the trousers into our bedroom," she said. "But I was hoping you might help me because naturally I am not that familiar with men's clothes. And if you were there to help me you would be seeing me in just chemise and pantaloons, just as if I were a boy too. How could I stop you looking at my botty? You would like that, wouldn't you? And it is so fiddly undoing all those hook and eyes at the back of my dress. And, imagine, I might even have to take off my stays. Please come and help me."

"Judy," I finally managed to speak out of a choked throat. "To see you undress is the very essence of my dreams, but where can we go where we will not be discovered? This would not just be throwing down your skirt if somebody comes."

"So you *are* going to let me try the trousers on." She giggled. She was so pleased with herself. "Tommy, I am sure I shall think of somewhere, somehow."

I should have pushed her down and done it. Had her. On the carpet. Over the table. Would she have screamed the place down? I doubt it. Would she have cried out? Several times, probably. If we had had to go to St. Michael's and she with child, what would it really have mattered? Except to the old women. Except she was my cousin. Or second cousin if you must have it exact. Family. And a virgin. A virgin. And she must have the best. God, why have you done all this to me when I was trying to bring her to Your table immaculate? Oh, nothing counted for You, did it? Because we had uncovered our nakedness to each other, even if we were mere children. You said nothing. Put it all in the scales and relentlessly let the pan go down, as compassionate as a judge in his scarlet and ermine. And his black cap.

You must be thinking that the hot breath of passion was all we ever did. Not so. Christmas was coming.

Captain Nelson of the *Harvey Birch*, burned in the Channel by the *Nashville* on her way in, appeared before the magistrates in the Guildhall in an aggrieved, bad-tempered attempt to get a search warrant to take aboard the *Nashville* because he said his chronometer, barometer and ship's papers had been stolen. He did not succeed. The crew of his ship were transported home in the *SS Hansa*. He would have done better to go as well. Our magistrates, well experienced with cases of assault, theft, putting chalk in the milk, pick-pocketing etcetera, would not have wished to steer into the uncertain waters of neutrality, piracy, recognised belligerent powers and the rest.

There was shopping for presents, alone and together for obvious reasons. I found myself watching Judy with her bonnet and muff, poring over this or that in shop windows and counters in serious discussion with her sister, hurrying over street crossings, keeping skirt hems out of the mud, without myself being throttled with lust. I was content that I knew what was beneath, warmed with tenderness that I was allowed this knowledge and thinking this looked as if it might be the happiest Christmas yet. Looking back as calmly as I may, as we were then hand on arm, I think it was.

The Bell seemed to be drawing an increasing number of Confederate sailors from the *Nashville*. They were making it their territory ashore. We were surprised to find how few of them were genuine natives of the Southern States and those there were, were mostly the petty officers who kept to themselves in the bar parlour. Many of the lower deck men were Irish, one-time fishermen, I suppose. There were many Britons, some of whom were ex-Royal Navy, and with a scattering of others representing half of Europe. It reflected on the almost total preoccupation with agriculture in the South. Precious few unemployed seamen were lounging about on Southern quays. Indeed, we who were behind the bar, in a manner of speaking, listening and hearing, slowly realised what little industry and manufacturing there was in that part of America. There was cotton and there was tobacco - how did they think they could resist the thrusting, populous, industrial Yankee States?

The men in the Bell might have joined for a bit of adventure or perhaps, more significantly, for pay that was double the going rate on the waterfront at Charleston. And the prize money they thought they were going to get. But when I remember that motley, mercenary ship's company, I still feel surprised how others like them valiantly fought for their employer on the *Sumter*, *Florida*, *Tallahassee* and the rest; and in that holy terror the *Alabama* - until she sank under them over there off Cherbourg. Ah well, what Englishman can altogether resist the cause of an underdog. And I think that the Irish are not the only not-altogether-peaceful tribe.

The strange thing was how these tribes seemed to have smoked the pipe of peace while on those neutral decks. Old Joby at first looked askance when he heard the brogue in the bar, but there was never any trouble, and if an Englishman got too pissed to stand the Irish helped carry him back to the ship. Seafarers learn to live with each other, and one stays away from causes of strife.

As the days towards Christmas rushed by, I drove Ma and the Day sisters and the cook at the Bell to distraction, sticking and licking my finger into various delicious mixtures destined to be Christmas cake and plum puddings. They tried to get rid of me by sending me on expeditions to gather evergreens to make Christmas wreaths and decorate the houses. More than once I mutinied and insisted Judy came along to assist, and she was grudgingly assigned to me for the afternoon.

I remember one occasion on the Common. She had scrambled up one of those mysterious banks you find in the middle of the woody areas there and was trying to reach some holly with a particularly fine show of red berries. Early sunset was beginning to turn into evening gloaming but there she was, breath steaming with the cold and a bright rose on each pale cheek, still seeking to add more to her already crammed basket. It was just a stupid impulse.

I called out quietly to her, "Lift your skirts for me, Judy," just as I had so many times in our lives before.

I never thought she would do it. I expected, "Not blooming likely!" appropriately attributable to that Bloomer woman. Or "No, it's much too cold," or even the plaintive "I can't: someone will see." But she looked right and then she looked left, and then she stooped and drew her clothes up above her knees.

"Satisfied?" she asked and let it all fall with a laugh without waiting for my answer. Her boots would need drying for days they were so caked with mud.

"No," I said.

"You never are. What a pity," said she quickly. "It's time to go home now, Tommy. We've got such a long way to walk."

We carried our gatherings through the Bell, calling out our hellos, and into the back yard to stow them temporarily in the coalhouse there. It was as we left in the gloom that she touched my arm to stop me, took my hand, glove and all, and using her other to raise her skirts at the side, drew it up right into her crotch. I fondled her as best I could for a moment or two. Whilst we were so close it entered my mind to attempt to kiss her but she immediately turned her face away. After a little while I heard her sigh shudderingly a couple of times and she whispered hoarsely, "That's enough, Tommy. No more," and she thrust me away. Now I think of it, it seems she never liked being kissed whilst she was showing me her person. It was almost as if it got in the way or was somehow inappropriate.

It was an odd thrill in it's own right, this separation of our real and secret lives. Also, and I hope you will not be too shocked, it seemed to me that now Judy had desire for her Exquisite Sensations up there, almost as much as I did, and she was a woman. Sometimes I am haunted that I had lured her into evil, indecent ways and aroused unwomanly passions in her. If I told Judy of this she would simply laugh and take my hand, as I have just described to you. Or reveal herself, uninvited. This usually swept away all doubt, but it stored up wrath for her as well, as you will see.

Christmas dinner was to be in the dining room upstairs in the Bell for the sake of space. Later on, all would gather at Mount Street for a Twelfth Night party. No celebration of New Year's Eve and the coming of 1862? No indeed, for New Year's Eve in the Bell was a question of all family hands to the pump. And yes indeed, because it was one of the jolliest evenings of the year. No one minded if the 'staff' were seen to have a glass at their lips occasionally or to join in the gales of jolly singing, as long as the change given was more or less right and expensive bottles were not let fall.

I suppose it was because of the presence of our newest clientele, or that portion of it that truly had their roots in the great troubled land across the Western Ocean, that certain events caught the eye as one scanned the newspapers. Yes - I had time now to scan the newspapers.

It slowly filtered across to us that Captain C Wilkes USN, our unseen tormentor in the *USS San Jacinto*, who was at first acclaimed in his homeland for his action, was now increasingly being damned by fainter and fainter praise, as anger spread in Great Britain and the implications of his action began to emerge.

A couple of Royal Mail steamers were commandeered by the Admiralty, and Southampton streets once again heard marching feet as reinforcing troops for Canada sailed for Halifax.

And then, damned if they didn't do it again early in December, when the *Eugenia Smith* was stopped by the *USS Santiago de Cuba* and some other rebel official was fished out of her. I blame it on captains who have been too long out at sea myself. Not only do they become ill-informed but they really do begin to believe they have godlike powers.

Then, out of the blue, Prince Albert died. The good die young, don't they? Not only the good, I assure you. I suppose people like us, not living in the centre of Society, even became a little bored with Albert's virtue compared with the goings-on of some of those who had preceded him. But give the man his due, he did a difficult job well. It must have been hard to have to keep his mouth shut so much. If the Queen was heart-broken -and I've known that starless night myself that no one can share - then the rest of us were genuinely sad that a good man had crossed the bar so soon. It was only later of course, much later, that it crept out about how he probably kept us out of war by toning down the messages old Palmerston and Lord John Russell wanted the Queen to sign. So we were a bit gloomy and thoughtful for a while. But then, Christmas was coming.

I have no need to take you through a blow-by-blow account of that Christmas. I was near the verge of having drunk too much to go to the midnight service of carols on Christmas Eve. I was hustled across French Street by a Belle at each elbow, being given little shakes at intervals to demonstrate their public indignation at my condition. I turned my head the while to blissfully contemplate in turn the beauty of my... custodians. I even remember trying to make up a statement of compliments for each of them that ran a grave risk of being too personal by far. Fortunately I stumbled on the cobbles. Inside St. Michael's I cheerfully bawled out those carols I knew by heart and threatened to doze off on my feet during those I did not. The hymn sheets were far too blurry to read. I also needed a surreptitious lift at the aforementioned elbows to get upon my feet from my knees when required, to avoid an undignified climb up the back of the pew in front. Funnily enough, and I could tell because the vibrations of it were transmitted from hand to elbow, it was Rachel who got a fit of the giggles first. I saw it made her bosom shake, so I looked at Judy's and hers shook too. I wished we were not in church. And so the virtue hardly gained by my piety trickled away because I had looked at my cousins' bosoms.

Ah, even so, this faintly disgraceful memory now seems like a distant shaft of sunlight in a life of dark and threatening cloud.

No sooner did we shamble home to Mount Street than we seemed to be walking back again for Christmas Day, roast goose and plum pudding. I do not think anyone reached the Christmas Morning Service.

Because the Christmas Season was the most lucrative of the year at the Bell, our big family party was held on Twelfth Night, when New Year had come and gone and the world was more or less back to normality. It took place at Mount Street because by then all who lived and worked at the Bell were sick of the sight of the place. Of course it filled the little house behind the shop to overflowing, but somehow this guaranteed the jollity of the occasion.

I was still accepted as the (now rich) layabout at home. An extension really of being on leave between ships. If I thought about it, which I often did, I could have pinched myself in case my solvency was but a dream. It was barely two months old.

Being around the house I was content to while away the time 'making myself useful', which is what everyone else called it. So I ran errands - well, condescended to stroll rather - for this and that. Beat eggs. Stirred the cake mixture. Tried my hand at making the marzipan figures to go on top. I noted again the beginnings of interest and a strange satisfaction with this elementary cooking. I suppose then it seemed to have no purpose and led nowhere. A rich young man was hardly likely to embark on a career as a cook. Little thought I then that it would be the saving of me.

The party drew near and one morning I was lounging in the kitchen with a newspaper, warming my shins near the range, while Judy who had come round to help was cutting out pastry for mince pies.

She spoke above the small sounds her work was making. She said, "Tommy, I know how we can do it, I think..."

"Do what?" I asked unguardedly.

"Oh, you know. It."

"What It?" I said, still without thought.

"Tommy, stop it. You are being stupid on purpose. You know very well what I want to do."

I felt a knot grow in my stomach. She had on a dark dress with a starched, frilled apron and she was not wearing a cap so my eye was taken by her glossy hair on her bent head. In fact she looked beautiful, like a young woman from one of those paintings the Dutch used to do.

"Judy," I said. "I still find it an absolutely revolting idea. I can't bear the thought of you wearing trousers. You look so pretty today and the notion of you deliberately throwing that away to put on men's trousers - it's really indecent."

She lifted her head and scowled at me. "You don't think it's indecent when I lift up my dress and you look at my pantaloons. They are just cotton trousers really. Why is that different?"

"I don't know why it is, but it is. It's just... it's just that your pantaloons and your petticoats are you. Pretty and female. You. And trousers are not you. I just hate it."

"Oh, don't be such a spoilsport, Tommy. I only want to wear them for a minute. I just want once to be able to dash round the house and not feel my clothes catching on every drawer knob and table leg. Oh, do come on, Tommy. Let me. Please."

She tried guile. She drew the top of her apron over her head, un-knotted her neckerchief and leaned over me.

"Look, Tommy. Look at my titties. Do not they look nice now my stays push them up?"

I looked and the sight shook me like a gust of storm wind. You may think it strange if you like, that I was so moved by those little, white, wobbly, raspberry-tipped breasts, but if I could have them again I would not exchange them for all the black watermelons from the whole Caribbean. Have them? I never had them.

"Please, Tommy. Please," said she, wheedling.

I managed to look away and said nothing. Then she was really angry. A woman scorned for the first time, maybe?

"If you will not listen, Tommy, I swear I will never, ever lift up my dress for you again. And I'll be a proper young lady and I'll tell your ma if I even catch you looking at my ankle. I'll scream. I will!"

In a world of black, brown, yellow and willing women, the seafarer had come home willingly to the servitude of this skinny little thing. Her threat was like a gust of Arctic cold and you standing there in your shirt. Of course I gave in. The only place in the world worth having then was near her.

The plan, such as it was, revolved around the Twelfth Night party games and forfeits.

I do not know how far away in time you may be, reader. A party now includes firstly eating especially enticing foods, secondly alcoholic drinks; and thirdly, entertainment. This latter ranges from conversation, through performance - when, for example, persons may sing songs or play upon the pianoforte - into playing games that in the cold light of day seem ridiculous but under the influence of wine are perceived as pleasurable. Games like 'The Mad Maharajah', who must not be given food with any name that contains a certain prohibited letter; or team games such as a 'Mime of Information'; or types of Charades. I am not instructing you on our social habits so I will leave it there. The thing - or sting in the tail of it - is Forfeits. Comic penalties are imposed on the loser or detected cheat, for the entertainment of the company. For instance, the subject of attention must at least attempt to submit to be tickled by everyone. Or repeat the words 'iced ink' twenty times in rapid succession and so on.

"What about them?" I said as she excitedly rattled through her memories of such things.

There was a long pause and then she launched into her Great Idea.

"Last year, while you were away, I went to my friend Emily's party and there were games with forfeits. (I knew the girl Millie. She was pleasant enough, but the father was a bookie.)

"And?"

"You had to dress up in men's clothes if you were a female, and ladies' clothes if you were a man. Then you had to go next door and ask the time. It was all right. They knew somebody strange might be coming."

The light dawned on me. In fact, it rapidly became as bright as day. Here indeed might be Judy's opportunity. My heart sank. She wanted to do something that was disgusting to me. But there was that gold at the foot of the rainbow. She had promised - very well, suggested - that I might see her undress and indeed assist her. And I would see her body below the waist without the least trace of concealment.

I do not expect you to understand. This was a unique young woman in her passions - in the country, nay all Europe.

"Ma will never have it," I said. She smiled a smile for herself only.

"I can get round her."

"And how are you going to be sure you get that forfeit?" I asked. "You have to draw them out of a hat, I seem to remember."

"I shall cheat," said she serenely. "And before you ask, don't ask! Oh, Tommy, you are a lovely boy. Would you like to see my bottom? I'll do it properly, over the chair with my clothes all up over my back and you can look and look."

With hindsight, I think we were both as addicted to it as if we were addicted to laudanum. Or perhaps it was only me. No, it was not. So, I think all people at some time must have contemplated dangerous waters in actuality, imagination or dream. This was the upland stream in summer, scarcely flowing amidst the tussocks of grass and banks of damp moss. Now, come December, it is a yellow-foamed, roaring torrent, still not very wide, but how deep and how strong? Yet you have to wade in to cross.

In a resigned way because life was out of control, I saw the days flow past to the party. I watched in faint amazement as an initially scandalised Ma was beguiled. I forgot that she probably visualised Pa in skirt and bonnet navigating a few feet of Mount Street. I heard Mrs Coulson next door give a roar of laughter as Judy explained. I remember Rachel becoming very prim and busy as the matter was progressed, not meeting my eye.

"But what of the upper half of you?" I argued sourly with Judy. "You might have on my trousers but you can't go out in your camisole." I was surprised to observe that she shuddered at the thought and found it pleasing that she retained a sense of modesty toward the rest of society, but it was also clear she had anticipated it

"One of your shirts. A good big one," she replied.

Oh, she had an answer to everything. She had planned it all. My parents' bedroom was to become the official changing room, with various garments of various sizes laid out ready. But it was my room that was really to witness her transformation.

The evening and the hour came. Several of the ladies had been unable to resist dressing in their crinolines and the little rooms seemed to be full of skirts. We must have a bigger house. They must have a bigger house.

They had roasted chestnuts from the kitchen range. There was mulled wine and whisky punch to drink. There was a multitude of small delicious things on plates to eat. The volume of conversation increased until you had to raise your voice to be heard, after which it increased again and was punctuated with laughter. My new fancy waistcoat began to feel superfluous and it was with relief I saw Pa take off his coat. We were not so grand then. As the spirits ascended to my brain, I began to enjoy myself. Early on, I had been low with the fear that we should be discovered. Now it seemed rather a lark that I might witness my dear cousin, my wicked darling, disrobe with all these unknowing people close by.

So after there was singing to put everybody in good heart, then began the silly party games with cries and clapping for the winners and moans and groans and the occasional good humoured boo for the losers. There were bursts of laughter, more raucous now, as the forfeiters made asses of themselves.

It was time to ostentatiously button up my waistcoat and replace my coat, announcing that I must just take a turn in the street for a breath of air, but not before catching Judy's eye.

It took but a moment to slam the front door when the little hall was empty for a moment and then sneak wildly and would-be quietly upstairs, trying not even to breathe. Having gained my bedroom, I waited. A brand new pair of my trousers, my favourite fawn and check, lay waiting across the eiderdown with a set of scarlet braces. Beside them lay a fancy shirt. I could not bear that Judy's adored crotch should rest upon anything not entirely fresh and pristine and I relished the thought that soon I might put them on myself with a trace of her sweetness intimate with me. How much better to have thrown her down on my bed on her back than brewed up this madness for myself.

I listened intently to the hubbub below. "Ohhhhh," they all went suddenly. Then I heard high above them, Judy's voice followed by a male voice, probably Pa, shouting, "Hoist with her own petard. Hoist with her own petard." Then there were light, running steps up the stairs and to my door. There she was, her pale face flushed with more excitement than seemed called for, so I thought.

"I told you so. I told you so. Here I am" she cried and gave me a real kiss on the lips, which I thought a mite strange with what we now had in hand. I have never forgotten it, nevertheless.

She spun round and turned the key in the door. "Quick. Quick," she said, ringlets swinging and chin on her shoulders as with arms behind her she fumbled with the back of her dress. It was a beautiful dress, silk, a secret present for the moment, from me, because we thought the matrons would disapprove if they were given earlier notice. My fingers were as handy as sausages with the hook-and-eyes as it gaped over her white shoulders, and worse as I reached her underwear, for it made them tremble. She jigged up and down with impatience under my hands and I was beginning to notice that I did not like the hurry, when we heard other steps on the stairs and we froze. The footsteps crossed the landing. We heard a door open and then a voice, which called in puzzlement, "Judy?"

"Oh my God, it's my sister. It's Rachel," whispered Judy almost under her breath. "What'll we do? She'll come here next. You must hide."

"Hide? Where?"

"Oh, I don't know. Behind the curtains? No. The wardrobe? No. Under the bed. Quick! Quick!"

And there was I, diving under my own bed like a frightened rabbit through a hole in a hedge. Not a second too soon. More footsteps and the doorknob rattled.

"Judy? Where are you? Are you in there?"

"Yes, Rachel. I'm just coming." She turned the key in the lock again and the door creaked open.

"Judy? What are you doing in here? This is Tommy's room, isn't it? I thought the clothes for the forfeits were in the big bedroom."

"He wanted me to have some nicer ones. If the forfeit happened to me, of course."

"Why didn't he put them with the others?"

"He didn't want to get them muddled up, I suppose."

A pause. Then: "Where is Tommy?" Could that be suspicion creeping into Rachels' voice?

"I don't know. Perhaps he went to the Necessary. Oh, I know. He wanted some fresh air and went outside for a walk. Quick, Rachel, give me a hand to get out of this dress. I can't reach properly."

"You've done pretty well. That's why I came up. It's a lovely dress. But I knew you would have a job getting out of it."

It was cramped under that bed. I was lying on my side and the floor was biting into my hipbone. Judy's feet were right before my nose. I tried to ease my position.

Clang.

Oh God, it was the accursed chamber pot. I think it was only somebody as keyed up as I was, who would have noticed the tiny pause while Judy's mind worked.

"Sorry," she said.

Thus I lay there as imprisoned as in hell with the tortures of the damned being applied. The quick sounds of female fingers in fabric. The dress billowing in front of my nose as it came down and was whisked away. Oh, a white silk petticoat with lace hem, which fell round her feet, and another and another one, both cotton with *broderie anglaise*. Then, for a second, just the little lace-trimmed legs of my desired's pantaloons. She had worn her best petticoats because of me, I was sure. She was not a one to short change.

"Sorry," she had said. Not as much as I!

Chapter 9

Making regular observations from a bar stool in the Bell over that month of Christmas 1861, I detected a slow change in patronage from what one might have expected in an obscure inn on the edge of a district of poor reputation in downtown Southampton. The sailors from the Nashville were part of it, but not so exotic once one became used to their uniform because they were mostly British or Irish. No, there were others. Gentlemen (or so they seemed) would come into the public bar, and let their eyes sweep over its inhabitants in the manner of seeking a person. Then they might buy nothing at all, or perhaps a measure of spirits, drink and leave. One or two would linger, affable enough if one engaged them in conversation, unless one expected anything more than the most mundane of small talk. Sometimes they were obviously Englishmen, at others there would be a ghost of an American accent and foreign-cut tailoring, and sometimes there was the full Southern drawl. Often, they did not engage the eye when chatting, in a way that could be annoying and almost enough to make one say or do something sufficiently outrageous to concentrate their attention, especially if drink was within. Otherwise, no matter what they said, they likewise watched the world visible in the reflection of a barroom mirror.

Occasionally, it was clear I was talking to a Confederate officer, ashore in plain clothes, for whatever reason. It was a Lieutenant Bennett usually. And, yes, there was a regular one. That man. Oh yes, he must make his entrance. A

Paymaster or Assistant Paymaster I thought; something of the kind. He had a beer-belly and was swarthy. Not a 'touch of the tar-brush', you understand, but a Levantine air and one of those chins that never look clean-shaved. And yet he had plump, white fingers. I would feel faint surprise when I considered his temporary lodging, because he seemed to me the type who would take good care to keep a hundred miles between him and the sea and shot and shell.

I was young, the world was interesting, and if the world in miniature in the pub failed to entertain me, then my attention went again to the Belles of the Bell, as was but natural. Now I guess that I was rubbing shoulders with agents of who knows what, the Union, our Government? Men come on business, who preferred not to be seen climbing the *Nashville's* gangway? There was a spice to life in the Bell back then.

You see, the *Nashville* had been lying there for the best part of six weeks. She went into one of the dry docks and came out again with her bottom strakes a little better suited to the Atlantic. Rumours abounded that she had taken on board a consignment of Enfield rifles, and for such a thing to be allowed it seemed to us that money must have changed hands somewhere, not including their price.

But what was she waiting for? It had been made plain to Captain Pegram that the structural alterations and rearming he desired would never be allowed by Britain as a neutral power. But the repercussions of the abduction of Mason and Slidell, the Confederate diplomats, from our old mail packet *Trent* continued to rumble and we were seeing the British preparations for war with our own eyes. We thought that was what Pegram was waiting for. Why take a chance on the Atlantic - at the worst time of the year - and the US Navy's blockade, when patience might provide almost an escort home by the Royal Navy?

That lasted until after Christmas, when the United States Government released the two Confederates, and almost as soon as we had digested that news (the first transatlantic cable had failed), they were actually passing through the town when the Royal Mail's *La Plata* docked. And still the *Nashville* stayed in her berth.

Judy was very inclined to tease me in secret about the humiliating debacle I endured under the bed during the Twelfth Night party. Even when she was on duty as a barmaid, at times there was a look in her eye and a smile not far away from her lips that made me sure she was thinking about it again. And laughing at me... And yet what I had been participating in was so private and so forbidden that, if word of it escaped, it might have brought the roofs of Mount Street and the Bell crashing about our ears, and both of us put outdoors. Or so it seemed to me then. Now I realise that when the immediate dust had settled, the families' actions were likely to have been to bring about the situation so desired then. They would have thought it better to marry than to burn; marry before something more shameful befell.

On January 11, Roderick arrived via the shop in Mount Street, almost indecently early during breakfast and in a state of high excitement.

"Have ye no heard?" he said.

"Heard what?" said I through a last mouthful of bacon.

"Ye cannot have heard, that's clear. How can it be that I away in a little place like Shirley get the news, and you sitting here downtown don't know?"

"Know what?" I said, wiping the grease off my mouth. "Will you take some coffee?"

"That there's a bluidy great Yankee warship anchored in the river not far from the Point. She's called the *USS Tuscarora*, they say. I suppose the name is after one of their Red Indian tribes or sumthin'".

She was not 'bluidy' because she was painted a drab grey. So strange for a warship. She was not great either, not in the sense of the black-and-white wall of a British ship of the line, because she was only a steam, barque-rigged sloop. Not unlike the *Saucy Jack* of recent memory. But the sea and the sky dwarf all Man's works when put against them. Even through a telescope from the Platform she looked small down there off the salt marshes of the Point, which obscured the lower part of the hull. But you could see a blob of bright colour blowing on her gaff - 'Old Glory' was marching once again into our lives. No one seemed to know exactly how long she had been there, but whereas most ships arriving in the port thankfully drew their fires, smudges of smoke from her funnel showed she was maintaining steam. She was anchored on the port side of the Itchen fairway and, if she chose, there would be no coming or going from our Docks! Tweedledum had found Tweedledee!

Excitement was compounded when ferries coming back from Cowes in the dawn next morning reported that one of our steam frigates, *HMS Dauntless*, had quietly come up Southampton Water under the cover of darkness and was now keeping a watchful eye on matters from just above the Royal Military Hospital at Netley. In the event, the eye was too far off and insufficient.

The day after, I had come yawning down to breakfast at not too outrageous an hour, say at a quarter to nine, when, of all people, Pa came hurrying in, his eyes positively bulging with news.

"I've just had that Mrs Franklin in the shop," he said. "You know, Mr Hodges' housekeeper." I must have looked blank because he continued, "Mr Philip Hodges, the Dock Superintendent. Oh never mind, your mother would know who I mean. And Mrs Franklin says there was some sort of trouble in the docks last night."

"Oh come on, Pa," I said. "There's always trouble in the docks at night. The seamen swallow a skinful of bitter beer and then fall off the gangway. Or else they fight or some such thing."

"Ah, and that's where you're wrong, young mister know-all," said Pa, shaking a finger at me. "Mrs Franklin says they was all woken up when the peelers came hammering on the door in the small hours. And it seems they'd apprehended a shore party creeping about close to that rebel ship *Nashville* that's still in there." Ma had come in by now and we both goggled at him.

"Shore party? What sort of shore party," said I.

"What's a shore party?" asked Ma.

"Well, I don't know if you don't know," said Pa. "There was four of them, it appears. Three sailors and an officer. And all of them armed to the teeth. Cutlasses and pistols and all. And they'd got other things. Hempen tow and tinderboxes. And they had cans of lamp oil!"

"You mean… you mean that these were Yankees? From that *Tuscarora*?" said I.

"Yes, of course that's what I mean," said Pa. "What did you think I meant? They reckon they were going to try and burn the *Nashville*."

"Burn that ship? Here? In the docks? But this is England!" said Ma. "They can't do that sort of thing here. They're nothing but foreigners. I've never heard anything so disgraceful in all my born days!"

Of course it made quite a lot of sense when one had digested it. Captain Craven, the Yankee captain, must have known that his arrival would bring the Royal Navy to the scene for the sake of the Neutrality Act. And having seen no men o' war in the Solent or on his way up Southampton Water, he'd made his attempt during the one and only night he thought that he'd got.

He was quite right. By mid-morning there were armed matelots from *HMS Dauntless* patrolling with the coppers round the docks.

The Battle of Southampton Water, eh? That would be something to tell your grandchildren.

Young men and war. Particularly young men who have never seen war, or felt real pain, and who are young enough to know that they are going to live for ever. What could distract them from such excitement but young women?

"Psst." I do not know how else to record young Judy leaning over the bar and whispering breathily into my ear. "Tommy, I want to tell you something. I'll be off duty in a minute or two. When I go, come round and I'll see you in the tap room."

War was fine but it could not give you that tightening feeling low down in the stomach that a young woman could. And I was somehow sure that she was not going to ask me to bring round an extra sack of potatoes tomorrow for Cook. It was as though she was dashed with some undetectable, irresistible perfume.

She called "Goodnight, everybody." She did not do that every night. I counted to a hundred fairly slowly and sneaked through the flap in the bar, closing it behind me and not looking at anyone.

If I wish to remember Judy, most often it is this image that I conjure up. There she is waiting, one shoe peeping out from under her dress while she idly turned it on its heel. To-and-fro, to-and-fro. Her dark dress and white apron. And again her big, white, frilled cap upon her dark hair surrounding that pale, oval face. Staring into nothing. Waiting. Waiting for me? Waiting. Not what you anticipated, dear reader? No, this is peace and warmth. Not one of those fevered images of the vice we were both addicted to like laudanum. Then, as you know, Judith would disarrange her clothes and indecently expose her body in a kind of silent rage at the world. And because of who she was, I thought I could not ease her as Pretty Polly and her ilk had eased me. No, nowadays and for years before, summoning up those images is to call the bright flames of hell and to taste the ashes for ever and ever. And it is not fair to Rachel.

I stepped quietly up to Judy but a little behind her. She must have heard me. I put my hands round her waist, spread my fingers and pressed them a little against her stomach. I took a chance. Sometimes she did not like me to do that but this time she leaned back against me. I kissed her neck and somehow she turned her head and kissed my cheek. It seemed a long, loving moment, the end of which, well...

She squirmed away and then turned to face me. "Tommy," she said quite conversationally. "Tommy, I am sorry for what happened to you at the party and I am sorry if it made me laugh. It was only a little bit." She paused. "Tommy, I want to make it up to you. I'll take off my dress while you're looking, and I know how we can do it. You'd like that, would you not?"

My thoughts moved like lightning. "Shall I bring some trousers?" I asked carefully.

She caught my eye. "So that I strip off my petticoats too?" I had thought that I was carefully keeping my features immobile. "So that *you* may strip off my petticoats. Yes. Thank you, Tommy. I would like to wear the trousers again for a little while although I know you do not like it very much. They make me feel so free." I do not know why her voice sounded a little bitter.

Thus the arrangements were made. I cannot remember the exact details of it. Uncle Joby would be out visiting the brewery. Rachel had an invitation. It was Cook's afternoon off. It was tomorrow. Thinking of it, I remember I would rather it had been a few days off. Next week, perhaps. Not tomorrow. Tomorrow was somehow a swollen rivulet after rain, racing towards a culvert. No time to prepare myself for the earth-tremor of seeing my cousin without dress or underskirts again. All the fantasies of febrile, youthful years suddenly real and arriving. Tomorrow! I remember I tried to swallow and nearly choked.

I was sure I should not sleep, but I did and awoke feeling very well. I had an indolent morning, took dinner with my parents and when the hour approached I left for the Bell. All the way there I was sure people were glancing at me as they passed because they knew my secret and what was in my smaller grip and what it was for.

The Bell seemed deserted when I arrived, in an unprecedented way for a public house. The door opened easily as ever but the bars were uncannily empty. I would describe it for you now as like something I read ten or eleven years ago of how the Prussians marched through Paris. All the great streets and squares of the French capital were deserted, the citizens penned safely far away by their own army. So the passage and the stairs and the parlour of the Bell were empty, although I could hear the sound of washing up somewhere in the distance. So were the stairs to the bedrooms. I paused on the landing and listened: and really, I heard nothing. It seemed unwise to call out. The door of the sisters' bedroom was ajar. Ridiculously, I tiptoed over to it but could see little through the crack. Fearing some unpleasant surprise, I pushed it open.

Judy was sitting on her bed. She had even put on the same green silk dress as she had worn to the party, but she wore no shawl or kerchief and her white shoulders were bare almost... almost as if for the axe. Otherwise, she looked such a model of the demure young girl of our time in the middle of the century with her glossy ringlets, and hands folded decorously in her lap. Although, like shawl or kerchief, she wore no lace mittens as she sometimes did. It flashed through my mind that she had kept her fingers free for the fiddly work with hook-and-eyes and buttons. And her shoulders? Did she expect that I would ask her to uncover her bosom? Or was it to misjudge in her such cold-blooded preparations. Women can be surprisingly matter-of-fact at such times and it did not take long for Judith the demure to become Judy of the glittering eye and hectic flush as she performed the unmentionable. Even a little keg of gunpowder could have uncontrollable consequences.

She smiled a wisp of a smile to greet me but quickly turned her gaze upon the grip.

"Those are my trousers?" she asked. Her trousers indeed!

"If you put them on, you shall have them. I will give them to you," I heard myself saying. Oh, my wonderful fawn and check trousers. But she smiled rather a sad smile.

"And what shall I say if my sister finds them? Any explanation will be worse than the truth," she said.

I said, "Why not tell the truth, but not the whole truth? You could say you wanted to try them on and I left them for you."

She laughed then and shook her head. "Can you imagine the lecture I might get on modesty and womanliness? I don't think so."

A period of silence and growing tension came upon us. Judy broke it.

"Before I do it… Before I begin...before *we* begin. Would you like me to lift my skirts first?" she said brightly, as if she were inquiring whether I would like another cup of tea.

God knows, as you do, God help me, that I loved to watch her raise her skirts: the billowing fabrics, the rustling materials and her hands and fingers busy with female work that was never intended for the eyes of men. Except me, I believed. Perhaps she yearned after our own, special normality.

But, "No, thank you. I must teach myself to wait," I found myself replying in the same spirit. It felt as if it would be greedy under the circumstances. "But I would adore a glimpse of your titties. If it were not too much trouble, of course."

"But when my dress is off, you... Oh, very well. If that is what you would like."

She stood and then came close to me. She averted her eyes, then pulled the front of her dress a little from her chest and I bent my head and looked.

There they were, the white, white swellings of her little breasts. I looked and looked and, maybe, it might have been that I saw her nipples harden. But she giggled with that sound in the nose, much more attractive to hear than to describe, took her hands from her dress and turned round. I contemplated her back. She waited a moment and then turned her head.

"If I had a lady's maid, as I will one day when I am a real lady, I would expect that she'd start to get all those little hooks and eyes undone," she said over her shoulder.

She made it sound so normal and welcome, as if she undressed to please me at least three times weekly. I became overwhelmed by the gift she was bringing me. So I clasped her in my arms and pushed my nose in amongst her ringlets. Instantly I felt I was in the wrong. That I had infringed this strange dichotomy we had. That the things of our bodies were separate from love and kinship, company and society. But she did not chide me for my confusion as she sometimes did, refusing me a kiss while she was uncovered, or sweeping my hands from her bosom if she did kiss. She merely waited quietly, unresponsively, and then I became aware that she was reaching behind herself to unfasten the top of the dress. My great clumsy fingers followed where she had led and so I found the top of her camisole with thin blue ribbon worked into it, and her stays and laces felt beneath.

"Oh Judy," said I foolishly. "However would we do you up again if we unlaced this and then heard someone coming?"

She considered this calmly whilst again continuing to assist me unfastening.

"Push everything under the bed where you were," she said succinctly. "I don't need them. I only wear them to keep all these old women quiet. And so that you will not be disappointed to see a young English lady in her underclothes without there being everything there. And I said I would take off my dress and my petticoats. Not appear to you in a... in a state of nature!"

I put my arms round her again and we both of us laughed out loud at our wickedness. And just above the swell of her posterior, which I have to say frequently brushed against me, we came to the last of the fastenings.

"What now?" I asked, with difficulty.

"I must take my dress off or it will be creased for all eternity," she said in a small voice.

Part of me longed to watch her disrobe; this dream, this fantasy of the crawling years of adolescence. Yet part of me was reluctant to break this sweet period of intimacy, with Judy in my arms with her unfastened dress and her bottom pressing through it against me. I could feel its warmth by now, through all our clothes.

"Shall you let me see you undress when we are married?"

She sighed. "As a married woman, should I have any option? But should not my dignity as a married lady mean that you wait downstairs until I am ready?"

"No!" I said. "Not even on Sundays."

She laughed and twisted away. "Now you must go and sit on my bed. And sit on your hands," she commanded.

"Oh... Judy!" I complained.

"Yes! Tommy, Tommy, you bad boy. All this long time we had the rule, 'if you can see you mustn't touch'. And I asked you if you wanted me to pull up my skirt first so that you could put your hand up and touch me. And you didn't. Now you can just sit and look. Promise?"

I sighed a big mock sigh and promised. Also I thought that a rule that allowed me to feel under a lady's skirts when those skirts were gathered together upon her hips, but not when she wore no skirts at all, should not be all that hard to break.

"Tommy, I'm going to do it now. I must. We have not got all day. Are you ready? I'm going to do it now."

She was steeling herself for the act, I could see. How strange it was that it should remain such a mountain to take off her clothes in the gaze of a man, a man she had known all her life - and that she should have known all the rest of her life - and who knew well the most intimate parts of her person. It must have been a reflection of the gulf between childhood and the adult state, a gulf we were hardly aware of.

"Go on, then," I said quite forcibly, for my body was responding to the idea and actuality before me in a fashion that was almost pain. And she did. One moment, fastened or not, the green silk covered her. The next she had pushed it down to her waist and, quickly, with one or two more deft pushes, it billowed and was on the floor, and she was stepping away out of it. And there she was indeed, all white in shift and stays and camisole over it and her petticoats down to her ankles, and hardly a square inch or two more in the light except that her arms now were bare. She looked at me sidelong without a blink and without a smile. Emotions were cascading over my being like a Channel sea on a glittering sunny day.

Somehow I managed to say, "Oh, Judy... Judy. You are... you are... beautiful. Magnificent!"

She looked at me with suspicion. "Nonsense, Tommy," she said. "I am in my underclothes and my underclothes are not pretty. They are not meant to be looked upon. They are there simply to keep me warm and keep me decent... when you let me! I've taken off the beautiful dress you gave me and here I am in what I wear every day and you say I'm beautiful and magnificent?"

I groped about my mind for words. On the one hand I was almost choking with desire for her. On the other, I was searching for words to match feelings that were the familiar province of no man.

"In some way they take a glow of you underneath them," I managed. "Your chemise and stays and shift from your darling titties. And your petticoats and pantaloons from your beautiful, beautiful, invisible legs."

She seized upon this at once. "How do you know my legs are beautiful? You've never seen them. I have never shown them to you."

I seemed to recognise that note of brittle excitement creeping into her voice. It was something I recognised there when she spoke and was about to show some secret part of her. Judy's carnal excitement.

"I'll never show you my legs. Never!" she asserted. But in my wickedness I thought, *Oh yes you will!* At any rate she came a step or two nearer.

"Please let me see your titties," I pleaded.

"You have seen them today already," she argued, but she tugged at the neck of her clothes and there they were, pushed up, as she said, by her stays and more naked than they had ever been. The image will still come in the night and drive away sleep entirely. They were milk white and not very big at all, but round and with thrusting strawberry nipples. I knew they were there but they were ever a delicious shock to see again. So uncharacteristic of the public life of my lady, and so in keeping with her private self. I remember a little blue vein that showed through the skin on her left one. I could not resist from palming them. She seized my wrists hard but then her grip softened and in the end she did but hold me with the tips of her fingers. This she always did, no matter where about her person my liberties had been allowed, so that Judy too might enjoy, but pluck me away if pleasure threatened to overwhelm her.

"Now, now," she said quite gently. "What ever became of not touching what you are allowed to see?"

She did not push me off but bent forward a little more and then I felt her fingers busy at her waist. Perhaps this was the moment that the separate portions of her nature began to blend together into the woman, alas for me. I knew what she was doing but I asked anyway, to make her say the rude, forbidden words.

"I'm taking off my petticoat," she whispered, and I felt it suddenly slip down from her.

"You said I might do that," said I.

"Oh Tommy, I'm sure I never did," said she, lying; but she helped me find the right bow in the right tape and, the second one, it too finished up around her feet on the bedroom floor. I reconnoitred a little and had a surprise. "But this is your silk petticoat," I said, basing this on an occasional pleasant acquaintanceship on Sundays. "And isn't it supposed to be the top one over the others?"

"You know much too much about ladies' underclothes," whispered Judy. "Do you mind so very much? Isn't it a little bit like the wine at Cana?"

Did I mind? I minded not at all. It drove me to gathering up the warm, slippery stuff of it and driving my hand up to her crotch. She was in pantaloons. I do not remember if I was in anyway disappointed that she had not chosen pantalettes or drawers for this encounter. Perhaps it was too much even for Judy, looking in her wardrobe in the cold to choose a garment that, after she discarded the last petticoat, would leave nothing between herself and me. Somehow she knew. She leaned against me and I quite roughly palmed her mons and thrust deeply within. And thrust and thrust until her pants became damp and warm like I knew from many a time before with the girl. I went then to undo the tapes of the petticoat at her little waist when she gave a sigh and began to tremulously collapse as if her legs would no longer carry her. I had noticed she had begun to jerk or shudder momentarily whenever my knuckles or fingers even brushed against her. This I knew could not be hysterics or the vapours, for she made no other sound nor struggled. She sank down as if she could do nothing of her own volition, not on the bed but onto a sheepskin that served there as a bedside mat. I caught her in time and eased her down so that she did not fall. Her eyes were closed but the lids trembled as though at any moment she might open them, and her lips moved although I could hear nothing from them. Her cheeks, rather than pallid, as indeed were their wont, had taken on a striking rosy flush, which faded, then returned before my eyes and indeed spread down over her neck and bosom before fading again.

I do not know to this day whether I made a decision that, cousin or not, affianced or not, virgin full of magic or not, I... we... could go on no further in this way. Or whether it was nothing more than a young male swept away by the sight and scent and touch of a young female.

I suppose I was wicked to assume that she still possessed the faculty of refusal. When I laid hands on the last of her underskirts she made no demurral so I raised it and let it fall over her upper body. And there she was and my eyes devoured her. I saw a little knot of pink ribbon at her waist and knew that it was not the waistband of the petticoat and I unfastened it. I pulled down her pantaloons and felt shamed to recognise they smelled of lavender. Oh, her legs were exquisite to me. So slim and well formed in calf and ankle, her upper thighs were curved and strong. Quite unexpected.

I had never in all the years seen her naked legs. Only a minute or two ago she had said I never would. Now I sweated at the thought of them clasping the small of my back.

She tossed her head from side to side and gave a little moan as she felt her pantaloons slide down and go, but she said nothing and did not open her eyes. She wore black stockings with a white, lace-trimmed garter for each. With her petticoat spread out around, suddenly I saw her as the great white opium poppy with its white petals and black centre. Her body hair down there was so dark, and in that second I thought the neatness of her mons and her 'Jade Gate' were quite adorable. A secret to be cherished for ever.

I kicked off my shoes and was just taking down my breeches and actually in the act of laying myself upon her when it happened. I do not know what it was. Something touched me, whether it was her body, or my clothes, or her hand, I know not, but it was upon my rigid manhood. Like an over-tuned violin string, it broke. Oh Lord God, I 'shot the bishop'. An endless, childhood decade of lust, love and longing, dreams and dreams come true was too much for it and me. Oh God, you Bastard.

Have you seen a dead man floating head down with his face in the sea? I have. So I lay upon Judith, uselessly spent, sodden with shame and degradation. She, poor sleeping princess, awaking from her trance, was first afraid that I was ill, then perplexed and finally disgusted.

"Tommy," she demanded. "What is that wetness on my petticoat?" Then: "Tommy, did you make that mess on my petticoat? And at last: "Ugh! You are absolutely, absolutely disgusting. I never thought a young man could do anything so revolting. It's my best one. What am I going to do now? How am I going to wash it without somebody asking what I was doing? Where can I hide it away until Monday? But I must rinse it through first. Tommy, you are never, never,

never to do anything like that ever, ever again or I won't speak to you. Ever!"

So... I was one of the wealthiest young men in the town and there I sat on the floor in disgrace and disarray, and I was the poorest because none of it counted. And she was still a damn virgin. So I was still unable to explain. God won the jackpot again.

So, good, patient, distant reader, if you have read this far in the hope of a first hand account of a Battle of Southampton, here is the story of the loser. The victor is dead.

Chapter 10

I presume, my friend removed in time, that you are still patiently or impatiently awaiting scenes of battle. Masts must reel and groan as they are shot through. Spars, great wooden blocks and cordage, tons of them, shall fall out of the sky onto shouting, screaming men. Cannon must bellow - and I can assure you that the reports make the ears ring, and the surge backward of the gun from the recoil is so sudden and savage as to stop the bravest in his tracks when he first sees it. All this you shall have, if you will bear with the slowness of our time, surely, compared with yours.

But our battle of Southampton was more amateur and spontaneous and its date for the newspapers, if not for the history books, was 21 January 1862. Thursday.

The *Tuscarora* had been crouched beside the mouse hole for twelve days by then. There had been polite, social scratchings behind the ears and polite elevations of back and tail in response. There had been warning political admonitions, which had been heard with a cocked ear but never a deviated eye. Not for a moment.

The apprehension of the shore party in the vicinity of the *Nashville's* bow was apparently to be overlooked. Captain Craven called officially upon the commanding officer of *HMS Dauntless* and took wine. Captain Craven called upon the Mayor and the Mayor accepted an invitation to inspect the *Tuscarora*. Captain Craven proposed firing a salute in appreciation and memory of the deceased Prince Consort. This was declined because of the stated wishes of the Queen.

We all thought how disappointed Craven must have been not to be able to make it essential that the ship's company of the *Nashville* considered their position to the measured sound of gunfire and its rolling echoes from close at hand.

How the social engagements must have galled Captain Pegram, but the position of a representative of a collection of States in revolt against their national government was perhaps beyond the social pale. The *Nashville,* for all her immaculate naval spit and polish, had been called 'privateer' and even 'pirate.' Pegram could only console himself with attending and returning invitations to private hospitality, of which there were not a few. There was sympathy for the South; the traditional English sympathy for the underdog and the way the Southerners looked on themselves as Cavaliers assailed by Roundheads. And then, of course there was the business of cotton.

The cat occasionally tried the old stratagem of wandering away feigning boredom. *Tuscarora* up anchored and dropped down Southampton Water, to anchor again near Calshot Castle. Sometimes she would actually go as far down the Solent as Yarmouth. She must have been hoping to tempt Pegram into making a dash for it out through Spithead. I have often wondered how whoever it was left to watch the *Nashville* was to get a message to *Tuscarora* if the Confederate vessel showed any sign of getting under way.

However, the mouse, big though she seemed, knew she was still a mouse with only her pair of little six-pounders, and would not budge. And before long, just off the Point, *Tuscarora* was back at the hole.

I confess that much of this part of the account is culled from newspapers and rumours circulating around the town; some confirmed later, some not. It was January with its cold rains, its sleet and its short, gloomy days. If you went to the end of the Royal Pier, for most of the time the Yankee war steamer was in her place. If not, the fishermen and Isle of

Wight ferrymen knew where she was. You became used to the situation. However, even though people went about their business, interest remained high. There was always the prospect of fighting a few hundred yards from the town, with large guns and shot and shell going who knows where. Or a wreck sealing off the port by going down in the fairway. Of course interest remained high. It was indeed difficult for some to understand why the Government did nothing more, apparently, than leave a frigate loitering at the scene, although there were rumours of activity at the forts at Calshot at the entrance to Southampton Water and Hurst Castle where the Solent finished near the Needles rocks on the westernmost point of the Isle of Wight. I made the ferry trip to Cowes twice to see what might be going on, only to witness *HMS Dauntless* and the *USS Tuscarora*, with their hands going about their daily routine of cleaning, painting and running repairs; whilst the *Nashville*, discerned if at all, was a funnel and masts amid funnels and masts up behind the big chimney of the dock pumping station. The rest of the journey consisted of being hunched under greatcoat, scarf and dripping hat brim, watching the dismal winter shores and the usual traffic of the port passing by. Recommended only by necessity, believe me!

One point, which might be of interest, was that it emerged that the *Nashville* some few years ago had actually done duty as a mail ship, running between New York, Le Havre and here a few times. This might explain why she had appeared dimly familiar to me when first I set eyes upon her from our old ship *Trent* last November.

So the stalemate continued. Thursday evening is usually quiet in the pub trade. By that time of the week many of the regulars of the Bell were contemplating pawnbroker rather than pint. Friday was payday but Friday was tomorrow. I had intended to stay home but I had finished the newspapers; Mr Dickens' and even the town's darling Miss Austens' books temporarily lost their charms and I was risking a night of poor sleep by dozing before the parlour fire. Before I could be overcome, I dragged on outdoor clothes and took the short walk to the Bell. It was about half-past eight. Rachel was on duty as barmaid and was single-handed. Thursday evenings were quiet.

There were a couple of regulars with pints before them, occasionally puffing their pipes and staring at nothing, and the usual sailors from the *Nashville* in a corner, noisily playing cribbage and dominoes. All lower deck.

Rachels' face brightened when she saw me, and she came to converse a little and to serve me. I took a sip of brandy and water.

"Are you all well?" I inquired.

"Well enough. Tommy," she replied. "Papa is in the parlour with the paper." We both smiled at that. Uncle Joby was as likely to be beneath the paper as reading it. "Judy says she has a headache and has gone to bed early." Poor Judy. Normally her health was robust enough.

So we spoke of this and that, whilst I thought her a beautiful young woman but pale beside my Judy. However, I thought I detected an element of strain in her expression and demeanour. The first thing that came to mind was that she knew something of the debacle of my attempt to debauch her sister, for I suppose that was what it would be called. But Judy would never tell. We had been uncovering our nakedness to each other for a decade. More than half our lives. The times when little Judy might have run to someone to tell them that wicked Tom had looked up her skirt had somewhat passed. No, something else was troubling Rachel. So I wheedled and persuaded and in the end she told me.

"It is those boys over there. They trouble me, Tommy."

"What? Has one of them been saucy to you?" said I, swelling up with youthful honour and pride.

138

She smiled briefly. "Oh, all of them. All of them," she said. "I'm not such a sobersides. I take it as a compliment. It can be fun to flirt a little. It is because it's fun. It is because I like them. Most of them. It's what they stand for. It's wrong."

"A lot of them stand for the money. They are getting double the going rate. And then there's prize money," said I.

"It is not them: the British, the Irish, the Germans, the Swedes. It is the true Southern boys. They call me ma'am and take off their caps when they talk to me. They tell me about their homes and families and they are such a long way from home. Tommy, what is this war of theirs all about?"

"They say it is about their States right to join the Union if they want and to leave it if they want. To run their own affairs the way they want," I said, but she interrupted me.

"I know that's what they say, Tommy. But they don't say that the affair they want to run their own way is slavery. People should not have to work for other people as though they were beasts of burden. Nobody will say it but that is what their war is all about, isn't it, Tommy?" She was right, of course. I remembered what she'd said when, some considerable time after, old Abe Lincoln got round to saying that 'somehow' slavery was the cause of the war.

About twenty to nine we heard voices outside and the front door opened noisily. It was a double door, of which one had been left bolted by whoever had opened up. It was Thursday, after all. Now a rowdy group of men were pushing through it and the bolt was dragged protesting from its socket across the floor, furrowing the sawdust. The old men with their pipes turned their heads. Rachel stood up on her toes and I narrowed my eyes to see better. More sailors. Sailors who had been drinking somewhere else by the red faced, sweaty look of them. Strangers' faces. And a different kind of sailor. They wore blouses with sailor collars with a star at the corners. My first thought had been that they must be from the *Dauntless* but they did not look right. These were not Jack Tars. Of course! These were from the Federal ship, the *Tuscarora*. When they came closer, indeed the ship's name was written in gold on the black ribbons round their caps. Johnny Reb and Billy Yank were staring at each other across the Public.

I turned to Rachel. I tried to speak urgently but not too loud. "Let me through the flap. Now!" I said. "And run upstairs and get your father just as quick as you can."

To my horror she merely gaped at me. Then at least she pulled the bar flap up.

"For God's sake, Rachel," I hissed at her as I struggled to bolt the bar opening again after me. "Go and get Uncle Job, quickly. Can't you see? That *is* the American Civil War, standing in your pub!"

She wasn't a publican's daughter for nothing. Now that she understood she whisked through the door in an instant, letting it bang to after her. I heard her feet drumming up the stairs and her voice calling urgently as she went. I got my coat off, leaned my elbows on the bar (where one instantly soaked up some spilled beer onto my first bespoke shirt) and put on what I hoped was a genial expression of welcome.

"Now then, gents, come inside if you're coming and put the wood in the hole. It's still January. And what would be your pleasure?"

Some asked for ale, without enthusiasm. Most demanded scotch, without water. Of course there was one who tried for bourbon.

I had a vague notion that if I could safely draw them up to the bar, past the group from the *Nashville* in the corner, then if I could entertain them I might be able to keep them there. There were about a dozen of them. The trouble was that I was single-handed and fast as I could be serving them, it still left a rearguard looking daggers at the Southerners. I heard two pairs of feet clattering down the stairs towards me, much as Wellington heard the approach of the Prussians at Waterloo. Joby appeared in a peculiar mode, bent forward, so that I was the only one to see the substantial cudgel he was concealing under the bar. Rachel had only her white-knuckled fists ready.

It began with loud remarks made by one group, designed for the ears of the other. The name 'Manassas', tossed about by the Southern men with laughter and swaggering, brought about the blackest of looks from the Northerners. I knew it was a battle last July that had turned into a Federal rout, but I don't think Joby realised the inflammatory nature of the name and he did nothing.

"Molasses?" I heard him mutter under his breath. "What's all this fuss over molasses?"

"It's not molasses, Uncle," I whispered as loudly as I could. "It's the battle of Bull Run. The South call it 'Manassas' because it was the nearest town. It is the North call it Bull Run." I saw his expression change. He picked up his stick and gave the bell a hard, single stroke. The noise subsided somewhat.

"Now then, gentlemen. Let's keep the party friendly. You're on neutral ground here, so if you cannot agree then keep quiet about it. Or go!" Job's voice cut through the confused sound. I thought he had done it. The angry buzz went down. People came up to recharge their glasses, avoiding catching the other's eye. I thought we had nipped it in the bud.

Even when I first heard the banjo start up, I remember my first reaction was relief. The tune was one we had all heard before in there. It was a bouncy, cocky little tune. Something about the 'Bonny, blue flag with but a single star.' They were almost singing it under their breath but then I heard the bit about 'for Southern Rights, hurrah' and felt my heart sink. It was like taking a lucifer to lamp oil.

"John Browns' body lies a-mouldering in the grave..."
I'll say this for it; it was a good song. Somebody wrote
some more uplifting words to it and the Yankees called it
The Battle Hymn of the Republic. It was certainly the call
to battle in the Bell.

I felt it coming; it was quite inevitable. The chord on
the banjo. 'Dixie' at full volume with stamping and table
thumping... Looking back, that window-rattling volume of
sound resembled the sea after a storm, beating on a harbour
breakwater. A wave would crash against the wall in white
water and recoil, only to make the sea coming after it into
a tower. So for a moment 'I wish I was in Dixie...' was
on top and then 'His soul goes marching on' overcame it.
Such music inflames men, especially drunks. The spark was
struck at the bar. And of all people it was gentle, serious
Rachel who struck it.

One of those tall, slightly stooping, bony-faced men - a
Yankee - shoved his way to the bar and bought 'hisself' a
'seegar'. Taking a match from the dish on the bar, he lit it,
dragged a lung-full of smoke from it and, full of bravado,
coughed uncontrollably into the face of one of our genuine
Southerner sailors. Now, it was a youngster trying to be big
maybe. But it offended another touchy young man, and the
fat was in the fire. The *Nashville* man wiped his face with
his handkerchief. Then he shouted after the first, who had
turned to return to his seat, something like, "Hey, Yank,
you could surely do with a Southern lesson in manners."
The reply was of the order of, "I don't need no lessons in
manners from any dirty Secessionist." To which the retort
was "Nigger Lover!"

Driven at last by her beliefs and the peaking tension,
Rachel, who had attended Abolitionist meetings occasionally,
suddenly screamed at him "Don't call them that! They hate
it!" and swung her hand at him to slap his face.

I remember that slap from long ago. Unfortunately, it was the face next to the Southern man's that she slapped, who swore, dropped his pint and hit the smoker in the mouth, breaking the cigar, the sparks of which went all over his uniform. It also knocked him backwards onto his fellows, with more spillages and more rage.

Job snatched up his stick and beat a tattoo upon the bell, bawling at the men to desist, which of course they did not. In an instant the drinkers became a mob of red-faced men throwing punches at each other. Deplorable as it was, the situation was not unknown to the Bell. What was unheard of was that the bony Yankee, pushed in the back to regain his feet, as he recovered, had in his hand a pistol! It was not a great big thing like our navy colt revolver. It was small and shiny: a little two shot Derringer for a waistcoat pocket or a reticule. I was paralysed by the sight of it but Job was not and swung his cudgel at it. Whether the man was seriously trying to shoot someone or just frighten them was of no import because it went off before it fell clattering onto the floor. There was a bang that made our ears ring and a bottle of Madeira on the shelf and the mirror behind it flew to pieces and we behind the bar were showered with wine and glass. The smell of Madeira always brings back the scene to this day.

I have read that the explosion of the French flagship *L'Orient*, blowing up during the Battle of the Nile, silenced the cannon for several minutes. The same happened to us and there was a stunned lull for a second or two whilst the customers examined themselves and others for bullet wounds. Then the fighting began again in earnest. Pots and bottles flew. Window glass cascaded. The marble and cast iron tables crashed over, sometimes onto their users who fell with them. The torrent of spilled drink began to challenge the sawdust with puddles.

I looked on in fascinated disgust as Murphy, rated as coalheaver in the Confederate Navy, a man who knew the Southern States intimately as far as a quarter of a mile out from the Charleston waterfront, rammed a brass spittoon down over the head of a flailing little Yank, plucked it off and laid him out with it. Only the young are so hugely entertained by such a sight.

At last I listened to what Uncle Joby was shouting into my ear: "Tommy, go out the back door and get the coppers, quick!"

"I can't leave you here with Rachel on your own. We must throw these blackguards out," I screamed back.

Joby shook his head. "What? You, me and my daughters? We haven't even the potboy. It's too late. We'll barricade ourselves in upstairs as soon as you've gone. You get the constables. Go on. Run!"

I turned about and sped through the door behind the bar and collided full tilt with that man, that gross assistant paymaster from the *Nashville*. In the frenzy of the moment and the unexpected impact, it never occurred to me to ask him what he was doing there, only to yell at him to get out of the way. Nor did I take notice of a flicker of movement on the stairs that I saw out of the corner of my eye. Out into the fresh night air, into the alley beside the pub and into damp, dim-lit French Street.

What now? There were a few hurrying shapes along the pavements, the usual smell of stale fish, and alley cats running about like moving shadows. It was Thursday evening. A couple of the local *filles de joie*, who had been despondently loitering under a gas light conveniently opposite, had now come together in alarm as the uproar from the Bell grew louder and, seeing me rush into the street, scuttled away into the shadows by the church. Not a sign of a policeman, of course.

The best plan seemed to be to get into the High Street and run towards the Bargate where the Police Office was and hope to meet a constable on the way. Before I could act on it, I heard a single bellowing voice making itself heard above the din in the Bell. Suddenly it was like the breaking of a dam. Men ran and fell out of the pub, picked themselves up and began to run helter-skelter down French street. It was dark and they were dishevelled but they were mainly the *Tuscarora's* men. I pressed myself into a dark doorway because I could see hands grasping broken bottles as well as chair legs and so forth. And as they ran after their adversaries and countrymen, the real Southern lads gave a whooping, yelping cry that somehow froze the blood. It was as though they were the Gabriel Hounds, the wild geese crossing the sky on a winter's night. Windows flew up and open along the street and men and women shouted, to hear for the first time in our Old World the famous Rebel Yell from the New.

Pounding feet were soon to be heard coming from the other direction as well. And flashing lanterns seen and blowing whistles heard. Much too late for the bar at the Bell.

The distant shouts and running feet died away and I went back to the bar. A bomb might have gone off inside.

"Don't suppose the insurers will pay," surmised Uncle Joby, sucking hard on his pipe as he looked around. "It's a wreck all right but it ain't a shipwreck. And there's all those items written small at the bottom of the policy that's excluded: insurrection is it? War? Does their blasted Civil War count as war?"

With all that money lying in the bank that I did not really know what to do with, I made the offer to make all good. After all, Uncle Joby had been kind and generous to me when I was a child and then again there was Judith...

It was as though someone had read my thoughts. "That will not be necessary," said a voice with that Southern drawl we knew all too well by then. A man, a gentleman aged about forty, with luxuriant side whiskers came in through the battered door and walked slowly towards us, his feet crunching over the glass-strewn floor. He smiled and bowed to Rachel and holding his topper in his hand spoke the words again to Joby.

"It will not be necessary, landlord, to argue with your underwriters. Nor take up this young gentleman's offer. I will make all good. Just get an estimate from your builders and tell them to proceed with the work and send the bills to me. Here is my card."

We were amazed, flattered that a gentleman, even if he was a Southern Gentlemen, should take such a benign interest in our affairs. We gaped at the card, which was that of a Mr J. D. Bulloch, care of a business with an address in Liverpool. But Mr. Bulloch was still speaking.

"Of course, you do not know me from Adam, but perhaps this will engender trust..." He held out a little wash-leather pouch. Joby took it. It was heavy and clinked.

"The only thing I ask," continued Bulloch, "is that you do not publish abroad my interest here. And also that when they come creeping back, you look with an indulgent eye on the *Nashville's* men. I shall have, er, reasoned with them and I think there will be no more trouble. In the Bell, at any rate. You will be under guard.

Ridiculous though it was, I felt a little disgruntled that my money was put to no use. But the mood soon passed.

With the Bell closed for repairs, it seemed at first to me that there would be enhanced possibilities of being alone with Judy. The excitement of the melee had driven the thought temporarily from my mind, but within a couple of days I was desperate to have a rendezvous with her. I was as addicted as ever to the vision of Judy disarranging her clothes and letting me see the intimate parts of her body. But I was also now most keen to rectify any bad impression the incident during our last encounter might have made, whether she really understood what had happened or not. I had decided that cousin or second cousin or no, virgin or no, I must have full relations with her or somehow things would go wrong. The sight of her uncovered nakedness for the first time had unseated me, but now I had looked upon her, and seductive and alluring as I found her, had always found her, now I thought I could take it within my stride until I had mounted her and initiated her into the joys and pleasures to which the West Indian girls had initiated me. Such hopes for my skinny little Judy!

But with people round about with little to do this was not so easy. Judy too seemed less compliant and inclined to prevaricate, which fuelled my fears. I pressed her and on the Monday, early in the evening before supper, she took a lamp and I took a candlestick and together we crept into a dusty attic.

"We must be quick. They want me to help with supper," was the first thing she said to me. Was it unfair to think I detected disinterest? But she lifted her dress readily enough and swept her petticoats to and fro to provoke me as she usually did. I wanted everything and asked to see her tits but she sighed and said there was not time and lifted her first petticoat.

"I'll let you look at my bottom today. If you want to," was my comfort.

I could not complain. But her fanny was covered and she would not take down her frilled pantaloons though I asked her and complained that now I had seen her legs what would be the harm in it?

"No," she said in a light, bright little voice. It was not unreasonable. It would have meant untying all her petticoats first with our fingers stumbling over each other in the doubt

147

of who was actually doing it. "We must hurry, we must hurry," was her excuse.

I put my fingers into her crotch, pushing them into her linen and just for a moment I though she might deny me that as well, but no. She was hot and damp in a moment there and I felt her body jerk a little, two or three times, as she dragged herself away from them.

From my distance now in old age, with the water long, long gone from under the bridge, what would you have had me do? What would you have done in your brave new world? What would your women have done? Would it have been rape or would it not?

And I hesitated.

"We must *go*, Tommy," she whispered at me and let her skirts fall. I felt suddenly frantic.

"But you promised me," I hissed in return.

"Oh…" she said with a trace of exasperation. I felt a spasm of fear. "Oh, Tommy. Just for a moment then," and turned her back. "You do it. You lift up my clothes," she said over her shoulder, after a moment.

But I did not want that. Not to see in a passive way, like noticing the petticoat hem of a girl sitting opposite in the omnibus. That was what was making me fearful. I wanted her to give me the private moment.

"No. No. No. It's not the same!" I exclaimed. "You have to give it me."

"Oh, Tommy," she said again as if she was weary, but she leaned a little backward and reached down to take handfuls of her dress to draw up, catch and gather on her hips so that her petticoats began their white shine in that gloomy room. And after them, a little shadowed, her legs in their white pants and how tight and white they swelled over her bottom. Because of some trick of the light the two little pearl buttons there seemed to glow.

We had not gone beyond but perhaps it was as well after the last time. Next time, then. So I put my hands into her warm, soft clothes and then ran them over her nether body and was content. Poor kid. As we left the attic, tiptoeing, coming again to light, I thought for a moment her eyes seemed moist.

***

Pa knew Mr Bowyer through the Freemasons. Mr Bowyer, or *Captain* Bowyer, was one of the pilots to the port. Pa spoke to me late on the Thursday evening when he came home from the Masonic Hall.

"You've got plenty of money," he said to me, standing with his back to the parlour fire. "Go down to the Royal Pier tomorrow and see if you can charter a launch or something, for early Saturday morning, and you might see something you'll never forget."

Of course I pressed him to say what it was all about. He let fall that it was a tip from Captain Bowyer and in view of Captain Bowyer's profession it was not hard to guess the nature of the 'something'. I was sworn to mention nothing of it to anybody. I managed to get an exception made for Roderick, who was summoned by messenger - an urchin from Pepper Alley with half-a-crown.

God, how I dislike early mornings. There always seems to be what we call 'a lazy wind'. One that goes through you, rather than go round you. Either the sun has just come up and shines chilly red gold at you or else there is an interminable pall of grey cloud. I remember steaming ten days to the west under such cloud before it grudgingly allowed a few streaks of sunlight through. Also, anything significant at sea, such as a new port or landfall always happens at dawn. At root, to be fair, it probably is not God's fault. It is the desire of those standing the morning watch to get to their breakfasts at the appropriate hour. And in my calling, I know very well what that means! But at least one is not on deck.

This was February and still half-dark at breakfast time and we were very much on deck, or something like it. We sat there on the damp seats of the launch, treasuring every stray eddy of heat from the little upright boiler and funnel, feeling the gripes of stomachs filled with nothing but black coffee, and wondering why the world fights for money when all it buys is this.

Southampton Water stretched out its broad, empty, mist-blurred road before us. The exciting road to everywhere, but not at dawn in February. It was only as we passed the last of the mud banks at the Point that the significance of the emptiness sank into our sleep-dulled brains. *USS Tuscarora* was not at anchor there. Nothing. No sign of her. Only a few vague, dark shapes in the distance. A coasting schooner and a few local fishing boats.

"Where's the *Tuscarora*?" I asked the launch skipper. He hunched his shoulders and shrugged.

"Don't know. They say she slipped early yesterday. She drops down to Yarmouth sometimes but the word is that somebody saw her going out past Hurst Castle. Some say she's going to coal at Portland although what the hell for, I don't know. Some fellows from the P and O boat as got in last night were saying there's another of these, what's-its name, Confederate warships as gone into Gibraltar. Burned something Yankee in the Strait as bold as brass before she went, too. They could see the smoke for miles, they said. Heyup, who's that then?"

A much bigger launch was coming up from astern. A much faster launch too, from the white 'bone in her teeth', and in a hurry, judging from the smoke streaming away from her funnel. She swung out a little before she came racing past us.

"Why, is that no the *Sprightly,* the Harbour Board's tender?" said Roderick. He was right.

"And there's Captain Patey, the Admiral Superintendent's man. Look! Leaning out of the wheelhouse window. What the hell's going on? 'Ere, Garge, shovel on more coal," said the launch skipper.

We were well down the Water by now. You could just make out Tichfield Haven, with that little sea wall where the Meon flows out, on the port side. Calshot Castle was ahead and to starboard. My father, back turned and hunched against the wind, was recovering and waking up as well because he called out and pointed. There was another white bone of foam under a ship's bow showing through the misty murk whence we came, although the ship herself was hard to see. The skipper screwed up his eyes.

"Oh ar; thought so. 'Ere she comes. That there Con-fed-er-ate. Looks as though you might get your money's-worth today, young gennulmen."

It was her, of course. *CSS Nashville*, God help her if He ever helps anybody, but with her popguns bravely cleared for action and the gun crews standing by. I can even remember seeing a man of exceptional height standing there, shading his eyes and staring ahead, with a rammer over his shoulder like a musket. She came past us just as we both rounded Calshot Castle. She was running flat out, her paddle boxes streaming like waterfalls and the floats beating the water in low continuous thunder. I was thrilled!

We were pitching into the choppy waves as we left sheltered water when her wake hit us and left us bouncing crazily. Poor old Pa groaned and threw up and even I, the hardened old salt, felt my stomach heave. The skipper braced himself with a foot against the gunnel as he clung to the tiller.

"'Ere, what about the speed limit? What about the eight knots?" he bawled indignantly after the *Nashville,* the wind whipping the words out of his mouth. The same wind blew *Nashville's* great ensign out stiff, with her circle of stars and her red and white bars. Maybe she was on Satan's side but she still made the heart leap to watch her go.

We were all of us out on a greater stage now. The Isle of Wight spread out before us with that spire visible in the huddle of roofs at Cowes. Eastwards spread Spithead. There were dark, indistinct shapes, which were boats and barges working on the new forts for the seaward defence of Portsmouth. They call them 'Palmerston's Folly' now that they are only just finishing them all these years later, but they made sense enough then.

But where were the Yankees, if anywhere? The *Sprightly* seemed to know, well ahead now and steadily steering toward what? And there she was. It was my turn to point and shout now. There was the *Tuscarora*, just west of Cowes and hard to see in her grey livery against the dark land. She had sent down her topmasts and no sail was set anywhere. Looking through my pocket glass I was sure she was cleared for action. I could see the long gun-ports for her pivot guns open, and even the cluster of figures round the rifle gun forward. She was making very little smoke but there was steam pouring from the safety valves, blowing round her funnel. It was so white and voluminous seen through the glass that it seemed strange that she was too far away to hear its roar. She was not alone. From where we were she looked as if she was being overlapped slowly; and she was, because she was being leisurely circled by one of our ships, the steam frigate *HMS Shannon*. I swept round the glass to see what other players might have made their entrance. There was something making its slow way out of Pompey with a lot of smoke. High sided and black and white and big. Good God, a battleship was steaming out - we learned later it was *HMS Trafalgar*, all eighty-six guns of her. Off Osbourne, a shape appeared familiar to us from many a description and many a drawing: our first ironclad, *HMS Warrior* was there! The 'Black Snake' was steaming dead slow but steaming westward. Surely she is still remembered? First of so many?

Thus it was that when the moment came, in spite of all the earlier carping that 'something must be done', the British lion awoke. He stretched himself, yawned (showing a great many teeth), lifted a paw and put it down again, and did not even bother to growl. And cat and mouse hastened to go their ways. Long may it be so.

Rather less fancifully, the *Nashville* paddled furiously on, her white wake a long curve to the westward as she made her escape down the Solent. Our launch bobbed and splashed and the engine rattled after her a while, far enough for the wind to bring us a snatch of whooping and jeering as the *Nashville* passed the fuming *Tuscarora*. And then since it was clear that no gun would be fired, we remembered that it was still a chilly morning in early February and we turned for home.

It seemed to us that the mistake Captain Craven and the *USS Tuscarora* had made was that whilst he had been careful not to leave British territorial waters during his coaling expedition to Portland, he had left the port area of Southampton. Thus it was that when those in charge of our affairs realised the situation that was threatening to develop, Captain Patey had raced in front of the *Nashville* to warn the *Tuscarora* that the twenty-four hour rule now applied. That meant that the Federal ship could not leave in pursuit of her prey until a full twenty-four hours had elapsed. Discussing the matter months later, Captain Bowyer told Pa that the *Nashville* was to have been blown up rather than have her taken by the Federals.

We were at our midday meal in Mount Street when there came a knock on the door. Ma rose and answered it and arrived back in the kitchen, Uncle Joby following her with an anxious expression on his face.

"You never took young Judith with you, did you?" asked Ma. We looked at each other and then "No" we all chorused.

"What's happened?"

"Well, I don't really know," said Uncle Joby. "I missed the dratted little wench this morning and I thought she must have gone with you, although she never said anything. She probably thought I wouldn't let her go. But if she isn't with you, then where is she?"

Chapter 11

I remember a little old clock that I believe my father brought from Tisbury. After it had come to me, many years later somebody stole it from the hotel. I was not really disturbed at first. My reaction was 'Oh, the police will soon catch the thief, whoever it was, and will bring the clock back.' I noticed people glance at each other but say nothing.

And for an hour or two this attitude was still reasonable. I expected Judy had gone off on impulse to see a friend. I said as much and I accompanied Job back to the Bell, where we found Rachel ironing. We asked her where Judith could possibly have gone visiting. She sat down and thought, and then wrote down four or five names and addresses on the back of an old grocery bill. I knew all these names vaguely. Girls of about her own age and an elderly couple she liked. Even the beginnings of concern sharpen the senses, don't you think? I caught a fleeting expression on Rachel's face, which made me think for a moment she was remembering another address. She caught my eye and looked away. I did not give it much heed.

Rachel said she was coming with us, but Uncle Joby told her to stay at home. He said that it was quite bad enough not knowing where one daughter was, without having another one wandering about. Judy would have put her tongue out at him as soon as his back was turned, because for all her longing, Judy was not a lady. So Judy did not have a lady's maid with her when she walked abroad.

We split the addresses between us. I took the two furthest ones: the old couple in Thorner's Charities and the second in East Park Terrace. I remember, as I set off up the High Street, how the high grimy bay windows, and Bargate's grey old stones in the winter light coupled with the odour of the old beneath its arch, brought a lowering of the spirits.

Nothing. Nobody had seen her that day. Uncle Job had done no better. We went back to Mount Street for an anxious family conference. Where on earth was she? One or other of us would glance at the window. It was not that late yet but already the grey light seemed to be ebbing. Young Judy was going to find herself in hot water when she got back. All the horrors came creeping as the shadows lengthened and the daylight faded. Horrors that of course happened only to other people's families, not ours. Of course at this state of affairs nobody mentioned them. Those who had risen very early to watch the *Nashville* sail were by now tired and inclined to irritation with the lack of consideration shown by Judith for going off somewhere unannounced and then staying late without thought for the worry she was causing. Yes, it was better to stick with that conclusion. Judith could be self-centred at times. She was probably chatting and taking a second cup of tea somewhere at an address we had forgotten but which would be as plain as a pikestaff when it was revealed. Since no one knew where, it was obviously pointless to aimlessly wander the streets. Better to stay put and let her come to us.

And yet the worm of anxiety was beginning to gnaw at my guts and it drove me out again. I found myself walking Western Shore Road with the Arundel Tower and the sooty old arch supports of the town walls behind me. The daylight was fading fast now and I looked along the long curve of shore to where already a few signal lights at Blechynden Station were to be seen.

I was not so far, I suppose, from where my narrative began. My thoughts flowed from there, back near the West Gate. How cold and dark and deep the lapping tide seemed. I remembered the latest occasion that Judy had lifted her skirts for me and that she had seemed a little unwilling before and a little distressed afterwards. But then that had happened before when one or other of us had had an attack of conscience. But we were addicts. We might try, but sooner rather than later Judy would crave her Exquisite Sensations, and I... I longed for the absolutely forbidden pleasure of observing a young girl disarrange that most archetypal of female raiment, to allow me intimacy with the most secret places of her person. I confess that the recollection of experiencing such revelations shakes me to the core even now. Would that others could have made that sacrifice of modesty for love, for with it I felt I could have sired a thousand children: surely as dangerous a phantasy as that of any opium eater? In the cold of the night I have managed but two, and in this world of fevers and consumption, fear we may yet be left alone. But away with this useless might-have-been.

I looked at the cold waters under a cold twilight and wondered. Surely she had not been that distressed, ever. But conscience still called up that cold, awful fear.

Thank God the repairs to the Bell were still not quite completed. Playing the jovial host that night would have been a task from purgatory. As it was we sat in the parlour, Uncle Job, and Rachel and I, listening for a step or knock whilst staring into the fire. There were bottles enough to hand with their easy comfort. I believe we found them all tasteless.

At the chimes of midnight Job sat up and pulled on his boots. "I'm going to the Police Office," he said.

"I'll go with you," said I, but Rachel caught my sleeve.

"Oh no, don't leave me here alone," she pleaded.

So Job went alone. Perhaps it was as well. Some of the officers are quick to detect those who know more than they would admit to.

Murder? Suicide? Abduction to white slavery? The mounting fear of those next few days, the ball of lead in the pit of the belly, could never be forgotten by any of us. Mud smeared and soaked, somehow Job and I searched the foreshore almost as far west as Millbrook. By the time we had done it and then trudged back to the old town we needed warming in hot, hot baths in front of the fire, with whisky forced past our chattering teeth. We felt we must search in those neglected parts where the police did not have beats and others had little recourse to, and so we wandered deserted little wharves and tumbledown sheds along the banks of the Itchen, left behind by the iron works and shipyards of Northam with their bigger and bigger ships.

One must remember with gratitude the regulars of the Bell who knew us all so well. Those who were hale and hearty, and not bound away to sea, who tramped out with us or for us. And there were certain others who slipped away into the nearby courts and alleys, asking questions that only they would get answered. Ah, Judith, there are worse things to be than an innkeeper's daughter in times of trouble.

One or other of us visited the Police Office three or four times a day to ask if any clue or anything had been discovered. They got to know us so well that the official face put on a friendly smile when it saw one of us approaching yet again. Nothing. Nothing.

It was they of course, after a day or two, with much circumlocution and clearing of throats, who raised the question of lovers and elopement. But this was not comprehensible to us. It was only when this possibility was being discussed later between us back at the Bell, if only to dismiss it, that I saw or thought I saw, some agitation crossing Rachel's face.

I did not immediately question her or even approach her. The rational part of my mind scoffed at any such idea. My emotional mind quailed at the very consideration of such a thing. Such subterfuge: such a betrayal by someone I had known and been close to almost all of my life and all of hers seemed monstrous. To even consider such an idea caused an increasing sensation of nausea until I put it from my mind.

It was much easier to endure the sights and smells resulting from the dragging of lakes and ponds even as far away as the Common. Nothing except drowned kittens.

I recall that I wished to avoid Rachel but that it was impossible in the terrible turmoil of those first days. I tried to stay away from her, I did not know why, except a feeling that she would tell me something I did not wish to hear. Inevitably, she caught me alone within hours.

"Tom, I do know how distressed you are. We all are. But there is something I must discuss with you. You remember that Papa asked me to go through Judy's things to see if anything is missing or if there was a note to be found?"

I nodded.

"I searched her wardrobe and chest of drawers again when I could think properly, and I believe some things are missing. I can't find some of her summer dresses and, well, other summer things. Of course, she might have thrown them away or given them away. I do not know what to tell Papa. I was thinking about winter things when I looked the first time. Tommy, I'm truly sorry to say it but if she has run away, why has she taken things for the warm weather?"

It occurred to me to ask if her toilet things had gone too. Rachel replied that they had not but after a pause asked the question, "Suppose, Tommy, just suppose for a moment, that she has run away. However wicked it might be, if her toilet things had gone, a search for her might have begun sooner. I do find it hard to believe that my sister would deliberately leave us in such anguish of mind. Wondering whether she has had some terrible accident, or been murdered or abducted. But she might have done."

A question swam up slowly but steadily towards the surface of my mind. I knew that I was never to be allowed to rummage through Judith's things myself. What reason could I possibly have given? The opportunity to enter the sisters' bedchamber unseen and search it undetected was remote. However, the question if asked might lead into dangerous waters, but somehow, something said to me that it was relevant. And then I realised that I had indeed the perfect disguise.

"Rachel, did you find a pair of gentleman' s trousers when you searched through Judy's clothes?"

She looked at me as if I had suddenly addressed her in Hindi.

"Gentleman's trousers? Tommy, did you say gentleman' s trousers?

"Yes," I went brazenly on. "You recall, she borrowed a pair of my trousers for that ridiculous game of Forfeits at Christmas. Fawn colour and checked. She would not give them back. It was some sort of joke to her. Did you find them?"

The shock slowly left her face. She had not, she said. She was an up-to-date young lady really. At least she could name the garment without blushing, although she would not quite catch my eye. And what did it mean after all that, if they were, in truth, not to be found? If her sister was right, could she have given them away like the other missing garments? No, Judy would not have done that. She would have returned them to me. Were they closely concealed somewhere? Had she been giving herself a guilty thrill by putting them on? For a young girl to undress before me just to give herself the indulgence of trying on men's clothes might suggest a powerful urge. But then Judy had been showing me her body since she was a mere child. She had lifted her skirt to get the last bull's-eye in the bag from me. If my trousers were not somewhere to hand, then the possibility, the *possibility* was that she had taken them with her. But why? Disguise? I had to be sure.

"Should I run and tell Papa that some of her things might be missing?" asked Rachel.

"Not for just a moment," said I. "Please could you first search once more and see if you can find my trousers?"

"Oh, bother your trousers, Tommy," she cried. "My sister is missing. Maybe she's... maybe she's even dead. And all you worry about is getting your wretched trousers back!"

I put my hand on her arm. She seemed to look at it with surprise.

"Please, Rachel," I pleaded. "Please look again. It's not just the return of my trousers. It might be a real clue as to what has happened to her. I promise I'll explain when you have looked." And then a thought struck me, very hard. "And when you've finished, could you just take a quick look in the attic?"

Her voice floated back to me. "Which attic? There are two of them."

"The back one."

"It's empty."

"Please, Rachel!"

I do not know how long I waited respectably below, fretting. Then I heard Rachel's step coming slowly down the stairs. She was carrying a medium sized brown paper parcel. It was neatly tied up with string and with a pang I saw how like my Christmas present it looked. Judith was always neat about that sort of thing. When she reached the bottom Rachel regarded me keenly.

"How did you know it was there, Tommy? In the back attic."

"I didn't."

"It is addressed to you, Tommy. Why would she have left it in the back attic? What on earth have either of you had to do with the back attic?"

"I don't know," I lied. "Suppose it was because she wanted it found later rather than sooner?"

"But it might have been months. Are you not going to see what's in it?" She pushed the parcel into my hands. It was much lighter and more amorphous than I had expected.

"Here they are," I said heartily. "Here are my long-lost trousers."

Rachel looked at me doubtfully. "I still think you should open it. There might be a message or a letter."

Yes, indeed there might. But from what I had deduced from the feel of the parcel, there might be a message of another kind. A message, stimulating, terrifying, humiliating, that I felt I would rather die than let Rachel be privy to. But of course, like any woman, she was eaten up with curiosity. I would have to open it. It came to me that to stick as near to the truth as possible might be the best course.

"Rachel," I said, trying to look straight into those honest, puzzled, hazel eyes, "I think such a letter, if it is in there, might be very personal to me. Is there anywhere I could be alone for a little while, while I open the parcel and look for it?"

Of course she readily understood. Or thought she did. Anyway, she agreed. I was ushered into the parlour and she went out and closed the door. Mind you, from the sound of her steps she had not gone very far. I got out my knife and cut a slit in the brown paper. It was entirely what I had expected. Even a faint scent of lavender rose at once to my nostrils. It was her beautiful, white, silk, Sunday petticoat. I put in my hand groping for a message. How cold the silk felt now against my fingers. Mercifully, I touched paper at once and drew it out.

My dear, dear Tommy, I read. *If I could only cut myself in two so that I could stay with you as well, I would. Try not to think too badly of me. Or perhaps it would be better if you forget all about me. Judy.*

Such things take a little while to sink in. At that moment all I felt was relief that I might well now be able to keep from Rachel that I was familiar with her sister's underwear.

The enigmatic nature of the gift perplexed me for a long, long time. Was it a discarded chrysalis of the beautiful butterfly now flown away? A sneer: a memento of the time before that man was shagging her, so lightly tossed away now? (Pray, pardon my crudity, distant reader. When something rare and beautiful falls, it is more disgusting than the behaviour of some well-known trollop.) So why not send some old thing nearing the ragbag? A despairing attempt to think of any gift - anything - that might help to heal the wound? She did her best; it was her best. I think that is what it was, and have thought so these many years.

As I went to rejoin Rachel, I comforted myself with the thought that at least Judy was not lying face down in a ditch somewhere.

"I do not think she is dead," I said heavily. "We must go and find your father."

On the way I managed with difficulty to stuff the parcel into the pocket of my greatcoat.

Uncle Job was staring out of the new bar parlour window, mechanically polishing glasses. I told him about the parcel and gave him her note. Firstly he sagged with relief. Then he suddenly flushed a peculiar red brick colour.

"Then where has she gone and why has she gone? The bitch!"

Words rose to my lips to protest at this epithet. Then I thought of the agony of mind she had left behind for so many, these hellish couple of days. She was his daughter. I said nothing. I went home to sleep the sleep of exhaustion. No. Thin, unrestful sleep, with dreaming that was feverish and of the flesh.

It seemed hardly any time before I was back at the Bell. I had been summoned by one of the snotty-nosed St. Michael's Parish boys before I had finished the morning wash and shave. I nicked my chin from haste, of course.

I was ushered into the parlour where Uncle Joby had asked to see me. Ascending the stairs, I suddenly began to be alarmed. It was reminiscent of being sent for in the Free Grammar School days. The thought of Judy's petticoat now thrust deep to the back of a seldom-used drawer rose to mind. Could they possibly have known and were they now going to blame me for her absconding?

I sat there listening to what Job had to say and there was a period before I realised he was talking about something entirely different. For a moment I was relieved, before the sense of what he was saying penetrated. That Rachel had come to him late the night before and tentatively voiced the impression - no greater - that, recently, Judith had been talking more and more with that ill-favoured paymaster from the *Nashville*.

I remembered the man then, and I remembered him on the night of the fight, where he had had no right to be. Behind the door of the bar as I had charged through.

It was a little like listening to a play. Hearing the actor's words but knowing they were not real. My head began to hurt. It ached, but as well it was as if somebody was ramming down a crown of thorns on it. I do not care if you think me a blasphemer. Then I threw up the miserable bowl of porridge, which was all I had time for before I came out. I recall Job and then Rachel as well, mouthing words at me, telling me not to jump to conclusions. But I knew. Somehow I was sure. I remember a glass against my teeth and brandy spilling into my throat making me cough. I remember as though in a dream being passively led across the room. Being arranged upon the couch and covered with a travelling rug. Hearing more coal being shovelled onto the fire. But nothing was real. After a while Rachel walked me home to Mount Street and I was put to bed in my cupboard-sized room.

But after a few hours, there I was awake again. Where had they gone? I climbed back into my clothes.

Job had been systematically dispensing drink on the house whilst questioning the regulars. Every day they hopefully came by the Bell to see if it was open again. Now they found a notice announcing that it would be business as usual soon but in the meantime there was an open door and an unexpected welcome.

It seemed unlikely that Judith had been able to remove herself and been taken aboard the *Nashville* without it being noticed. Job had had some premonition and I was there to witness the revelation.

"Well, I came up to the bar and 'e was leaning over it 'olding up the service as usual, chatting to 'er, and I 'eared 'm saying something about Liverpool, that 'e was going there; because I remember I thought to myself, Good riddance to 'm, if 'e weren't there, holding up the service to a thirsty man..." So old Ernie rambled on.

Liverpool! The very name brought down dismay upon my head. It was a great northern city and seaport. Miles and miles of thoroughfares and streets. Tens of thousands of houses, great and small. Docks and basins and wharves stretching miles along the river, the Mersey. Ships of all kinds packed together and leaving for the whole world. All totally unknown to me. A maze, a labyrinth, a jungle - into which that loathsome creature effortlessly moved, with his poor prey held in his salivating jaws. You think it strange that I who knew the Caribbean, the Gulf, Mexico and the ports and harbours thereof great and small should be so weighed down by the thought of a city in my own country? Well, Southampton then, with our one dock and pleasant streets and parks, seemed but a village to Liverpool. A couple of hundred miles of Old England, further far than Barbados. And, should I journey there, where oh where to begin to search? I recall my very knees seemed to sag at the thought.

And then I remembered. Bulloch! The man who, as well as paying for the repairs, had implied after the breaking up of the Bell that it would never happen again; that in some mysterious way we were to be protected. Had he not come from Liverpool and had some business there? What was it in Liverpool, from which these Southern rebels came and went like wasps from a nest?

"Blockade runners," said Joby when I made him privy to my thoughts. "They say there are dozens of ships up there that break the Federal blockade. They brings in cotton and baccy and takes back guns and gunpowder. Built specially, they are. Fast and shallow draught."

Need I remind you that one of the principal strokes of war the United States Government was using against the Confederate South was a naval blockade of all the Southern ports? But ports were many, if shallow, and the US Navy of those days was small in numbers and deep of draught. Add the vagaries of the sea, fog or storm - many runners got through.

Was this what that swarthy pig intended? To drag our Judith across the Atlantic to who knew what back street or shack? Or set her up in some room in a Liverpool alley to enjoy her until he sailed away? The thought of those greasy hands interfering with her brought on the nausea as ever. Disgusting. Intolerable.

Bulloch had left a card. Where was it? Job had it. There it was. J.D. Bulloch, care of Fraser, Trenolm & Company, 10 Rumford Place, Liverpool. Surely it was at least somewhere to start. Uncle Joby was not too sure. He scratched his bald head reflectively.

"Well, he has done handsomely by us..." Builders' bills had been sent away to Liverpool and only copies of receipts had been received. "But, lad, it wasn't done for the love of us and the Bell. I suppose it would be no strange thing for some merchant of Liverpool to have business in Southampton, but why would someone the likes of him be hanging round a pub of the likes of this? No. He's not just one of these Southerners over here. He's got some special charge for these Confederate States Navy men, as they call themselves. His gold stopped me making complaints all over the town. .

His gold kept light from being thrown over whatever it was they'd been using this place for. He's done us no harm but if you go bursting in there accusing one of these Confederate officers, or even some warrant officer, of kidnapping my daughter then you might get a nasty surprise. He may not then turn out to be the upright gentlemen he seems."

"But that man may have lured away our Judy," I cried out. "And where else have we got to start looking?"

"It seems very likely that that be so," rejoined my uncle. "And if he has, I'll beat him to within an inch of his life if I can catch him. The poor sulky little dreamer ain't grown up yet, that's for sure. And it's not just that she isn't twenty-one. What I'm saying is, it may be hard but we've got to go careful. I've got to think around it and talk around it, not least with your father. And I think the best way you can help at the moment is to go home, Tom. Go home and sleep on it until tomorrow."

It seemed to me then that I had the hardest task of all. To do nothing. I must have been already several steps on the road to madness, because I was of a sudden assailed by the desire to confess it all to him. That his daughter was more grown up than he thought. That she had tits and a bum and long legs for such a little creature. But I choked it back down and got myself out of the door.

Round and round in parlours and kitchens went the discussion. Nobody believed she was dead now, although she could still easily have been strangled and thrown down in some coppice somewhere. She was alone with that foreigner, who no doubt had ruined her, and when he had had his fill and sailing day came, would abandon her somewhere to starve or something worse. There was the question of depriving Job as a widower, against his will, of the company and support of a daughter. There was family honour. Nobody said anything, but questioning faces were turned in my direction. If she was found and brought home, would I be prepared to accept soiled goods? I had a vision of throwing her into a bath and scrub, scrub, scrubbing her with a brush until she screamed for mercy and then scrubbing her some more, so I supposed I might. The thought of what they might be doing together was as though she had flung herself headlong into a trough of excrement. It was unbearable and I had to learn to steer my mind away from the notion so that it did not deprive me of breath.

If there was to be an expedition to Liverpool, who should go? Myself, of course. Job? He would have come, but he needed to stay in Southampton in case the theory of where Judith had gone proved mistaken. Pa? He had never been nearer to London than collecting Covent Garden vegetables from the railway in the small hours (the Railway Age was still a source of amazement to him) and would have been completely at a loss. I had visited London with Ma when I was small, as much for the ride on the train and the sights of the railway as anything else. Once, I was dispatched as a messenger to Austin Friars in the City with a package precious for some reason. I came away overwhelmed by size and populousness, and dark with suspicion at the cost of everything. I have never liked London, although with money to spare on hansom cabs door-to-door for shopping and pleasure, I suppose it is tolerable for a short visit. At the time, London was the first great obstacle, or so it seemed in my lowness of spirit, on the road to that dark city and seaport crouching on the northern horizon. But I could not go alone so I rode out to Shirley to speak to Roderick.

He had lost little time since abandoning RMSP Co and the sea. Lower courses of brick for his forge and engineering works were already laid, while he lived in comfortable lodgings close by until his house was built. The purposeful way in which he went forward was, I felt, an uncomfortable contrast to my own aimlessness. I had mentally prepared myself for him to say that he was too busy building his business to accompany me on my Forlorn Hope expedition to try and find Judy and bring her home. But he listened attentively and when I stammered out my request for his support he replied, "And when shall we begin?" What it is to be young and convinced that you are immortal and invincible.. Of course he knew us all intimately but he never said as well he might, "Mon, ye do understand she might hate the sight of ye if you bring her back?" For me, I considered it a possibility, but one so low on the scale of probabilities that I could dismiss it from my thoughts. Repeatedly! We might have seen the ocean but we had seen little of life.

It took a few days to prepare. Clothes, baggage, visits to the bank, visits to the ticket office at the Terminus Station. First class tickets! Pa was appalled. So was I, a trifle, when I recovered from my attack of braggadocio, although it made sense. It was still March, which can be a miserable month for rain and cold. I knew second-class carriages had glass windows by then, most of them. But we were going on a long journey: sitting on wooden seats and freezing in our greatcoats in semi-darkness was not necessary. Perhaps it was where we intended sitting that at least finally drove us into purchasing a reasonably good top hat for each of us, even if we did not yet really feel as if we were toffs. A more unsuitable type of headdress to wear in a coach with five foot of headroom was hard to imagine.

"An' do ye have the slightest idea what ye'r goin' to do when we get there?" Roderick had an ability to take up a conversation exactly where it had been broken off inconveniently a few days previously.

"There is something Rebel, something to do with the Confederacy, going on in Liverpool," I said, trying to think aloud.

"That man who's lured her away, why did he not leave with the *Nashville*? Why did that Bulloch have the card with a Liverpool Company?"

The more I thought about it the more I became convinced that Fraser, Trenholm and Co. was the lock and Mr Bulloch was the key to Liverpool. I daresay it was because otherwise we had nothing. But another idea came unbidden to my thoughts.

"You know, I think when we pack we ought to take some of the old clothes as well. The gear we used to take for going ashore for a run."

Roderick's eyebrows shot up. "I thought we were past all that. I thought we were young gentlemen now. What would we want all that old stuff for?"

Inspiration came to me. "Disguise," I said. "Suppose we have to keep an eye on this Fraser, Trenholm place. Who's going to notice another couple of men with business ashore, or hanging around to sign on or something, in a seaport like Liverpool?"

He still rolled his eyes at me. "D'you no think I should pack a pair of overalls as well? Just in case?"

Of course it was ridiculous. We were setting off on a matter of family pride, family honour. Or to save a headstrong girl from herself. Or even me and my pleasure? No, never! Why should the possibility of packing a few relics of the old life somehow bring a lift of heart? The first since she had gone.

"Well, meybe that's no such a bad idea." I tried to imitate his Scots accent back at him. "I'll just put in a couple of wee white jackets m'sel. Just in case, y'know."

"And ye've no answered my question yet. What are we really going to do?"

"Make it up as we go along, I expect," I said, and thank heaven he asked no more.

It was a strange, silent little group that stood down on the station platform to see us off. There stood my parents, leaving the shop in charge of the boy just for once. Judy's father. Her sister. There was something right and proper about it, as though we had gathered for a funeral and were now departing. Conversation was stilted and of unimportant things, as the engine hissed and its smoke went up to make the glass and iron of the high roof even sootier. That little group of the two families waiting and watching us there put a seal of righteousness on our expedition, our punitive expedition. Young girls must not dare to leave home without their father's sanction. A cloud of steam obscured them for a second and the thought came into my mind that young girls should not be taught to lift their skirts for Exquisite Sensations either. I felt a spasm of fear that, because of that, the authority of our mission was flawed and would fail. Even as I looked again into the faces of her father and her sister, the vision of Judith gathering her skirts onto her hips, away from those pretty limbs, the while her grey eyes looked past you, brought a stiffening.

I felt sudden fear, I remember, and at that second would have run for it if I could. But the station master himself in topper and uniform raised his hand to send us on our way, the engine gave a throaty chuff and its great driving wheel slithered a moment then seized the shining rail. The floor beneath us was no longer solid but free, and our house was built upon the sand.

Chapter 12

The descent through the tunnel from Edgehill Station to Lime Street in central Liverpool was, I thought, reminiscent of entering Hades, although I did not remark upon this to my engineer companion. Of course, it was not all that steep. The perceived sensation of precipitousness was probably because one knew the famous gradient was there. Since the locomotives of those days could not cope well with this gradient, the line of carriages was allowed to roll down the slope by gravity, controlled by a massive cable paying out from a revolving drum. As an additional benefit, passengers were spared the stale fumes and smoke of other tunnels, which were such an ordeal to the timid. Just consider the tortured chuffing and wheel spinning. The fog of steam and the rain of smuts. When time came for them to leave again, the cable was hauled in by a big stationary steam engine back to Edgehill. Perfectly in order. Nevertheless, we looked out of the windows as we rumbled past our old-fashioned locomotive with its polished dome and its tall, brass-rimmed chimney that had brought us all the way from London Euston, now only fuming gently as it rested, with the same sort of emotion that the souls descending to the classical underworld must have looked at Charon as he turned indifferently away from them and boarded his crazy ferry boat again.

So we came out from under the high, complicated, curving roof of the station into Lime Street itself and there was Liverpool. Dark red brick and stone and grime except where it could be scrubbed. On the right hand across the cobbles was magnificence to rival the glory that was Rome: the pillars of St. George's Hall - although I do not suppose Rome was so sooty. Victoria is Empress now and slavery built both, I suppose, in different ways.

Liverpudlians: prosperous bellies well stuck out under watch-chained waistcoats above broadcloth trousers inside frock coats beneath tall black silk hats. Thin women with thin brown shawls over their heads and coarse grey skirts, getting out of the way of overdressed, overweight matrons. Darting through the throng, the grubby barefoot children. The blare of a ship's whistle from not far away, yet not a feel of the sea. It made me look up at the sky for seagulls.

"Have ye given a thought to what we do now?" inquired Roderick. Of course I had, but enclosed in our compartment for eleven hours we had never been on our own. I had a low fever of suspicion about me and imagined Bulloch's agents listening from every slumbering form hunched in a corner seat and every jostler in the stations during the acquisition of a sandwich box or foot-warmer.

"Because if you have not, I have." His idea had been the name of a boarding house apparently treasured by generations of engineers sent to the Mersey, and he had reserved rooms for us by telegram. There was nothing, therefore, to do but pile ourselves and our luggage into a cab and trot and rattle away through the noisy thoroughfares to a plain house in a quiet street. It was plain inside too, but scrupulously clean and starched like its bedclothes. The landlady knew her clientele, it was clear, because the first thing one clapped eyes upon on entering the hall was a notice on the wall above the umbrella stand absolutely forbidding the wearing of oily steaming boots another inch forward into the house. Irish stew with dumplings, and then crisp sheets wafted us early to bed, away at last from railway sandwiches and a night of dozing with the jolting and the clacking of the wheels, the stations with clanging milk churns, the stops for water every thirty miles and the stops for no apparent reason at all. It was a wonderful thing, the Railway Age, to us, but there is always room for innovation, such as the corridor and (would you believe it) er, conveniences. And now... dining cars!

Next morning, having come down to breakfast in rather less splendid clothes, not unnoticed by the landlady I would add, off we went to spy out the land.

All towns are sooty because all men must have fire. This city had been putting up factory chimneys for a century while Southampton decayed gently as a spa. Liverpool knew that muck breeds money. Coal and cotton cloth, along with everything made by fire from metal, poured out of the country into the ships, crammed three and four and five deep into six miles of docks: the Albert Dock, the Salthouse Dock, the Prince's Dock, the King's Dock, the Queen's Dock, George's Dock and George's Basin and the rest of them. Southampton had but our Outer Dock, our Inner Dock and our Town Quay to earn our promise as a 'Steamship Station'. We had the High Street and Above Bar but here in Liverpool, wide streets lined with rich shops in tall buildings led one into another, William Brown Street and Chapel Street, Ranalagh Street, so on and so forth and on and on.

Somehow we went downhill, past the little back-to-back houses of the dock labourers, conveniently near their work, to the shore of the wide grey Mersey. And across the grey wavelets - where from a similar vantage point at home I would have seen fields giving way to the New Forest trees - here I saw the slipways and graving docks and heard the cacophony of the John Laird shipyard in Birkenhead and I knew not then that I had scales on my eyes as I looked upon it.

But not far from the water we did find Rumford Place.

That first day we paused around the corner and planned what we would do. Then we walked firmly but not too fast past number ten, quizzing it from the corner of the eye, and passed on.

It was an elegant enough three-storey building, quite new, with a central passage to the courtyard within. The big brass plate was still new enough, polished as it was, to have clear letters spelling out Fraser, Trenholm and Company. Who Mr Trenholm might be and what he did we remained blissfully ignorant of, and it was just as well or we might have taken to our heels in earnest.

"So there it is. What do we do now?" I asked.

"Find the nearest public house," Roderick said. I was not well pleased with this and showed it. Sinner I undoubtedly am, but I do not imbibe with pleasure until evening.

"No, no, laddie," he said, seeing my look. "We have a couple of quiet pints together and see what we can see. And see what we can hear if you like, as well."

It was not that much of a place, as I remember. The floor needed a scrub and the bar and the tables needed a wipe. Some of the paintwork was peeling and the ceiling was stained almost orange with tobacco smoke. The beer however, was cool and nutty. It was too early to be full. There were a few men in pairs drinking and talking, leaning on the bar or seated at the tables. I particularly remember the fingers of the landlord, which were swollen and stiff from some rheumatic disease. He held the pot with his fingertips because he could not bend them. And the fingers on the bar of the man beside me as I bought the first round. I noticed them too. Several of his nails were missing, the nail beds still had traces of dark dried blood. That was thrashing canvas aloft some howling night recently. The other nails were filthy black. He was a seaman right enough.

I made to take up our beer from the bar where the landlord was still pushing the pint pots towards me with his claw-like hands. I glanced at his face, as one will, and nearly died of shock because it was Judy.

Only for a split second, but with that solemn, searching expression of hers. It crossed my mind to wonder if she was soiled, irredeemably soiled now under the green dress by that vile man's greasy hands. Or whether her skin was still white and her petticoat hems still not draggled.

Then I found myself on the floor. On the floor with all these people stooping over me. Then I recognised that seaman who had been next to me, and Roderick, a couple of strangers, and then the landlord, who squatted down and with surprising skill was ramming a glass of brandy against my teeth with his damaged hands.

I choked and coughed at his firewater and contrived to sit up, was then dragged up and propped up in a chair.

"He's had a fit," said the seaman with the broken nails.

"Och! Away with ye. We came all the way from London yesterday. He's still just a bitty over-tired or somethin'."

I managed to intimate that I, too, was still among those present. The conversation slowly began to include me again as it seemed less and less likely that the performance would be repeated. And it wasn't, not then, although it still afflicts me now from year to year and drives me to the brandy bottle when it does.

Still shaken by the visitation, although I now perceived it was some trick of the senses, it had nevertheless served to introduce us to the other patrons of the pub.

"Are you from London?" the seaman asked in the nasal local accent.

"No, Southampton," I blurted out and got a kick from Roderick on the ankle under the table. The man glanced at our clothes.

"Been at sea, have you?"

"Mebbe," said Roderick cautiously.

"Looking for a ship?"

"Mebbe."

"Only, putting two and two together and making five... You're from Southampton where there's been the uproar over this *Nashville* ship that's in all the newspapers. You're in a pub that's just round the corner from Fraser, Trenholm and Co., and I just wondered if some little bird from the *Nashville* or something to do with it said that there might be a bit of money to be made up here."

"Money?" asked Roderick with eagerness. (Dear God, as if he hadn't broken the bank at Monte Carlo.)

"Well, there are certain owners, skippers, whatever, who are paying over the odds."

"For doing what?"

The man shrugged. "Haul a rope, shovel coal, empty a piss-pot... you know."

"No, we *don't* know."

"No? I was sure you did. Why, sign on a runner."

"A runner?"

"A blockade-runner. You know. Cargo of rifles or boots, or whatever, outward-bound. Nip past the Union blockade outside Charleston, say. Come home full of cotton or tobacco. There's hundreds of ships in Liverpool doing it. Fast. Specially built for the job some of them. From over in Lairds Yard, a lot of them were." The fellow winked and tapped his nose. "And for some who's really greedy there's more." He leaned across to us in beery confidence. "I could tell you of a ship, ships maybe, where they're paying *double* the goin' rate."

"Double? And what the hell are they expecting you to do for that?"

"You're not Navy men, are you?"

"No, Royal Mail."

"Pity. Even so... You ask around... careful like. A ship called the *Oreto*. Brand new: still fitting out. They put the sticks in her about a fortnight ago. William Miller*'s* Yard in

Queen's Dock. The whisper is they'll be paying double. Nip in to old Fraser, Trenholms if you're interested. Tell 'em I sent you; Jeb Duff."

As we walked away from the place, I felt dissatisfied. "Why did you get into a conversation about ships we do not want? I just want to find Judy, argue it out with her, make her see sense and get her home again. If I can."

"Aye, if you can. She probably thinks she is having the time of her life, getting herself taken up by these oh-so-gallant Rebels. She always had a restless nature. But as for them, the more we know about them the better we know where to look. If she's here in Liverpool at all."

"I thought we would just be watching the office. You one day, me the next, if you like. For that devil paymaster. Or Mr Bulloch. So we could follow them. Him."

"I think that yon Mr Bulloch might be pretty fly about being followed, and we are not detective police. If he thought someone was following him I would not put him past pistolling the culprit. And suppose the paymaster had been ordered not to go near the office because he is known as a Confederate naval officer? And why would Miss Judith go in any case. And how many people work there if we are to follow them all home. How long have we got? No, I think we should spread our net as wide as we can. For the present."

We got ourselves through the grim maze of Liverpool's dockland to Queen's Dock that cold, short afternoon. We could see over the wall that there were ships on the slips but no masts and spars to be seen. Hanging round the gate trying to see what was within without attracting too much attention, we were almost swept off our feet when the works siren blew and a tide of men who had just knocked off came unexpectedly running round a corner and out of the entrance. After a few minutes the mob was followed by some more sober fellows walking. Roderick spoke to one of them.

"Have ye a vessel building here called the *Oreto*, by any chance?"

"Oh aye, the Sicilian Job, and if you believe that you'll believe anything," replied the man. "Except they've taken her away somewhere. Some say she's up in Toxteth Basin - and what for? I'd like to know. Have a look for her up there, mate. Ta-ra!"

Next day we trudged out there. Have you noticed how towns peter out in a semi-rural mess of isolated, run-down cottages, lonely rows of runner beans, discarded broken vehicles (some obviously being used as chicken houses), old horses grazing and so on? We eventually found Toxteth Basin in this sort of wasteland. I thought it was a timber yard at first, seen from a distance with the stacks of wood piled high. However, as we walked towards it, we began to make out masts and yards behind the timber. A brig nearest us and another ship beyond, barque-rigged it appeared but peculiar in appearance. There were very tall lower masts, which must have spread enormous courses. If your time has forgotten sail at sea, I mean that the foresail and mainsail nearest the deck would be obviously large and therefore have taken many men to handle them. A big crew? To trade in the Mediterranean?

There was some big dog barking hoarsely and incessantly in there. It seemed more ominous as we got nearer. I do not like large dogs and do not understand those who do.

There was a fence not a wall around the place, and we at once discovered some broken planks where we could effect an entrance. We stole through a space between the lumber stacks to reach the quay beyond. The basin must have seen better days but now in places the soil had slipped between the rotting, green-slimed piles, leaving the facings marooned in a foot-wide channel of water. Plant life grew in every crack and crevice. Ropes trailed ribbons of green seaweed. Here we discovered the brig, Swedish, evidently newly relieved of

179

her cargo and now apparently deserted. Beyond her, moored stern to the quay Mediterranean fashion, was a ship that was grossly out of place. In that decaying, stagnant puddle of a dock it was easy to see she was brand new. In fact, one of the first impressions she made on my senses was the smell of new paint. 'To be payed within and without board with three coats of paint' her specifications would probably have read. It was black paint: black to the waterline with nothing of the Royal Navy's cheerful red and white-lined boot topping. There were two small, thin funnels between fore and main masts, black too, not buff. Why quote the Royal Navy's colour scheme? I was only young but I had seen a lot of ships and loved them like some will love a horse, and in my mind this one spoke 'warship' although there was nary a gun to see. Portsmouth not Southampton, said an inner voice. Not some great black-and-white wall of a thing. Not as big as *Warrior* by far. A sloop, that was it. An auxiliary steam sloop. What pigmy players they all were, compared to the Royal Navy's battleships. Unusually for me, fool for any ship, I did not like her looks and never did.

There were men carrying things aboard. There were carts at the bottom of the gangway. Big wooden things in them that had a half-dozen fellows struggling and swearing as they pulled them up the narrow incline. We goggled at them, hoping for long cases that might be full of rifles. Or powder kegs - not that we had ever seen one before. Gun carriages in pieces? Round shot? No, only the wares of the butcher, the baker, the candlestick maker. Like any ship preparing for sea. The dog continued to bark incessantly throughout our observations and we suddenly became aware that its location and volume were altering. It was getting nearer and then we saw it straining at its collar whilst its handler, fortunately unwary, called it harshly back to heel. Time to creep away.

Lying in my alien if comfortable bed at Miss Taylor's boarding house, it all went round and round in my mind and I could not sleep. It was all very childish, these mental pictures of the new black ship, remembering the old *Trent* back home or wherever she was, and the *Amazon* that caught fire, and the *Nashville* of course. And where was my best friend, my childhood friend who was sad sometimes but whom I had been sure would be happy with me soon?

How had we all become drawn into this alien conflict? What did we care? A country or states or whatever, with people coming the nob on the backs of blacks? What did that mean to us? To me or Judy? Summoned thus, I saw her face in shadow but I could hear the rustling of her clothes and in this childish dream my body stirred. Afterwards I slept. Ah, but it is a lonely vice.

I shall never love Liverpool. Not just because of the grime. It is those endless crowded streets we walked. And so often, there, just a few yards further on, was Judith - except it was always a stranger turned her face.

One morning after, when it was my turn to loiter fruitlessly in the neighbourhood of Fraser, Trenholm's, trying to keep my back to the March winds, I saw Roderick hastening towards me and waving to catch my attention.

"Gone. She's gone," he panted out. He could have meant Judy. Of course it was the ship.

It was not that far to the wide, grey Mersey. We stared out. There was shipping as ever. Tugs towing flatties out of the docks and, as I remember, quite a few small coastal sail. There were several dark shapes with smoke out on the skyline. I borrowed a glass from an old man. One was obviously Cunard's *Scotia*, which was expected, paddling in from New York. The other might have been the *Oreto* but it was too far to be sure. I asked the old man when I returned his telescope. The name *Oreto* meant nothing to him but it was the new one from Miller's gone out on trials, he thought.

"Black job, is she? With twin funnels? She'll be back for teatime. If you come down 'ere again half-past three to four. Before it gets dark. You'll see her."

We did. Oh yes, dear reader, we did indeed. We arrived back on George's Dock Parade in front of the Baths about twenty minutes to four, and five minutes later we would have missed her. She came up quite close in and swept past so that her smoke blew over us. I have said I did not like this ship; nor did I. But they are all swans when they begin to move and this was no ugly duckling to begin with. I think of her now as I would a beautiful dangerous woman, although the two skinny funnels were a blemish, like a mole on the cheek or a cast in the eye. A pleasure, but likely to leave with your purse while you sleep. Not so inappropriate for a vessel brought forth from Maggie May's city to help herself to other people's property.

She was sliding past when we saw that there was a group of people standing right aft between the wheel and mizzen mast. Toppers and bonnets; not unusual to entertain guests if you are going to have an exciting day at sea doing engine trials. Seeing how fast she can go. And there she was, amongst them. Judy. I was sure. And before I could think I started to wave, until Roderick seized my arm.

"For Gods sake, mon. You a eejit? If she sees you she'll go to ground or make a run for it or they'll do somethin', even if it's finding a clergyman. If they've no done that already."

Go to ground? Run away? My mind resisted it. Surely this was my girl, of my family. Someone I had known most of my life and all of hers. Someone you did not expect to knock on a door if she came round. Someone who came to Ma with her woes. And yet the sight of Judy (I had no doubt at all that she had seen me, too), standing rigid there on the deck of this war steamer secretively built by strangers and foreigners for purposes that were absolutely nothing to do with us, for the first time really made my soul scream. I recoiled from the thought that she had done all this. She must have thought of me yet still begun to pack her bags. Even though she knew exactly where I was and what I was doing, she must have looked both ways along French Street to be sure that I was not coming along before she stole away. She might have permitted hands touching and lips meeting with that disgusting swarthy creature. It had been the act of a spy that ponders on the hospitality received from these new friends and still picks up his pen. This was deceit that smiles in one's face, knowing that the gaolers are on their way. This is the blow that is so easily, safely struck at the face of trust. These things may not need saying but I need to say them, even after all these years. Hotelier I may be but seafarer I was, and God may forgive unfaithfulness to those away on the deep sea, but we cannot forgive, and we cannot forget.

You weak women, with your littleness of soul.

Judith had created with her own hands this betrayal, this gulf of a hundred yards of murky Mersey water between myself on the shore and the black ship steaming past. It was unbelievable but she had. This I knew for a moment before my senses reeled from it again, and the knowledge that in his squat tower God was beginning to smile. The spelling of Judas is not so different from Judith.

And what on earth were we going to do? We must do something. Poor silly girl. Up and down we go. See-saw, see-saw.

Chapter 13

Judy and I never had that emotionally cathartic meeting, that quarrel that might have cleared the air. No shouting or screaming, tears or slaps or half-restrained punches, scratching at faces or seizing by the hair. Perhaps we would have been able to go our ways in peace. Or perhaps not. Perhaps pushing her onto the floor and dragging her skirts up over her chest against her will for a change... Perhaps murder. How stupid it is to hang men and women for what they do in the grip of a hurricane of passion. Just for once Johnny Crapeau does things better. (There again, the French *understand* such things…)

But they knew they were guilty. That man put her aboard the blockade-runner. When I had got an address and we had found it, there was only a fish-eyed landlady who stared into space over my shoulder and denied it all, then said they were gone. By which time I was in such a passion that I pushed her aside despite her squawks and hunted through the place. I found a shoe I thought I recognised. When I clattered down the stairs I saw Roderick placating the woman with gold. She glared at me and I back at her, for at that moment I hated her for harbouring them. And he a foreigner.

"You're mad," she said at me, and perhaps I was. Perhaps in some locked inner room of my soul I still am. "She's sailed on the *Ghost*," she said with relish to wound me. And you could see immediately she knew she had said too much because her face changed and you could tell she was getting ready to whine, and run if I made towards her. Roderick gripped her arm, got her inside into the hall and then left her and closed the front door after himself.

"What is the *Ghost*? Where is she bound for?" I babbled as we stood outside on the pavement. Roderick took my arm now and propelled me away.

"Just in case the old biddy takes herself round to the scufters. Ye were trespassing or some such thing then, laddie. What would you do without your old uncle Roderick? And you were looking at the *Ghost* only yesterday. That paddle steamer with the two funnels in the Brunswick Dock. She looked as though she was ready for sea."

I recalled the ship with difficulty. "Do we know to where she was bound?"

A little tavern research was soon successful. Nassau in the Bahamian Islands. The Ghost was well known as a 'runner'.

"I must follow."

"Do we go home, then? The old company. Royal Mail from Southampton?" No, no, no. That seemed to me far too slow.

"No. I'll go on the *Oreto*."

All this is in as much of a feverish whirl as my thinking was at that time. To recall it in order to record it, conjures up again that sick confusion even now. To witness Judith standing on the deck of that damnable ship apparently of her own free will was more than my mind could encompass. I have discovered that the human mind, mine at any rate, is divided into two. Like a city wrecked by a great earthquake, one part slowly drags itself clear and painfully begins to rebuild, brick on brick. But while a survivor from that time lives, the incredulity towards events, the terror, the loss of hearth and home, kith and kin, remain forever vivid in that other part. Forever just at hand.

Roderick was not impressed.

"Hold hard, Tom. How d'ye know she's going anywhere near Nassau? She's supposed to be bound for Palermo."

"Jeb told me."

"Jeb told ye? You believe that wharf rat?"

"What reason have I not to? What could be in it for him? He tapped his nose and said I'd like the Bahamas. And I said, 'I know,' and he said, 'That's why you'll get the job. I told 'em you was Royal Mail.'"

"No, Tom. It was just a... a subterfuge to get inside the office and find out where the Paymaster lived. Not to sign on."

"Assistant Paymaster. Paymaster's mate, probably."

"What the hell does that matter at the moment?" He clicked his knuckles as he does when exasperated, opening and closing his big fists. "Anyhow, ye are no cook."

"Cook's mate."

"Mon, mon, they'll fuckin' kill you, they fuckin' will. When they find out ye know fuck all about it!" Ha!

I tried to get him to go home but he would not. I had to cajole and plead with him. Eventually I persuaded him that he must take the news home and also discover a way of getting some money to me at a Nassau bank. He said he would never be able to look anyone in the eye if he was not to hand when the crew of the *Oreto* discovered my culinary skills. He muttered away to himself about the follies of our situation for hours. But eventually, grudgingly, he agreed.

Of course it was a lunatic thing to have done, but if you are old enough to think so and have no memories of things foolishly done when you were young and on the horns of love, then your life must have been a dreary plain indeed.

***

So here I was again, beginning to feel that old familiar motion beneath my feet and with the sickly stomach and dry mouth and sore eyes from getting up so early, except now instead of the trays and teapots for my ladies and gentlemen, I was shovelling coal into this ugly great black stove in the

Oreto's galley. Quite apart from the odours of food driven out by the heat, it was new enough to smell of black lead and that was a curiously unpleasing smell. Beside me was the ship's cook, Hibert. Imagine some stout jolly fellow? This was one of the other kind, lanky and dyspeptic, who, when the meal is ready and served, sits on a stool in the galley, munching a cheese sandwich. A preserved cheese sandwich. A Suffolk cheese sandwich. Oh well, if you have been fortunate enough never to taste Suffolk cheese preserved in a cask for years, you cannot know what it is like. Its only merit is that it keeps well in a cask. He had a long, bony nose with a red tip as if he had a permanent cold. It was frequently adorned by a glittering dewdrop.

There were two large copper vessels standing on the stove. Cook looked at me.

"There's whiting in that there little crock, boy. Put a little of it on the cloth and give they coppers a rub up."

I could see my face quite clearly reflected in the metal and to me it seemed mad to be concerned with their appearance at this crack of dawn - but it was for him to say and me to obey.

"Then us'll fill them up wi' water and set 'em to bile. Be thee going to give the innards a rub too, while thee's about it?"

Some instinct for danger made me hesitate.

"No, thee ain't," said Cook, his eyes gleaming. "Thee must never be rough inside because there be a layer of tin on 'em. Never use nothin' as might be rough or thee'll ruin 'em and poison 'arf the ship's company, as like as not. Just a little soap and 'ot water in there. Thee'll learn, though I reckon thee's got plenty to learn. Give over that now an' gi'me a 'and with this here water. Thee do that one and I'll do this 'n." It was not a Hampshire accent, but close to.

Everything at sea seems to start very early. Early to bed and early to rise, although it never really agreed with me and there are not many wealthy seafarers. The ship oscillated a little beneath my feet and swayed rather than rolled, but it was so quiet. No beat of paddles. I was not then used to screw propellers. I thought about how the famous Liverpool skyline would be sliding past, grimy in the first grey light of dawn. I never liked the commercial, ostentatious place. I did not like the people with that nasal accent. And harbourers of sinners, all of them. 'It ain't the leaving of Liverpool as grieves me. It's, Darlin', when I thinks of thee...' Oh, Judy.

That chilly little wind. What could you expect? It was only March. It blew cold round my ankles even though I could feel the heat from the range on my stomach right through my clothes at the same time. I saw the dewdrop follow a jugful of water into the cauldron.

I looked up and there was Cook's collection of knives with wooden handles and brass studs in them, hanging from a deckhead beam and swaying a fraction from side to side all together with each other and the slight roll of the ship. I looked at the knives again.

I have never seen a victim of a successful or unsuccessful attempt at killing, excepting pigs, but I could guess at the copious quantities of blood that would result. And the frequent squalor of a merchantman's forecastle was not going to be tolerated by master or men of this *Oreto*, destined for the 'Mediterranean Trade'. I could hear the sounds of holystoning overhead already. A speck of anything unusual on deck or paintwork would be bound to be noticed here. But how does one kill without blood?

And what of the noise? It would require a practised assassin who could silently cut a throat in amongst the duty watch and the sleepers below, and whatever my purpose, I was not such a man. Nor did I even possess a razor. While that man lived, it was more than possible he might recognise me, so what small necessaries had gone into a new sea-chest for me, deliberately did not include a razor, for I was resolved to conceal my visage behind a beard. This was now all of thirty-six hours old! No murderer's mask as yet, although I had begun to look villainous enough, and all I could hope to add was that with rumpling of my hair I might be dismissed as just another dishevelled 'idler', the ever-so-humble Cook's Mate who kept below. But without my razor I might have disarmed myself.

The frustration of my purposes boiled over in my brain and the potatoes faded under a vision of Judy coming towards me with that abstracted expression on her face, as though she was not truly there, holding her lifted skirts about her waist. So she came in the flesh, once upon a time. Like a painted portrait or one of these photographs, blotting out my vision for an instant. (And she comes now still; at long intervals without warning. I have lost my seat on a horse from one such visitation.) Oh, how could I get that accursed man out of our lives? Natural justice should have decreed that at that moment I burned myself, but I did not, though I was wielding the shovel again. I did grind my teeth however, but becoming aware of Cook's interested appraisal, resumed the appearances of caution.

Sitting there in the morning, watching for the first wisps of steam to arise in the coppers, I longed for her petticoat, now! Now, even in this mysterious, threatening ship that appeared neither man-o-war nor merchantman. I wanted my brown paper parcel like I wanted my rag doll in bed in the dark as a child. I wanted to tear it open and, although I knew it must be all cold, thrust my hands into it just in case some warmth from her person lingered deep inside. To what a state women may reduce us. Particularly when we are at sea with little else to occupy the mind. All I could do was hunch my shoulders and hope my madness did not show.

Half-asleep again, I squatted down on the deck and leaned against a stanchion while slowly, slowly the water in the coppers climbed reluctantly towards the boil.

"They'm 'aving just coffee and bread with a bit of butter maybe, for breakfast today. Seeing as how it's sailing day. Drat that dang water. Why's it so slow?" said Cook.

189

I went on deck to the heads to relieve myself and in the hope that the fresh air might jolt my wits into activity. Everything at sea is to excess; gone, gone the smoke-hazed air of the city. The wind was so cold and strong it made my eyes water. Rubbing them I looked aft and was surprised to see a little group of females near the wheel. It was a shock considering what I had been about, for there was no privacy about the seamen's heads. Who could these be? There were no cabins for passengers in this ship. Was it sailing day or was it not? And were we bound for the Bahamas or were we not?

" We'm cleared for Palermo, that's what I heered," said Cook. "Mebbe 'tis a bit o' window dressing if thee mus' know."

I could make little sense of him then, of his dialect or his thoughts. Or of this crazy ship where nobody knew where we were heading. The women really did not matter to me then because I was sure Judy was not amongst them. But I wonder now who they were. Those ladies in bonnet and shawl who stood on deck in the freezing wind before the day had truly dawned, to be seen by any who wished to see from the Bootle shore or Prince's Dock Parade. And then bravely went down the ship's side on an accommodation ladder, and filling their shoes with sea water, scrambled into a tossing boat with New Brighton Fort abeam in the distance. All so the Sicilian Job looked as if she was going out for just another day of engine trials. Southern Belles indeed!

As for me it was back to the galley where I continued my murderous ruminations while I blackleaded, scrubbed, stoked and polished.

Some of the mess cooks grumbled that their messmates preferred tea or cocoa rather than coffee, which is what they got. British men-o'-wars' men earning their double pay in an American-style ship and still grumbling. I knew enough to tell them to take it up with their officer or the captain next Sunday. It was, in truth, a fairly easy start for me because there was fresh meat for the men, so the mess cooks only re-appeared well into the forenoon watch with their meat and prepared vegetables in the mess netting bags to be boiled in the coppers.

So I brooded in peace. Anybody that goes to sea knows it for a dangerous life. Half-frozen men fall from aloft and gear carrying away falls on them. And fair or foul weather, the sea gropes blindly on for us all. But how was I to contrive such a thing for a man who would spend his days with his ledgers and his fourteen ounces to the pound, in the paymasters cabin?

I briefly visited the deck again that morning to find us out of sight of land and with only a couple of hull down sail to be seen. Strange in waters teeming with the country's coaster fleet and only a few hours from the Mersey Bar.

It came to me in a lightning flash that, employed in the galley as I was, poison was the way. But only the paymaster's assistant must die. I drew back from the prospect of several others dying suddenly as well. I could calmly entertain the prospect of the horrible illness that man would endure. I could imagine with absolute detachment and calm the horrid stomach cramps, the vomiting (hopefully) of blood, the disgusting loss of control of his bowels, the panting grey-faced wretch lying on his side somewhere awaiting his end. He was an alien being, a moon-man who had intruded into our world and must be removed from it, so that we could be happy again. Two intermingling families once more as we had always been. The prospect cheered me. I decided he should have a dose flowing over, to put him down as quickly as possible, like the libertine mongrel he was... But I recoiled from the prospect of bearing off his entire mess as well. Quite apart from the humanitarian aspect of it, important though it was, it also occurred to me that a group all becoming ill together in this fashion might well suggest a trail that led back to the galley.

But as midday and dinnertime approached and bending in the steam over the coppers to find the metal-tagged victuals bag for each mess, oh it seemed such a broad and beckoning way to get near to his life. At any rate I determined to discover to which of the messes he was attached. It could do no harm.

That morning, Cook, knowing that I had not come from the Royal Navy, had collected our tots of grog. Since my next task was to collect together the 'sludge' - the fat that had floated up from the men's meat and which was one of Cook's perquisites - I had to decide whether to drink the rum first (which I should have done) to steel my hand, or to keep it until I had done the disgusting chore, as a sort of reward or compensation.

And so to dinner for us as well: boiled beef and carrots, cooked with a little more attention to detail and with even a couple of dumplings. Courtesy of the 'sludge', as Cook, who had noticed the expression on my face whilst collecting it, was not slow to point out.

I could not get my plotting out of my mind. I ran over the range of materials found in any ship: the paint locker, the bosun's store, the carpenter's store. Surely there must be something secretly and swiftly poisonous in a dark corner somewhere. What about wood alcohol for cleaning brushes? They said if you drank it, it turned you blind, but somehow I thought you had to take it for weeks or months before it killed you. In St. Michael's Parish back home, there were vagrants lying about in dark corners with bottles of the stuff, who were said to be drinking it. In which case it would be too slow, for they seemed to be about for weeks at least before the coming of the paupers grave.

We carried no surgeon at that stage of the voyage but there was a dispensary cabin. What might be to hand amongst the medicines? Would that man notice an overdose of laudanum in his wine? Or did it taste bitter? Then my mind roved again over my place of work. Not the knives this time. Cook had a set of copper saucepans, I think more for show than sauces. I remembered learning that cooking certain fruits and vegetables in copper pans could produce poisons that had seen off whole families - but which fruit and veg were they? It must be a reflection of Cookie's concern over the tin lining. It occurred to me that Pa might have known.

By the second day, glimpses of the sun in a cloudy sky suggested we were heading south. It must be the Irish Sea. This sank into far more experienced heads than mine and there was nothing to discuss between the quartermasters on the wheel and the rest of us. We also were still under steam. The greed for steam of the engines of those days meant a consumption of coal that made the trim of the ship perceptibly alter as days passed by and smoke poured out of the funnels. From the short sharp roll of the deeply laden, the ship gradually rose bodily in the sea and began an uncertain, top-heavy, slow, lurching roll. It would have been uncomfortable had not all possible canvas been set, which steadied her. I realise now that we were in a hurry to lose ourselves in the wastes of the Atlantic before being sighted by some lurking Federal cruiser watching Queenstown perhaps.

A day or so later I wakened to the piercing sound of the bosun's call in the dark and a shout turning out the off-duty watch. The motion changed disagreeably and there was a thunder of canvas overhead. Nervously I sat up. Had a Federal warship found us already?

"Go to sleep. Duff bosun," murmured a sleepy voice from another 'idler' two hammocks away. "They've heaved-to, to get the screw off and hoist it in. You're going to be a real bloody sailor-man from now on."

It was true. Although the furnaces were never quite allowed to go out, the rhythm of the engines and the eternal scraping of distant shovels was stilled and before very long there was a final clap as the sails filled again, the *Oreto* heeled, steadied herself, and began a balanced pitching up-

and-down over the seas. The galley, I recall, was forward of the foremast. The distant sources of heat dwindled too and the ship became pervaded by the sticky, damp air of the cold sea. Not for nothing were the cooks' perks of slinging their hammocks alongside the galley, and to hell with the odours of past cooking.

I shall never forget that crossing. There was a thick, grey, never-ending blanket of cloud that came out of the west, day after day after day. Occasionally the sun would break through a hole and there would be distant golden fans and pillars - but, it seemed, never over us. We had no gales or heavy seas. Just plodding on, on our way at, I suppose, ten or eleven knots over a pewter coloured, wave-carpeted sea under this leaden sky with never another sail to speak. In fact if topsails were seen we steered away. Unnatural. Seamen like to see other ships. Where are you from? Where bound? What news? Report me to my owners when you get in. So the whole world has not vanished while we've been sailing for weeks across this endless round puddle. Strange, this *Oreto*. Like a chrysalis found in a dark corner in winter.

I often lay sleepless in my hammock with the knowledge that this hated enemy was lying only a few dozen feet away from me. Sometimes I felt that surely he would sense such hatred and thus detect my presence. I remember once, having completed an errand to the wardroom pantry, I lingered a while only inches from him. I could even see his pudgy fingers with that swarthy wrist skin as he wrote in his ledger. How could she bear, with a skin like that, to let him touch her? Every time it must leave an invisible grease mark to collect dirt. How could she? I hastened away lest anger and violence suddenly overcame me. You see, as I have explained, his death was necessary. A necessary fact of life. I wondered how that skin would look with the life drained out from under it. But I had no intention of letting such a necessary event become an excuse for the mummery of my hanging.

Still desperate for a plan I even visited the larboard-side officers' heads. Closing the door - oh yes, it had a door - I looked about me and down through the seat at the churning wash below. But there was no surprising him and stuffing him down through there, especially with his corpulent person. Could it somehow be weakened so that the whole contraption would fall into the sea with him inside after a violent push? But its timbers were as brand new as everywhere, and the smell of new paint still battled with the scent of the sea heaving there below the seat. And I could hardly be seen taking a saw to it. Leaving in despair, I was caught by the Old Man, Captain Jimmy Duguid himself, who led me about the quarterdeck by an ear for a long time, berating me as we went. He pinched my ear most painfully but even as I yelled I laughed to myself within, thinking of what he might do if he had really known my purpose. And also it occurred to me at that moment that I could probably buy and sell him a dozen times over and I giggled out loud at the thought.

His reaction was to bend down and peer into my face. "Funny, is it?" he bawled.

So I got my face straight again. "I was taken short, sir," I muttered.

"Short; he was taken short! Lookie here, I'll haze you if I catch you in there again. That'll make you short! And make sure you wash your hands afore you touch any victuals."

Not so easy, but I managed to get a bucket of sea water from over the side without having the rope torn out of my hands. To comply exactly with his order somehow became a kind of prayer of gratitude that my murderous ambition remained a secret.

So we sailed on. It was not that we had been becalmed. We must be long past the Azores by now. No Gib, that's for sure. We were all on salt beef and hard tack now, although the officers would get a chicken to roast out of the coop for a Sunday. There was little else to do on a Sunday after the captain had been round so I'd watch Cookie roast the chicken in the side oven. I tried to see what he looked at when he drew it out to baste it. I noted how it smelled when he sniffed it. Saw how brown the potatoes in their roasting tin were when he turned them over. And before the steward took it aft we had an unobtrusive slice or two from underneath it with a potato or two.

"We don't get no wine to go with it and sure as fate they bain't having no bread sauce," cackled Cookie.

On and on. It became a sort of joke with some. "Where the fuck are we? Where the fuck are we?" they would say, peering at the horizon as their watch came on deck. *Wherethfukarwi, wherethfukarwi* became a sort of rallying call of the men, to be shouted out in bars and public houses to attract attention from latecomers from the ship. I'll bet it was heard ashore on that night in Bahia when she was taken. Imbeciles!

The weather was getting warmer and the sun made more frequent appearances. The waves lost their sharp crests and became languidly rounded. And dark blue, and the wash and bow wave whiter. One day, several clumps of weed slid by and on the morrow they were everywhere. I was surprised when it seemed this dalliance was not acceptable to Captain Duguid because steam was raised. Low green grey land lay on the horizon for a few hours and sometimes one could just make out brilliant white surf and a turquoise lagoon beyond. Some of the men were wide-eyed with wonder. I was not. This was never Sicily. It seemed now a joke to think that was where we might be going. I had seen something very like this landfall for years of my young life. I was sure these were the cays of the Bahamas.

We defaced the balmy air with smoke and stink as we approached at top speed. For us, it was like a coachman afraid of highwaymen, who whips up his horses to reach

196

some friendly inn as the shadows lengthen. Soon there was land whose skyline was broken by a distant spire. We turned and slid through an opening, with the waves and the wash whispering white onto coral close on either side. No sign of a Federal ship, so we might have saved the coal. We turned sharply again, heeling away from it into a long landlocked lagoon and saw a little town that straggled along the shoreline and I knew it was Nassau. Thirty-seven days from Liverpool Bay and I knew where we were. The roar of the anchor cable shook the whole ship. It was 28 April 1862.

There were two Royal Navy sloops with their shiny black sides and buff funnels above their immaculate white awnings. One was alongside and one was out on a buoy not far from us. Quite close.

And suddenly I looked about me and despaired. In that summer place I reeled because I had failed to do anything. That man breathed and lived, and I had made no attempt on him. I had dreamed of watching him slowly dying on the deck, writhing like a fish on the bank. I had planned to strike or kick him so that I could hear his petty screams of agony, so much more arresting when they are delivered by a man's voice. And I had done nothing. Judith would be hidden somewhere here. She knew the *Oreto*, of course. Would she have come down to the shore to greet that creature who must have somehow magicked her. Or stay away for fear that she might see me.

I did not like the *Oreto* but I grudgingly recall her as a good ship in a seaway. You get in after a long passage like that, feeling beyond exhaustion. You sweep the skyline of wherever you are with a dull eye and all you want is to sleep. Sleep? When your body is still trying to keep you on your feet on an ever-shifting deck, now still? Without the creaking of a wooden ship like she was? Dark. Stillness. Silence, except for the animal sounds of sleeping men all around you and the distant, slow trudging footsteps of the duty watch on deck, coming and going, coming and going.

Sleepless you lie and aware that every sleepless hour brings you nearer the time for turning out again.

Next morning, after breakfast had been dished out, I went on deck to see again the bright blue water and bright white sands, everywhere the green of palms and yet always with those lumpy grey-white clouds passing distantly in the tropical blue. There were plenty of ships in that harbour and alongside. Many were the raked masts and raked funnels: blockade runners, built for speed like yachts. The watch on deck were no longer about their mundane daily tasks although the scraped decks steamed in the early sun. The capstan was still manned by a few and the rest clustered expectantly forward and aft. There was a tug at Nassau popularly known as *'Old Smokey'* and such a vessel, dwarfed by a cloud of funnel smoke, was visible making in our direction. God only knows how old it was or how they had got her here but her funnel was almost as tall as her mast, with fancy metal fretwork round the top. Perhaps she had been brought to Nassau in pieces. Handlines flew, the anchor was already aweigh and with immense churning overside *Old Smokey* had us on the move. I expected to see the quays of Nassau slowly drawing nearer but it was soon clear that we were being moved to what they call the New Anchorage, even further from the town. With Royal Mail one became accustomed to heading in to the centre of affairs and maximum passenger convenience, useful for getting ashore oneself. Why were we so far from the town?

The bulwarks were high but I suddenly got a glimpse of a naval jolly boat passing close to the side. All very proper: boat crew's eyes staring aft, pulling together like a machine and an officer languidly reclining in the stern-sheets. And having a bloody good look at us at the same time. Suddenly, I felt like a small boy with stolen apples in his pockets when he sees a copper.

Apples? It is quite easy to stop thinking on a long ocean passage. Indeed, it may be one of the attractions of a life at sea. Now we had arrived in Nassau and amazingly, although I knew where we were, many of the men did not. As ever with this ship, nothing illegal had been done. Any ship owner may vary the order with which the ports on the ship's papers are visited, but when a hundred or so men who thought they had signed to go to Palermo find themselves somewhere else, then there is going to be muttering.

Then there was the ship herself. Disregard for a moment old Captain Duguid, the Board of Trade tonnage inscribed on the engine room hatch for want of anything better, and the 'Red Rag' up at the peak. Regard instead, bulwarks pierced for ports and surmounted by hammock nettings and indeed nowhere to stow any cargo. I suppose an eccentric millionaire may have himself built a yacht that looks like a warship without offence. Then said yacht unexpectedly turns up in a British harbour bustling with blockade-runners a few hundred miles from the ports that are being blockaded by the United States Government. Consequently, it is no longer surprising that there is interest in a jolly boat from Her Britannic Majesty's Royal Navy!

Chapter 14

We thought we were to lie at Nassau for a few days or a week, possibly. We were there for a good three months. After a long life I will affirm that the quickest way to alienate a group of people is to keep them in the dark about what is going forward. Obviously, there were unusual difficulties for the command of the *Oreto*. She looked like a warship from any angle, except for her armament. She had nothing, nothing more lethal than a pocketknife to her name. And great had been the pains that this was so, or she would never have got clear of the Mersey because the Customs would have seized her, prompted by the never-ending protests from the US Consul in Liverpool and the Ambassador in London. It was not permitted to recruit British subjects to serve in foreign wars. And if she was in fact a foreign warship, then to sign on a British crew was illegal. She moved as a floating legal fiction, registered as a British merchantman, under the British flag, with a British master for a voyage to Palermo. If we now discovered ourselves in the Bahamas, what business of that was ours? Owners were at liberty to alter the order in which ports were entered and we had signed for Palermo, yes. But the small print had mentioned some possible further voyages to the West Indies.

So what is ailing you, Jack? So you went to the West Indies and doubtless would soon sail for the Mediterranean and Palermo. You are getting double the money any other owner would pay you, so what's this grumbling? You are paid to climb rigging and shovel coal. Do that and shut up!

Such was the voice of authority. But where was authority on this ship. True, there was old Jimmy Duguid but always, it seemed, with a shadow: this man Low with his Southern American drawl and fancy whiskers, who was always at his elbow and who would walk with him, talk with him, together even on the captain's sacred reserve, the starboard side of the 'quarterdeck' (for *Oreto* in reality was flush-decked).

And no shore leave... *There's no shore leave in mid-Atlantic. There's no shore leave here. What's it to you, Jack?*

So we waited at this anchorage. We coaled ship from lighters and waited. Waiting for what?

Many of us stared towards the town and the quay and the beach. As the days wore on it became compulsive for me, and I spent most of my free time devouring the scene with my eyes. People ashore were slow-moving dots. The lighter coloured ones were mostly females. I would screw up my eyes trying to see them better. Sometimes I could borrow a glass and just make out bonnets and dresses, but nothing more. I could think of nothing else but that Judy might be among them. When would she come? Early when it was still fresh? In the heat of the afternoon? Surely not, even under a parasol. But I must still watch. In early evening when the people took a stroll as heat waned to warmth? Did she come to look at the little black ship with the black matchstick funnels? Or would she come when the tropical sun sank in the brief twilight and we were only a distant white riding light? Or would that man have forbidden her to go near the waterfront at all?

What would she be wearing here? Muslin frocks perhaps. Sweatily, I imagined asking her what she had on underneath, like in the old days. Before she had dirtied herself. Sometimes, in those days when we were out walking,

I would feel astonished that this beautiful, demure little lady with her bonnet and ringlets and her tartan dress down to her little shoes yet made me free with the secrets of her person. So petite and dainty but with that luxurious black muff beneath all… Was it really ladylike to have a fanny hill like that? Or was she, as she sometimes said so sadly, just an innkeeper's daughter?

She always seemed to know my thoughts and she would put on the look of horror and then a certain conspiratorial smile. I believed that there was no other like her in the world. Certainly not for me. A pearl beyond price, she was. How could I know that she was God's slowly, carefully built snare. And I believed He would heighten her lustre!

Well, I dare say, with the chilly vision of old age, it was a good deal more feral, furtive and fumbling than this. But cooped up in the *Oreto* in semi-tropical heat her image was torture indeed. This is what I am showing you. Most seafarers will know.

The privilege of slinging my hammock near to the galley stove now became a liability. I recall night after night lying there, unable to sleep because of the sensation of sweat trickling over my face and body. Cookie was in an amiable mood when I grumbled to him about my difficulty and put me up to applying for permission to move my hammock down a deck into the hold. There was even less air movement down there but somehow to be free of the immediate proximity of my crewmates was more comfortable, although the privacy made the phantasmic visitations like that above more intense. Sometimes I was almost ashamed to scan the shore for Judy in the morning, so outrageously had I made her image behave during the night.

As day followed day, Mr Low had much business ashore, the more so since I noticed the attention given to the arrival of the steamer *Bahama* a day or two after ourselves. Indeed a party of seamen and stokers, all big, strong and extremely silent fellows, frequently accompanied him in our longboat. Nothing we could do would prise out of them afterwards what they had been doing ashore. I also noticed that the few genuine American Southerners amongst us, mostly ex-members of the *Nashville's* crew who had turned-up in Liverpool, often seemed to serve as gang leaders.

Then they began to bring a few sacks and packages back with them on the bottom boards. Often it was stuff for us in the galley. Proper bread and fresh fruit. Dried fruit for duff and so on. Later, the items looked a lot heavier and were a struggle to get up the ship's side. That was when the boats from the British warships began to take closer interest. One or other of them would row round us several times a day, as well as putting out whenever they saw one of our boats moving. They stopped bothering with disguising their purpose. We were being watched. We became more frequently aware of the flash of a telescope lens catching the sun from a quarterdeck and of men still stationed aloft in a warship at anchor. We were being closely watched.

Also, British naval officers from HMS Bulldog and HMS Greyhound inspected us at different times. We even heard them laughing with our officers. Magazine, shell rooms: quite empty. Of course they knew. How could we have been still muddled about what she was? But she was still legal.

I have said before that great events at sea always seem to happen first thing in the morning. Talking in this vein to real Navy men leads them always to confirm this, as it is a good time to strike an enemy, when he is only half awake and definitely has not had breakfast.

It was in the morning watch of 15 June. It was pitch dark still, of course. You don't get much dawn or sunset in those parts and night and day are of equal length. I was shovelling the ashes riddled from the galley stove into a bucket, whilst Cookie was hunched unseeingly on a tall stool, holding his empty coffee mug and waiting for the water to boil, when we felt a violent bump. On deck, voices were heard and voices were raised. We inclined our heads to listen. Then there came a shouted command and a trampling of feet. We both stood up and I crept ridiculously on tiptoe towards the ladder to the fore hatch, ignoring a hissed command from Cookie, took hold of it, looked up and found myself staring at a bayonet on a musket barrel and behind it the red coat of a British marine. He stared at me, and I, open-mouthed, stared at him for a long second. Then I fled back to the galley.

"There's marines on board. There's Royal Marines on board!" I whispered at Cookie, who hit me a stinging blow upon the ear with a wooden spoon.

"That'll larn 'ee to take 'eed of what I do say. Bootnecks, eh?"

"Are we being arrested?" said I, rubbing my tingling ear.

"Course we'em being arrested. What do 'ee expect? 'Anging about 'ere like a burglar in 'is mask and striped jersey, even if we 'avn't got no jemmy. There's plenty o' deserted islands round yere where we could 'ave waited, whatever we'em waiting for. And thee just mind what I do say. Take thee pay and keep thee 'ead well down and thee mouth shut.'

All the hot day we looked at the 'bootnecks' and they looked at us. They looked extremely hot, with red shiny faces and sweat trickling in streams from under their shakos. After a while, I was sent by Cookie to find the nearest of them to see if he would accept a cup of coffee.

"Maybe he'll tell us what's going on if we wet 'is whistle,' was Cookie's idea. He wouldn't, and stuck to slaking his thirst from his water bottle.

"'E probably thinks it 'ud be scotch coffee," said Cookie. "I never sailed in no ship before that 'ad real coffee like this 'un. Maybe I'll sign on one o' they proper 'Merican ships one day, thee mus' know.' Scotch coffee was made by charring ship's biscuit black, then adding hot water and a spoonful of molasses. Some of the men had at first actually requested the vile brew.

So the day wore on as we self-consciously got on with the normal tasks under the marines' eyes. Of course, the buzz got about soon enough, that the captain of *HMS Bulldog*, Commander McKillop, had become convinced that our shore working party was bringing armaments aboard. Some of those men smirked at each other while the marines searched every storeroom and the hold. Nothing. They even tried to search the coalbunkers but, although they made a mess that caused the stokers to swear, they could not get very far and in the end convinced themselves that neither could have we. I know now that Captain Maffit, Confederate States Navy, our real captain-to-be, had been in Nassau since 4 May when he brought in the 'runner' *Nassau* from sea. But it was known, obviously, who he was and he was much too fly to go near the *Oreto*. He had observed the surveillance we were under and had probed it by setting up the shore party. Those heavy sacks that had taken such heaving up the ship's side had nothing more lethal than broken bricks and lumps of coral inside them, which had gone down straight into the ballast. We had the marines overnight whilst our people ashore went dashing round to see the Governor. But he decided that *Oreto* was a British-registered ship with no armament and seizure was not justified. Off went the 'booties', but instead of them we had Customs officers in a boat hanging around in shifts and looking at every single thing that came and went from *Oreto*. It occupied the minds of us all and was an escape from the boredom of just lying there twiddling our thumbs and sweating. She was a new ship and there were limits to how much of her you could re-paint or re-rig.

Then, I don't know how they did it but I think it must have been that they persuaded the Customs boat to take them, half-a dozen of our crewmembers got on board *HMS Greyhound*. So much for bottling us all up with no shore leave so that someone full of rum couldn't shout his mouth off about what was going on aboard. These men told Commander Hinckley that they had no idea of where the *Oreto* was going and also that someone had been ashore trying to recruit more men. That of course brought down the Foreign Enlistment Act like a ton of bricks on us. Old Duguid found out that these men were missing and where they'd gone and got into a rare old panic. He ran round shouting about raising steam and weighing anchor. The blokes asked, "Where are we going?" and he said, "Havana, for coal." The men looked at him and said. "What, with full bunkers?" Then they turned their backs on him.

It was sad really, because he wasn't a bad Old Man. Just out of his depth, if you will pardon me. I suppose, like the rest of us - even me - he felt he needed the money. What good had all that money in the bank done me? Where was Judy? No. Reality now was here, looking forward to being paid like the others.

Then it was another boxful of Royal Marines coming up the side, from *HMS Greyhound* this time, and that was that. Arrested and taken to court.

They moved us to a berth alongside, where they could keep a better eye on us. Of course, it was more convenient to walk across the gangway for supplies but it did open us to the curse of longshoremen: thieving. Whenever you are alongside, there are always strangers on board. If you approach them with your "Can I help you, friend?" it is always "Oh, I'm just waiting until the Chief gets back," or "I've brought the laundry on board for the wardroom and the steward has just gone to get my money from the paymaster." Maybe he has and maybe he hasn't. If you are watchful you can sometimes see your man sneaking hastily towards the gangway, but mostly life is just too short.

Things - possessions - began to go missing. So did a set of navigation instruments. It was a pity they had taken away the marines. We were stuck there for another fortnight. Our case of violating the Foreign Enlistment Act (this business of not being allowed to recruit British subjects to fight in other people's wars) was heard by the Vice Admiralty Court in the little whitewashed courthouse in Nassau.

Cookie thought that I was mad but he let me go a couple of times and I sat fanning myself with a newspaper in the wooden gallery, trying to keep awake and follow it all. I also was keeping an eye open in case Judith came to see what was happening to the little ship she had been to sea with, upon *Oreto's* trials, but she never did while I was in the courthouse. Back home, her sister would come with me to visit the ships, but to Judith they were no different from a house or a hillock. "How can you be so fascinated by a machine?" she once inquired crossly. She had lived near the sea for most of her life but cared nothing for it, except that it provided money in the pocket for so many. Although it made me sad at times, it was just one of those things about Judy. She cared no more for the pub.

Nassau is a small enough place. Just a main street parallel to the shore, with side streets running a little way inland. If I walked about, I thought I saw her in the distance just as before. And just as before it was never she. Sometimes I felt despair. I think she may have been taken to stay at some inland house amidst the palms and geraniums. I shall never know now.

If it had not been so long drawn out in the summer heat, the trial would have passed as a farce. At rock bottom the prosecution said the *Oreto* was a warship. A warship, which then turned up in Nassau. A warship, thus likely bound for the Confederate States from British territory, which was not allowed because it was not being neutral.

The defence said it did not matter what she looked like. She was registered as a British merchant ship with a merchant navy skipper and a British crew properly signed on in Liverpool. Her documentation as such was almost painfully correct.

Calling Commander Hinckley and several crewmembers as witnesses, the prosecution then asked, in effect, why are there a magazine and shell rooms in the ship but no cargo hold? The defence replied that it did not matter what these spaces were called or looked like. There was no ammunition in them, not then, not before, never.

They had to let us go, which, with great dispatch, we did.

The first thing was that the captain came aboard. I was not able to go to the last day of the trial. Cookie would not have it and I can see now why. So this man who walked across the quay - bounded across the quay might be better - was not known to me. I was carrying two pails full of spud peelings and the like, which I intended to dump ashore. And as it happened I was just at the head of the gangway when he appeared. This man in a linen jacket and a straw boater, worn at what I would describe now as a trademark tilt over his right eye, came clattering up. I suppose trying to cope with the weight of the pails and keep out of the way I was in the spot where a naval man on duty at the gangway would be and I was standing up pretty straight. I had a glimpse of a youngish, tanned face with the eyes set in wrinkles from squinting in sunlight over sparkling seas. There was a black goatee beard under a humorous mouth.

"Good afternoon," I got, with a rather off-hand sketchy salute in the air. And as I gaped after him hurrying away aft, a chuckle and a drawled, "Glad to be aboard," floating over his shoulder. I had no doubt at all that he was what we had been waiting for and that was my first sighting of John N Maffit, Confederate States Navy.

The arrival of Captain Maffit bore a resemblance to the effects of the Last Trump. A few souls ascended to serve on in the ship. The rest took their effects and descended to the quayside, not satisfied to hear that the ship had been cleared in ballast for St. Johns, New Brunswick, in Canada. Oh ye of little faith...

That left eleven of us to work the ship. Or was it twelve? Why did I stay? I must have been crazy. There was not a sign that Judith was in the Bahamas except that 'that man', the assistant paymaster, seemed to have much business ashore. But since we had spent so much time lying off and using boats, there was no way I could follow him. In any case, after all this time I had sunk into disbelief and despondency. There seemed nothing else to be done, so I felt I might as well follow my nose and see what the rest of the story of this strange ship might be. That it might be extremely dangerous, I recognised; but it seemed unreal and remote to a young man, like death. .

The war was not far off as it happened. Grey from distance, grey in paint, now there was a strange ship hovering outside the harbour entrance. Talk along the waterfront said she was the *USS Culver*. Not so greatly impressive, except that even half a gun was better than no guns at all like us. There were also rumours of something far worse. A big Federal steam frigate had been sighted not far away by several ships.

Do you see? It was us and them now. She was our ship. No, Judith would not have understood. And again there was this man Maffit. Occasionally you meet these people who seem to bring light into a room with them, who are never tired and always charming. You find yourself cheerfully following a leader like that anywhere.

We toiled through the day to ready her for sea, men and officers alike, sweaty and grimy, stripped to the waist. It was like the routine for coaling ship, everybody up - except that it was not coaling ship but everything else. Whatever one was doing, whenever you heard the bosun's call for 'all the watch' or a simply a yell down the hatch for hands, you dropped your appointed task and ran to help out where it was required. There were no steam windlass or capstans in those days. It was still just arms, legs and back power to work the ship. I often felt helpless and useless amongst the seamen but with a good-natured shove here and a shout there, even an occasional bellow to 'get the fuck out of the way, duff bosun', I too could squint up at the black yard ascending the mast silhouetted against the bright blue sky, amazed to discover that for the moment I was blissfully, blissfully happy.

I found it even accompanied me back down to the galley. We were busy enough there on our own account. To spare the hands time there were no mess cooks, so it was I who peeled a mountain of potatoes and chopped my eye-streaming way through a net of onions. For a while there was no sign of Cookie but then he re-appeared, struggling with a great bag of meat (cursing the flies that followed it that he could not swat) and parcels of suet, sugar and extra raisins. Dumping it with relief on the deck he ran a critical eye over my efforts.

"Cap'ens orders, if thee mus' know. Money I got for extra victuals. You scrape and slice them there carrots while I knock up some suet pastry and we'll give 'em a sea pie and a duff for afters they'll never forget. We'm short a' kindling and the danged wood-butcher won't cut us up some special. Go on, Tom, nip ashore and see if 'ee can see anything on the quay that'll do. An old crate or somethin', or we're goin' to be messing about in the dark tomorrow morning."

All I could find was a heap of palm tree leaves somebody had dumped. Cookie looked at them dubiously.

"Wal, them 'ull just 'ave to do, I suppose. If 'ee gets rid of the greenery, the stalks might do. An' lay 'em out in the sun to dry off a bit more."

Nothing loath, I immediately laid hands on the palm fronds but after I'd done two or three I was shooed ashore by Cookie for making a mess. One or two insects had flown out of the leaves as well: mosquitoes, maybe.

Crossing the deck I was nudged by several people in succession with gladsome tidings.

"Shore leave tonight!"

I could hardly believe it, for looking about me there still seemed so much to do. But in return, all hands sweated valiantly through the dogwatches until supper - and grog to give us a fair wind - and the ship was in pretty good order before most of us trooped ashore. Captain Maffit was a shrewd judge of sailor-men.

The one thing they had warned us never to drink was the cheap white rum that you could get in the little grog shops of the back streets, which largely served coloured men. Of course we had to try it. And even I went along with it, an old Caribbean hand. It was like a volcano erupting, that first drop on the tongue. There was a silent explosion that filled the mouth and then rivers of fire that flowed down everywhere, while the locals grinned wide grins in black faces and waited. I knew you stopped it there if you were wise, for there are many fine rums to sample without drinking gunpowder. But some were not and did not, as you will read.

Cookie was there. In the din of some bar, loud with piano, I heard myself asking where he was from. A little drunker and I'd have asked him about his accent. He glanced at me and his eyes, always slightly bloodshot, were more so now.

"Wareham," he said. "Down in Darset. Fuck it," tossed down his rum, flung his head back and roared out:

"Be I Hampshire, be I buggery.

"I be up from Wareham.

"Where the girls wear calico drawers

"And we knows how to tear 'em."

He wagged a finger under my nose. "I know where you'm from. You'm a bloody Hampshire hog, you are." He let out an amazing cackle of laughter.

It was the calico drawers that almost had me. How could he possibly have known? Fortunately, I was not so drunk that thought could not move on and inform me that it was the place I came from, not what I had been doing there, to which he was referring.

But the calico drawers had worked their secret spell. I thought of Judith's drawers and I wanted Judith and I could not have her. I could not have her even though she was probably hidden only a little way away in this small place. If she were here she would refuse me and hold her skirts down, that hellish punishment of other times. And even if she uncovered her sex to me, I could not have her because she was not to know what the parts between her legs were really for, apart from the Exquisite Sensations, until we had traipsed up the aisle to meet God. That was the only thing good enough for Judy in my eyes. After that she could know. We could take off her white garments at long last and put them with the veil I had persuaded her to lift so long ago. The magic would be over. That druidic magic that I most clearly remember from when she uncovered herself in that little wood on Southampton Common, when we were little more than children. That spirit, which conjured up letters and poetry, longing and exotic gifts from the far places of Earth and now which had escaped and was running wild.

Now I must have a woman! My head throbbed with rum and longing and with a desire that Judy should be made to watch me, to punish her for what she had driven me to. There were plenty of young tarts about in that bar. I remembered Pretty Polly in long-ago Jamaica. But to punish Judy I wanted a white woman. The white women there were raddled and gaudy. Enter Satan who bowed like a waiter and presented his suggestion.

She was 'high yalla', a quadroon or octoroon, I would guess, with an arrogant manner and, appropriately enough, a scarlet dress. Then came the devilish trap. As I caught her eye she reached down and took hold of her dress with both hands. Just some feminine need to re-arrange it, I suppose; but it was also the exact same manner that Judy used when she was beginning to lift her skirts for me. That settled it. She was suspicious of me at first because with my poor clothes she thought I might not have her price. But I had a pocketful of money - I had found the bank where the blessed Roderick had forwarded funds arranged from the High Street bank at home.

She led me upstairs to her bare little room. There was none of the French-style opulence one might have expected but the pillow and the little cloth were white and crisp and the towel to lie upon was pristine clean. She was beginning to unfasten her dress, but I stopped her and said that I wanted to have her clothed. I told myself that it was because I did not want to linger there longer than the business required, but of course beneath that I knew she would have to manage her skirts a little like Judith. She made a face and lifted an eyebrow but went to lie down as, practiced roué that I was, I turned my back to struggle out of my trousers. When I looked round, there she was on the bed and as I watched she slowly drew up her knees and slowly, slowly the scarlet dress slipped downward from her thighs. I sprang. I found myself as a starving man. Thinking about it afterwards I could have kicked myself because for a shilling or two more she would probably have lifted her skirt for me as I wished, before she lay down.

When eventually I returned to our table I was greeted with a respectful silence.

"That must have taken most of your advance of pay," at last somebody remarked.

I nodded and rolled my eyes to intimate that it had been utterly worth it. I was also peacefully aware of how the shackles of desire had fallen from my waist and now clattered futile about my feet. Damn Judith. Damn her calico drawers. Damn her for dragging me to this hole. I'm free. I'm free. Oh yes, free after a 'quick one' with a trollop. Free for a drunken hour or so whilst I kept drinking. One of life's more potent lessons, that. They didn't teach you that at King Edward's Grammar School.

I turned, thinking of telling Cookie about it, but he was muttering something into his glass, something about the captain's servant. I did not even know the man had brought a servant but captains often did. And this captain was Navy - well, Confederate Navy - but he had done many 'runner' trips into Charleston, they said, so he must be pretty good.

"Another bloody quean, I suppose," Cookie was muttering. I thought for one outraged, spirituous moment he meant me! And then the captain, which was only marginally better. But he didn't. He was quite drunk. Who cared what he meant.

We were in honour bound to be back on board before midnight. Some might sneer but most of us felt that we should not let our new captain down. However, there are always one or two who go too far. We were getting tired of Nassau, tired of rum, tired of black tarts (and white tarts, too, for that matter); just bloody tired. And our legs were tired. No one likes to be the first to suggest, "Let's go back to the ship," but a time comes when it's welcome.

We were lurching along with the blinding lights and the loud noises going past, holding each other up, when, in spite of all precautions, Cookie tripped up and went down onto all fours in the street. We hauled him, swearing a blue streak, up again and then turned back to see what he had fallen over. There was somebody lying half on the pavement and half in the gutter. Cookie went back and there was something in his demeanour that suggested he was going to give a smart kick or two to whoever it was had obstructed his progress. Whatever he at first intended, we saw him bend over the body, swaying, then he looked back at us and gave an incoherent cry. Peering closely in the gloom we discovered it was the AB, Jeb Duff. He reeked of rum and there was some blood on his face near his nose and he was unconscious, whether from drink, whether from fighting or whether he had simply fallen down dead drunk we did not know. We were worse for wear ourselves but somehow seafarers manage to pull themselves together, especially to deal with this kind of emergency. Somehow we picked him up and carted him along face downward and, pausing for a supreme effort, dragged him up the gangplank. We had enough sense left to decide that it would be unsafe to turn him in, in his hammock. So after someone unslung it, we let a mess table down and made a sort of berth with it on the deck underneath, turned Duff in on it and there we let him lie.

Chapter 15

When the bosun's call shrieked through the gloom next morning I sat up and jumped down feeling quite bright. The curtailed hours of slumber did not seem to matter at all. In other words, as I recognise now, I was still 'shaking a cloth in the wind' (under the influence, to you). We all were. How everybody else's breath stank of second-hand rum!

I blundered up the ladder and into the galley to be narrowly missed by Cookie with the wooden spoon. "All 'ands on deck. All 'ands on bloody deck!" he screamed. "Do they bloody want to eat or don't they?" With which he tore off his apron and was off himself. I noticed a glow between the bars of the range before I ran after him. He had got the fire alight and I wondered when on earth he had turned to. Then I wondered when on earth I had turned to.

It was a lovely tropical dawn on deck. And how bright the rising sun and the pink and blue sky were and how roughly the on-shore breeze ruffled my hair. Greenish black smoke was pouring heavily down from the funnels and rolling low over the town as the *Oreto* began raising steam: so we were not likely to be going anywhere for a couple of hours. In those days steam pressures were so puny... But even blowing landward the cloud must have been visible way out at sea. And there was that damned Yankee *Cuyler* again, flattered by the dawn, steaming about just outside the harbour entrance in an interested kind of manner, like another cat sniffing at another hole.

There had been a change in the Royal Naval presence over the weeks of our stay in Nassau. I understood they were a team of three. One conducts a cruise through an itinerary of foreign and British port visits, 'showing the flag'. One prowls the smaller islands and lighthouses, occasionally playing the locals at cricket and keeping a watch for anything or anybody out of order. The third has a period alongside somewhere for self-maintenance and repairs. So *Bulldog* had gone off on her beat and it was *HMS Petrel* now that was anchored near the entrance. She was just another barque-rigged sloop much as we were, with a telescopic funnel.

We had steam up and were casting off, indeed were singled up to bow and stern line several feet from the quay, when we were disturbed by a shout from someone pelting towards the ship, while another ran after him pushing a trunk on a trolley. We all stared crossly at him wondering who he was when Captain Maffit suddenly shouted, "John! What on earth are you doing here? I heard you had gone home to get married."

So of course we all heaved in on the bow line again and by this 'pier-head jump' acquired our Executive Officer, Lieutenant Stribbling, late of the *CSS Sumter*, trapped, so we heard, at Gibraltar. Better for him if we had gone too far to recognise him or hear him. Better for him to have stamped in annoyance and frustration at the sight of a dwindling missed ship. Poor young woman, his fiancée, whoever she was.

Anyway, we tried again and this time dawdled towards the entrance and anchored as closely as possible to the *Petrel*. That is not all that close, you understand. There has to be room to swing from tide or wind. But near enough to be able to see the people on *Petrel's* deck. Over the months, one way and another, we and the British sloops had got to know each other pretty well. We had almost become part of the scenery. It seemed that the *Petrel's* people watched us in a noncommittal kind of way. This was the ship of unknown intentions of which they had received a brief. What were we about this morning and was there going to be trouble? The Naval officers might saunter about *Petrel's* decks in their usual offhand, superior manner, but her funnel was up and smoking gently. She undoubtedly had steam. But mostly our eyes were upon the ever-moving *USS RR Cuyler.* Now we saw her broadside outline. Now that narrowed and her masts, yards and funnel seemed to fuse into symmetry and then of course began to diverge again. But was she coming on or turning away out to sea? But wait. Was the confusing image getting slowly larger or was that imagination? By God, it was not. She was coming in and I remember how my stomach turned over!

There is an immense delight, if meeting an adversary on neutral ground, to observe them, in their uncouthness, offending your host. Our Southern officers with their elaborate, old-fashioned manners must have taken even greater pleasure as the Yankee piled offensive gaffe upon gaffe.

Neglecting the Harbour Master of Nassau's instructions on navigation, she came in too fast, leaving a wash that soon had many small boats tossing uncomfortably and wavelets breaking amongst the piling of quays and upon the beaches. Most crass of all, she omitted or neglected to dip her confounded 'stars and stripes' as she passed *HMS Petrel.* I could easily imagine the faces of the Royal Navy officers growing redder and redder and their politeness becoming more and more icy. The Federal vessel then proceeded to circle us and the *Petrel* several times, which must be comparable to being discovered in somebody's garden trying to look in through the downstairs windows!

Two small bundles rapidly ascended to the *Petrel's* yardarm and snapped open, revealing a yellow and red and white signal flags. No response. As the *Cuyler* went round for the second time we could clearly hear an exasperated voice bellowing through a speaking trumpet. Indeed, we could see its polished copper flashing in the sunlight.

"*Cuyler,* ahoy. This is Her Britannic Majesty's Ship *Petrel.* What the devil d'you think you're doing? Kindly enter the harbour and anchor, or leave British territorial waters immediately!"

I have often wondered what had been in the Federal commander's mind. Did he think we might suddenly fire on him because perhaps our unarmed status had not been communicated to him as yet? It was only yesterday we escaped from court. Or was he one of those Americans who resented the impossible dominance of the Royal Navy wherever you were in the world? One who did not recognise his betters when he saw them.

So they went. They completed the third circling manoeuvre and then just kept going towards the harbour entrance. They appeared to be pretending that we were not there, that we did not exist, judging by their apparently averted faces. (Apart from some buffoon amidships who was vigorously waving his hat as they swept past, and who then suddenly disappeared behind their bulwarks as if seized from below.)

Or was there method in their madness, in that now Federal naval officers had seen close-to this suspect vessel that had come from the Mersey? I wonder if there is still a report in the intelligence department archives of the United States Navy.

We had been towing one of our whalers and, taking three quarters of our crew, no less, our captain had himself rowed over to *HMS Petrel.* He had exchanged his boater for a low-crowned straw hat but it still had the jaunty tilt over the right eye as he went up the ship's side and uncovered his head smartly in the entering port. The visit was not a long one but appeared to have been amicable enough. The British captain - they said it was Watson - took the unusual step of accompanying his caller to the side. I was watching through a borrowed glass.

"I'm sure I do not know whether I should address you as 'Mister' or 'Captain'," was the sense of what the boat's crew recounted afterwards of what they had heard. "But I suggest you go, and go now, while there is no hindrance. I dare say I cannot properly wish you good fortune but... a safe voyage should do no harm."

They should have held us for twenty-four hours but they did not. It was a convenient way of expressing their irritation with the United States Navy.

The *Cuyler* was distant now, still legging it towards the horizon, trailing smoke. We hands were merely puzzled at the time. I can still make my stomach sink again by remembering the sudden realisation that she might have gone to fetch the frigate, the *USS Adirondack*, rather than risk an action on her own trailing glory. Or possibly not. All from our poor toothless *Oreto*.

"I've told thee before to keep thee mouth shut," said Cookie. "You'm going to put the wind up the troops, you be."

When the *Cuyler's* smoke was just a smudge, we few, we very few, manned the capstan and got the hook up. And sweaty we were by the time it was aweigh, even in such shallow water. And then it was out of the harbour after dipping our 'red rag' to the *Petrel* who punctiliously replied. Ostentatiously, we set off on the usual course for Charleston but, with Nassau becoming a blur on the horizon, we turned off, putting Hog Island between us and it, and with a certain reluctance on our part, anchored. Such a short roar going out and such a long haul getting it back in.

To allow us to recover somewhat from our exertions they gave us a 'make and mend' afternoon. Right in the middle of it, about three, our nap was disturbed by calling all hands. A pretty topsail schooner came round the headland and made towards us. I remember vaguely having noticed her moored outboard of the steamer *Bahama*, which had seemed odd at the time because there was ample room for her to be alongside the quay, but I had dismissed it as a delivery of coal, or some other stores or cargo. Now she was definitely coming to us. *Prince Alfred* or *King Alfred* she was named. I forget which now.

A glance aft at the officers revealed no surprise. She was expected. She ranged up to us alongside and Captain Maffitt shouted across that he proposed to take the schooner in tow as soon as he got under way. Then of course for us there was tramping round and round the capstan, getting that damned anchor up again.

Heaving lines fly. A towing cable is passed, and off the pair of us lumber until in the first watch we were all called up again to anchor and secure the *Prince Alfred* alongside. Looking back at it, I am surprised now that they did not try to work us through the night.

In the morning we found that we were anchored off another uninhabited island. Green Cay on the edge of the Great Bahama Bank, they said. No sooner had the hands gulped down their porridge than it began. Penal servitude with hard labour for what soon began to feel like life. It would have been hard for any crew, but for the handful that we were it was back breaking. In the schooner's hold was the ship's armament: two bloody great nine-inch pivot guns and half a dozen smaller six-inch guns for the broadside, all rifled, and it was a pity that it did not make them a bit less heavy. Then there were the carriages for the things. Then there was all the ammunition.

So we toiled in the sun: officers, petty officers, seamen and stokers (all two of them) alike. If I think of that time, I summon up a vision of an elephant of a gun weighing three tons or more, suspended a little above bulwark height and placidly rotating a few degrees from side to side for all that we could do to stop it, while masts and spars groaned with strain and rope tackles thrummed and twanged alarmingly. The very ships themselves inclined amorously towards each other, like lovers mingling their hair, although the wooden hulls protested with creaks and cracking sounds. Those ships for the Confederacy were built of wood in Liverpool so that if repairs were needed they could go into any little port around the world and still find shipwrights who could tackle the job. Iron was still very new in those days and these ships would never know a home dockyard. And the great weight of the dangling gun entered my mind and memory. What if it fell? As the salt sweat stung my eyes I thought of God. He was not hunched in His tower now. He floated by, lolling on a cloud and sipping from a great horn cup. His grey beard flapped as He roared with laughter, bawling at us, "That's right, work! That's what I made you for, to toil and sweat, to labour and bend. Work! *Work*!"

At first the intention was that, normal ship's routine having been abandoned, all hands should work through the usual working day. Our position was precarious. All could see that. At any moment the *USS Adirondack* or even the *Cuyler* might appear, 'catching us with our trousers down', if you will pardon me. But men became exhausted and, drenched in sweat, would collapse, letting go of the rope tackle. The monster would jerk down a foot or two, putting the fear of death into us working below it, until we could take up the strain.

At one of the firemen's suggestion, we were given some of the salted, thin gruel that they used to stave off stoker's cramps in the stokehold. It may have helped and at least it was disgusting enough to be a diversion. On the second day we were all rested for ten minutes in the hour but, as over the day the temperature built up, it was not enough. Once we had taken delivery of the two big pivot guns it got a little better. Their carriages came over in bits, which had to be reassembled, but their weight by comparison was bearable. The six-inch rifled guns for the broadside were heavy all right, and took all hands to keep them from taking control, but there was not quite the same fear of them. I know the officers considered working us by night but it was not safe, for we could not see with a lantern to walk across a plank between the ships, let alone staggering over with a shell in our arms. I never thought I would be so grateful to be taken back to the potato peeling.

For eight days we laboured and on the eighth day Satan came again to me. It was all there in the twinkling of an eye, the answer to my wicked prayers. We were still working in a living chain: empty handed we walked over a plank onto the *King Alfred*, and, loaded with shot or shell or charge, we walked back over a second one.

I never found out for sure what that man was doing because it seemed wiser not to ask, but there he was in this boat, almost below me. Somebody said he had been sent ashore to look for fresh water, likely a fool's errand because the absence of it was probably why Green Cay was uninhabited in the first place.

We had transferred shell and powder for the guns as the priority. Now it was the shot, and I was just about able to carry one of these iron balls. I had had to put up with a good deal of banter and teasing - I was not used to heavy labour. It emerged I could deal with the six-incher's shot, so it was six-inch shot that I carried. It was imprudent to annoy anyone too much even the cook's mate.

Below me was the boat, with four of our badly needed hands cursing as they pushed and fended it off in an attempt to get space to use the oars.

That vile man had the tiller to steer.

Poison; razors; knife; contriving 'accidental' damage: all the plots and plans feverishly ruminated upon during the long, dark silent hours flowed smoothly through my mind like quicksilver - and out of it for ever.

Now was the time. Now was the opportunity.

If I dropped the shot directly upon him I could expect to see those black greasy curls split apart with blood, bone and brain. If it fell onto a shoulder from that height - twelve feet or so - it would break ribs and chest or arms and then smash through the bottom of the boat and this ruined thing could never then swim away. Even if I missed and it merely sank the boat, the wreckage might tangle with him and the ever-watchful water would drag him down.

How could I lose? After a little time and tears Judy would be lifting her skirts and taking my wrist in her small hand again to give her the magic of the Exquisite Sensations. Until we married, and then she would be mine, naked as a babe, or with her skirts up round her neck as I pleased. Would it be good to have her amidst her petticoats, through the space in her drawers and that thick black muff that had haunted me or taunted me for so long? It would be good to try. At last. And no evil done!

Ah ha. And, quicker than the eye could see, the flawed optimism of the thought flows through the brain. Not only to get us up the aisle in St. Michael's, but to lie two in a bed for the rest of our lives - and to lie. To shop in the High Street and walk in Above Bar like everyone else, but be different. To babble in fever, and yet say nothing. To be cast-iron sure never to take a brandy too many. To attend St Michael's, St Mary's, St Lawrence's or Holy Rood's every Sunday for ever and ever, face to face with the same unfriendly, accusing God wherever one went. To fall ill and fear death and confess nothing. And at the end maybe to stand naked myself, with Judith beside me when it did not matter anymore, and tell what I did before her face as well as His. Not for nothing is Satan the prince of lies. And whose is the first stroke of hell?

And why, oh my ever loving Father, would You not join us together? Why would You not?

And when it came to it, as once before, I could not make poor Judy weep. Even though I had known my cousin all her life, loved her, and still she turned out to be a deceitful bitch on heat.

Rejection had no sooner been my decision than for a moment of sheer terror I thought I really was in the power of hell, for I received a violent blow from behind. I turned my head to see what it was and became aware of an object falling and then saw a tall spout of water. I thought the strength of my hate had been enough to make what I had in my mind happen in spite of my will, but then I looked and I still had the shot in my arms. I staggered onto the deck and dropped the thing, which splintered the planking where it fell. I looked behind and there was that seaman, Jeb Duff. He had collapsed and lay precariously face down on the plank, an arm dangling.

Everyone was slow to accept the new situation. The boat's crew stared up at us, drenched, open mouthed and white faced, while the wavelets were still sloshing between the ships and spreading away over the blue sea.

Somebody behind me said, "Drunk again, is he? I wonder where he gets it from?" Then Mr. Stribbling's voice sounded louder above everything. "Look alive, you there! Secure that man!" And before we could think, we jerked into action.

I let the real seamen do it, balancing without thought on that damn plank as they retrieved Duff's dangling arm and then dragged him inboard. We turned him over on the deck and he groaned.

"Can't smell no drink," somebody said, sniffing ostentatiously. "But his eyes look a bit funny, don't they?"

"Course they look funny if he's been on the toot," said another. "Bloody bloodshot they'll be."

Lieutenant Stribbling pushed through, his initial reaction the usual one of seafarers.

"Is he drunk?"

"Don't know, sir," we chorused.

"Is he ill then?"

"Might be, sir." We had to do what we could for poor old Jeb. "His eyes look funny, sir."

Stribbling bent over the patient, looking closely.

"Oh, it's me legs. Oh, its me back," moaned Duff.

"I'm going to get the Captain."

The Captain. But no surgeon. Not even a surgeon's mate. So if anything is going wrong it's always the captain. You ought to remember that if he's giving you a rough time some morning, but of course you don't.

I was quite impressed with Captain Maffit when he arrived. You might have expected a sea captain confronted with a sick man and an unknown disease to fumble and move slow, but not our captain. He immediately felt the man's forehead, peered into his eyes and then pulled down an eyelid to examine it, looked at the tongue - not a pretty sight or smell from Jeb's nasty old pipe - felt his back and his belly and his legs and took his pulse. I saw him frown slightly, listen to his pocket watch and wind it a little and then count the pulse again. His face became quite expressionless.

"This man has a fever. You men turn him in. No. Take down his hammock and sling it up forward. Turn him in there. If there's anywhere cool below decks, it's up there. And his messmates to keep an eye on him. Try to keep him drinking. I'll take another look at him in an hour or so. Y'all carry on now."

Fever? A catching type of fever? But life was much more like that in those days, you know. There was cholera in St. Michael's parish tenements. School children vanished from their classmates because of typhoid. If God thought it was satisfactory, what was mankind to do? No, they took old Jeb forward carefully and Cookie made him a jug of lemonade. For the rest of us it was a double tot of rum.

Next morning after breakfast we sailed. It is easily said. All through the forenoon watch the handful of men set sail, little by little, mast by mast, beginning with the staysails, which were easiest.

About five bells, we found ourselves participating in a sort of crazy Christmas. We all had presents, doled out by that accursed man, fortunately as exhausted as any of us. I kept my now blackly hirsute head and face as averted from him as possible and he made no sign of recognition, flinging his bundles down at our feet, dull eyed. Inside were white duck jacket and trousers, a flat black cap, a black handkerchief for the neck, black socks and no damn shoes. No matter how toe-flapping the footwear we had - we had no cobbler amongst our handful - that was what we kept on wearing. We could go barefoot old-time-navy-style if we liked, but sooner or later you found that duty called you to run across the deck above the boiler room, which made you run a whole lot faster. And nothing on the feet in the galley was asking for trouble. But there was something unreal, a farce, a children's game of dressing up, about putting on the uniform clothes and looking at each other. Who were we trying to fool? Or fight?

Noon, and the Captain, First Lieutenant - I beg his pardon, Executive Officer - Mr Bradford the acting master, with the three acting midshipmen observing, shot the sun to obtain our position. I have never got over a primitive awe when I watch this 'ceremony'. To use the sun and stars to calculate where we are creeping over the surface of this world of water below has an almost druidical magic about it for me.

They huddled over the chart comparing results. I believe it was also to make sure we were outside British territorial waters. There was a small cheer. Then the bosun sent us off the deck in ones and twos to change into the new uniforms and to eat.

Come one o'clock - two bells in the afternoon watch - we were told to fall in, aft.

"Fall in, fall in," muttered Cookie. "I've been fell in, in better ships than this bloody toy." Fascinating to his hearers but he would never enlarge on what he meant.

So, come two bells we fell in: two untidy little rows aft of the six-inchers, pushed and shoved into line by the bosun and a couple of other men who surprised me by also seeming to know what they were doing.

Then the officers came up the wardroom companionway and formed a line athwartships. I supposed that we were probably meant to look to our front, but as this was the first time we had seen them in uniform, surely we could be forgiven for training our heads a little. They had on white duck trousers and a navy blue frock coat over a blue waistcoat, and peaked caps, of course. I have seen a photograph of Captain Semmes of the *CSS Alabama* in a grey uniform, but that was later on in the war. Our officers had all resigned from the US Navy and had simply changed the buttons and gold braid on their old uniforms, and a good thing too. Rather like my feelings about sailors with moustaches - whoever heard of sailors wearing grey? Bound to bring bad luck, that was.

One of the midshipmites had a fiddle under his left arm, I saw. So it looked as if we were going to get a tune. It was pleasant to see that one of them could do something, because as far as being at sea was concerned none of them knew their... backsides from their elbows, poor lads.

Then the Captain came springing up the steps and it must have been this servant of his right behind him. The one that Cookie thought was a bit of a nancy boy. When he got onto the deck too, this young fellow gave the Captain a rolled up piece of paper tied round with some dark red ribbon. The Captain threw him an elaborate salute and the kid sketched something in return and then, embarrassed, scuttled over to take his place at the end of our line where I could not see him so well. He was dressed in white duck and a black cap like the rest of us. I suppose there might have been something feminine about the way he held his arms and hands, and walked, until he got to his place and tried to stand up straight like the rest of us. I suppose it is not to my credit that I know better than most Englishmen exactly how a woman walks. The hair might have been rather long and the cheek more flushed than one might have expected but I doubted if he was much older than thirteen or fourteen. I thought him but a pretty boy who would probably coarsen satisfactorily when his beard began to grow.

Captain Maffit ran his eye over us all in silence. I felt a pang of anxiety and a fear of what might be to come. But I only had myself to blame that I was here.

Then he spoke to us. He told us that he intended to commission the ship into the Confederate Navy. It was time. Then a slight smile crossed his face.

"It may surprise you to know that I have never actually been present at such a ceremony myself and we carry no formal Regulations and Instructions for the Confederate Navy as yet, so I... we have had to improvise. I do know..." he said, waving at the sea around him, "that we cannot have a ceremony comfortably on the quay with the dear ladies looking on and giving us their support, and then march on board. So we will just have to do our creative best."

He went on to describe briefly the events that had led to the secession of the Southern States from the Union and their undoubted right, in his opinion, so to do under the Constitution. The Federal Government denied that right and denied the legality of the Confederate government, and that had led to this state of war between the States. There was never a word about slavery in it. Certainly nothing about extending it into the new States growing in the Wild West, which was one of the main bones of contention.

I had read that President Lincoln had denied that the war was about Abolition and that it was all the integrity of the Union that was his cause, but it still surprised me a little that there was not a mention of it in Captain Maffit's address. It came as strange to me because I had listened to plenty of Rachel's angry opinions on the matter after attending Abolitionist meetings at home, and she was quite convinced the war *was* about Abolition.

Captain Maffit spoke about the task of our ship, which was to injure the North as much as possible by attacking its shipping upon the high seas wherever it was to be found. That she was not a privateer but to be a properly commissioned war steamer of the Confederate Government, not a merely useful example of private enterprise and profit. Then he took off the ribbon from the rolled up paper and began to read it to us.

"Jefferson Davis, President of the Confederate States of America," it began. "To all who shall see these presents, greetings."

Jefferson Davis, eh? Suddenly, it was real.

"Know ye, that by the powers invested in me by law, I have commissioned and do hereby commission the vessel called the..."there he paused, "...*Florida*..."

So that was it. She was the *Florida.* Confederate States Ship *Florida*, to be exact. Not *Manassas*, as some rumours had had it.

Captain Maffit was reading on about the Ships, Vessels, Goods and Effects of the United States of America. I felt as if somebody had emptied a bucket of cold water over me. With my head full of little but the pursuit of Judith, I had signed on for a war! Well, it was too damn late to think of that now.

The captain finished and nodded. The midshipman raised his bow and one of the seamen picked up a kettledrum. I have heard *Dixie* played many times in my life, but with that squeaky fiddle, the breeze blowing away the notes and the beat being kept by just a tap on that drum, I have never heard it played with more menace!

The Confederate ensign, the circle of golden stars and the two red bars, was hoisted to the mizzen peak. Two fingers up to fate and fortunately a sea empty of the United States Navy. No more comfortable old 'red rag' and the Royal Navy never far away. We were really on our own now, double pay or not.

While we were having prayers led by Mr Stribbling, a man two along from me collapsed to the deck. I remember thinking at the time that I had heard that men on parade in the sun often collapsed.

Chapter 16

Have you heard this song? It could have been written for us and the *Florida.*

And in her hair she wears a yellow ribbon,
She wears it in the springtime, and the merry month of May, hey-hey.
And if you ask her why the hell she wears it,
She wears it for a sailor who is far, far away.

I find that after three months or so in a tropical climate, I begin to dream of a wet day in England with the cool rain trickling down the back of my neck. It does no good, of course. Out there the sun burns down pitilessly every day and there is a moist warmth, which invisibly floats to a few feet above the warm blue sea. Not a good place to take my turn coal-heaving in the bunkers. Not a good place for a man to lie in a fever.

We most of us did our best for poor old Jeb, although some were afraid to go near him. It seemed to me that if Miss Nightingale's young women at Scutari could look after the sick and survive it, so could we. We sponged him down with wet cloths and attempted to get him to drink while the Captain tried to ease the headache and the pains in his back and legs that made him groan, and toss and turn, with a little laudanum. There was nothing else.

Come about four days, he seemed to be getting a little better. He stopped burning up and rested easier, but after a day or so we could see his gums were bleeding and he started to throw up dreadful dark vomit. Then his skin and his eyeballs began to get yellow and we guessed what it was: yellow fever. Though some said he'd done for his liver with rum. Then he died so it didn't matter to him. It was over the ship's side in canvas with a couple of fire bars to keep him down.

This did not cheer the man who collapsed on divisions when the *Florida* was commissioned. But although he complained of the same symptoms, they were never as bad and after a few days he began to recover. Because he never went yellow it gave everybody the opportunity to suppose that maybe it was not 'Yellow Jack' after all.

"You'm better get your 'ammock out of that there 'old," advised Cookie. "Ah heard as it was something to do with bilge water as brought the Yellow Jack a-times."

There was a little water in the bilges. Building the *Florida* of wood back there at Miller's shipyard, even in 1861, had not been easy. It appeared it had been difficult to get together enough seasoned timber. They had to use some green timber and as a consequence she leaked a little. But she was brand new and the water did not stink. She was pumped out every day, but even when the pumps sucked dry there was always a little left. It still seemed healthier to me than sleeping on the same mess deck as the sick men up forward.

We had a day or so of peace steering west past the light on Lobos Cay towards Cardenas on the north coast of Cuba, where it was hoped to sign on more men. We went so close to Lobos that we could see what must have been the children of the lighthouse keeper running and tumbling down the steps in exact order of size, littlest first, to wave to us from the bright white sands of the beach. Foolhardy? Not us. Captain Maffit had been a marine surveyor in the old navy and what he did not know of the waters we sailed in, the reefs and shallows and channels, was not worth knowing.

Then, oh God, three more went down with fever and the *Florida* became a ship of frightened men avoiding each other's eyes. Fear of infection. Fear of every dark corner where some miasma could be lurking. Fear of the sea and fear of wind and what they might do if they discovered our plight, as hands to work the ship dwindled. And fear of United States ships patrolling the Old Bahama Channel like the Saucy Jack had done.

Can you think of worse to come? Linger with me a while. They left it a day or two because with sickness and exhaustion the men had their work cut out just to handle the ship. But the ship was now the Confederate warship *Florida*, flying the stars and bars, and effectively with her hand against every United States man o' war and merchant vessel, and every man's hand against her. That hand might come smoking over the horizon at any moment. With all the hope and proud boasting invested in her, it was unthinkable that she should be taken, haltered and dragged home to the North without a fight to the death, or at least a shot or two of defiance. Although, of course, in the end she was.

We had secured the big pivot guns in their places fore and aft of the funnels, and the six-inchers behind their gun ports. And very impressive they looked, for several of us, including myself, had never seen a big gun in our lives before. I was just a piss-pot emptier and I did not think the two knee-high pop-guns carried by the Royal Mail ships counted. And I would not have been able to fire those either.

There were British man o' wars men amongst us, trained with the great guns. One of them, one of the brightest amongst them, became in the eyes of the officers and ourselves, the gunner... acting, unpaid, maybe. He was outside the galley that morning, waiting for the coffee when Lieutenant Stribbling came by.

"Morning, sir."

"Good morning to you, Grimes." (Or Smith or Brown or Bloggs. But I think it was Grimes. AB Grimes.) "Come hell or high water, Grimes, somehow we must get gun crews together."

"Yessir."

"Maybe we should not run before we can walk. I intend that we should begin drilling with one of the six-inchers. I want you to break out a rammer and sponge for one of them. And fit the sights and quoins first."

"Yessir. Where are they, sir?"

"Now, that I don't rightly know. In the hold somewhere? Who was in charge of the hold? Ask him."

"I think it was Winslade, sir. He's got the fever. He's off his head with it, sir."

Dear reader, do you need me to go on with this? A search of the hold. A search of the ship. Amusement on the part of those like me who did not understand what was amiss. Explanations. Uncertainty. Slow, stomach-churning realisation. No sights. No quoins. No rammers, no sponges to be found anywhere. Mr Stribbling ordered another strict search. Nothing. Despite all our labour with the ammunition, for want of these things on the end of sticks, the *Florida* was as helpless as she was when she left Liverpool Bay. I wished to hell that I was back there. Not trapped in this joke of a navy. Yet how else was I to follow Judy, with the world so wide and she so small?

Poor old Stribbling. There was nothing for it but a heavyhearted walk aft to tell the Captain. The first we knew of it was when we heard faintly a wild cackle of laughter coming from the cabin. And next, a little laughter, uncertain at first, from a second person: Stribbling. I shall never forget the Captain of the *Florida*: amused in the face of disaster.

The devil knows where the equipment really was. Was it overlooked in the holds of *SS Bahama* or been left in the

Prince Alfred? We were out on our feet, all of us, after that frightful week. I suspect it was there that they lay.

I suppose things could have been worse. Even with false teeth we could overawe any Yankee merchantman we came across. And run from most ships of war thinking to catch us. The cardinal problem was the undermanning and we pressed on towards Cardenas.

The north coast of Cuba is screened behind an archipelago of islets, cays and reefs. Dull-eyed as we were, we could still wonder at the blue water, translucent as glass, with a white sandy bottom many, many fathoms down. There were tall dark towers of coral, some deep, some dimpling the surface as the little waves sucked at them. In our fatigue, we could still be thankful to the sure hand that took us through them.

Arriving off Cardenas, the yellow quarantine flag was dutifully hoisted to show that there was disease aboard but the fat Spanish pilot shrugged. There was yellow fever ashore as well. It was the season. Before long, thankfully we were alongside.

Most of these Cuban ports are much the same to see and are situated on the estuary where a river runs down from the hills. Cardenas is called the 'American City'. As well as the tangle of narrow streets, whitewashed walls, red tiled roofs, and domes and towers of churches, there were more heavily built warehouses near the waterfront. Visible here and there on the hilly outskirts amongst the dense, vivid green foliage were white pillared classical houses, more an echo of the American South than the *casas* of Old Spain.

"Lot o' Americans lives 'ere. Import, export; baccy, sugar, rum, railway lines, thee mus' know," said Cookie as a group of us clustered at the gangway entry port in the bulwarks, wearily contemplating the sights.

"What sort of Americans?" I asked. Cookie raised his hand and threatened me.

"I've told 'ee. I've told 'ee," he said. "We'm alongside, thank God, so don't look no gift 'oss in the mouth."

But would they be Southern Americans who would have been trading through New Orleans if they could? Or merchants from Boston or New York who might start telegraphing to bring the United States Navy down upon us before those tarpaulined shapes near the funnels could be uncovered against their ships?

Something of both, in the event. There was a visit from a Spanish Naval officer who startled the Officer of the Day (one of the midshipmen, nobody else could be spared) at the gangway by addressing him in colloquial American, if I may refer to it as such. He was an American doctor who had taken a post as medical officer in the Spanish Navy. Accompanied by Captain Maffit he came forward to inspect the sorry sight of our 'sickbay', which is when I saw him. Later, he made arrangements to remove our patients to sick quarters, but at the time he seemed to me to be as interested in the Captain as anyone and accompanied him back to the cabin to examine him before he went ashore. We soon found out that Captain Maffit was turned in with yellow fever as well. How that man had stayed on his feet until we got in I'll never know. And knowing he was off them gave me a moment of real fear because Lieutenant Stribbling had left for Havana earlier that day to try and sign on more hands and get a doctor. Which left a wealth of experience at the helm in Cardenas...

For a while I seriously considered jumping ship but speaking no Spanish and considering Cardenas as the back end of nowhere, somehow the ship was the devil I knew rather than the devil I didn't. Also there was the sneaking feeling of shame in letting Captain Maffit down in the moment of need. A captain is always in need of a good cook's mate, of course!

We grew to loathe that place. The ship lay in the sun, day after day, and each day she grew a little warmer and each night she cooled down a little less. If one went for a stroll when it was dark, hoping for refreshment, one found the heat beating up from stone and wall instead of beating down from a hostile sky. To endure a fever in conditions such as these was to encounter the pangs of hell rather than purgatory.

Then Mr.Stribbling returned from La Havana with twelve men and a doctor. There were eight seamen and four stokers. I suppose the men were a sorry looking lot, thin, dirty and ragged as they were. Rum-rats probably, to find themselves at a loose end in Cuba. But to us they seemed to be the Heavenly Host with St. Luke himself following on. The doc seemed to be a nice old boy who introduced himself cheerfully as G H Barnett, Acting Assistant Surgeon and, "I don't know whether I'm unpaid as well or not, yet," he drawled, running his eye over us. He was a real 'South'n Gennelman' too, from Georgia it appeared. Then he hurried off aft to see Captain Maffit and I doubt not that his servant boy was mightily relieved to see him. I had no business with the cabin nor he with the main galley, since there was a separate pantry and galley aft. I remember glimpsing the boy one time and experiencing one of those false impressions of Judith in the street that I have spoken about before. I had a momentary qualm that I had an element of perversion within me if this Confederate youth in his sailor clothes provoked it, but from bitter experience I knew that it never was she, so dismissing it from my mind I went about my business. Although I remember waking in the night with a craving for my petticoat parcel. Ah, those sometimes endless, sweat-soaked, sleepless tropical nights.

Think of how an owl or a hawk is mobbed by other birds. We could not perch there long. There was a US consul at Cardenas and soon there were Federal warships on the watch outside. Our poor Captain could still hardly stand, but a message from Spanish high-ups came, warning us that the Yankees were gathering and commanding us to move to Havana. Not that they gave a toss about us but they feared a US ship entering the port to attack us, or their boats arriving in the night on a cutting-out expedition. A subsequent row over a breach of Spanish neutrality might have been bad for business. Oh, I suppose I should not sneer. We all have to make a living.

Anyway, quite early in the forenoon watch on 31 August we heard the sound of distant gunfire and it was discovered that the Yankee ships were no longer visible. We had no idea what was happening but the important thing was that for whatever reason they had gone. All possible sail was set and steam was frantically raised. We slipped and went.

We heard in Havana that these Federal imbeciles had gone chasing and firing after a Spanish packet, identified no doubt as us because she had twin funnels. But at the time we went with hearts in our mouths, like a wounded fox making for another earth. Except that the fox had the armament of a rabbit. I do not altogether jest. Speed! With sail and steam the *Florida* could make thirteen knots, and it was only a few hours and we were passing under the massive ramparts of Morro Castle. Although looking up at them I wondered if we would ever pass out of Havana again.

The next thing that happened was we smelled the stink again. There was nothing to compare with it. The famous harbour is a deep, land-locked inlet with a narrow mouth. The tide is feeble and does not scour it, and the filth of centuries has drained into it. The water of the Tidal Dock back home is not beyond reproach but this brought men close to heaving. I look at the people ashore in such a place, the greatest city in the West Indies. The citizens, no doubt, think of themselves as urbane, cultured and sophisticated. Yet they live with this stink, untroubled.

I was fortunate, I think, to have a culinary errand for Cookie and spent an hour or so ashore. Narrow unclean streets, a maze of them. Churches everywhere and a jangling of bells. Black-cassocked priests, lots of them. Curious horse litters on high spidery wheels. The crowds about their business. The cackling speech. Oh, and the flies. Flies around the eyes of sleeping beggar babies left in baskets on church steps to attract alms. Fleas too, judging by the insect bites I later discovered.

Blank white walls, small heavily barred windows, and yet glimpsed courtyards and gardens bright with flowers and shaded with palms. I wondered where 'Vandal Eyes' was. Perhaps you will have visited Spain. Toledo or Valladolid. Much the same, but I had not been to Spain. Those streets had a certain threat for me, like a concealed knife, which made me continually look over my shoulder. They say Columbus himself is buried in the Cathedral here. I would like to have seen that but I did not know the way and there was no time. A seaman's story.

Regretfully, there was no coal. With apologies, it is not permitted to sign seamen. In any case there are none. It is the yellow fever season. There was nothing for us there. The Captain decided to leave as soon as we had taken on water and some vegetables. Into the setting sun we steamed, past the beetling castle and the forts, with no reaction. Denial of coal was today. Detention was possible for the Captain General *mañana*.

Rumour diffused through the ship in the evening like the land breeze. We were going into Mobile, in Alabama, in the Confederacy. But surely there would be a blockade by Federal warships? We were going to Mobile. As the *Nashville* in Southampton had been the first Confederate warship to come to Europe, now *Florida* was going to be the first of the Confederate cruisers to go into a Confederate port. Needs must, I suppose.

Four days it took us. Uneventful days with the blue water seeming to slide endlessly towards us, if you ignore more cases of Yellow Jack. Four days with fear growing in my guts like a stone. I noticed the ship change course once and later learned smoke had been sighted which might have been a Federal ship and we had turned away for a while.

"Should we not prepare in some way?" I pestered Cookie. "Is there not something called general quarters?"

"Why d'ye think I knows about it?" he replied, radiating suspicion for some reason. Then: "How the 'ell can we go to quarters with this 'ere 'andful? And what they goin' t'do when they gets there? Dang guns don't work. We're goin' ter 'ave our work cut out to keep 'er swimmin' and keep 'er movin', that's what, without tryin' to play battleships."

What we did get was morning drills in seamanship, especially in making and taking in sail, tacking and sending down spars. Although mostly I was a back and arms to be shoved and shouted at on deck; twice I was encouraged and threatened up the shrouds, sweating and at slow speed, to the maintop and out a step or two onto the footrope of the main-yard. Still, I was allowed to go up through the lubber's hole onto the top and I also swore to myself never to complain again about clearing up after some unfortunate seasick passenger. I am not sure to this day whether these exercises were to make a real seaman of me or to act as a diversion for the rest of them, because if not required on deck I was told often to assist the surgeon. Certainly those climbs have provided a lifetime's fodder for nightmares.

Being issued with a tourniquet by the wheezy old surgeon, with visions of mutilation and gore, was not encouraging either. About as encouraging as an inquisition upon us to discover anybody, anybody at all with experience as a carpenter or shipwright, to be entrusted with shoring up and leak-stopping. The look on Cookie's face as he overheard the candidate's crash course of instruction spoke volumes.

But there was not much else to do. The quarter-bill might assign me to assist surgery on the wardroom table but I was just as likely to be shovelling coal in the bunkers when the moment came.

And steadily, day-by-day the moment came sliding nearer. About mid-afternoon on 4th September we could see a smudge of land. Not tremendously impressive. Mobile Bay is not like Bournemouth Bay. It is more like Portsmouth Harbour with a narrow entrance and a marine lake within, although much larger. The entrance is screened by several small islands and, like so many of the Southern harbours, approaches and interior were shallow.

Drawing closer, and again rather resembling Portsmouth, the undulations of the spit of land to the east that is Mobile Point were visibly straightened by a rampart: Fort Morgan.

And there, at last, they were too. The blockading squadron. Three distant ships in line ahead, steaming slowly eastward to interpose themselves between the entrance and the unknown ship coming in from sea. I suppose it was raw fear because, looking at them, I found it difficult to take a breath. And then I found myself giggling, because behind them I made out the lighthouse on Sand Island. It took me back for a moment to a good old-fashioned singsong of a Saturday evening in the Bell at home. Everybody there and Judith looking disdainful as we sang. Do you know the ditty?

There's a tall and stately lighthouse, that the gulls use as a shitehouse,

now they're calling it the Whitehouse, in Mobile.

And there it was! There it was!

Cookie took one look at it all and made for the fore-hatch ladder, bawling. "'Ands to supper, 'ands to supper. Come and get it now if you wants something 'ot, cos I'll be drawing the galley fire." Will you believe me, we ate the damn stuff?

When we came up again, wiping our mouths, you could see the Federal ships more clearly. There was one of their steam sloops, like the *Tuscarora* in Southampton Water last Christmas. Then one of those spindly ninety-day gunboats of theirs. Then what looked like a schooner that they might have been towing.

I had to take my turn stoking, although I was so exhausted after forty minutes or so that they threw me out. I have never felt so hot. I was almost blind with sweat and could hardly hold the shovel it was so wet. In the end I missed the furnace with a shovelful and threw it all over poor old Duncan, which is when they ordered me out. I remember I was so tired I went up the ladder like an old man, one foot at a time, crawled over the coaming and fell down on the deck where somebody poured some salty water into me and some more in a bucket over me.

I lay propped up against the bulwarks for a good time but got back on my feet when I heard Lieutenant Stribbling shout to hoist the British ensign. I saw Captain Maffit sitting perched up on the quarter rail. He looked like the ghost of the man, still a bit yellow but with his straw hat at the usual jaunty angle and he was whistling quietly through his teeth. He was staring forward intently, stopping his whistling for a moment to give small alterations of course to the men on the wheel. I looked forward too and, Jesus H. Christ, I'll never forget it - there was the Yankee ship right in our path. And by God, we were going it. A lot of funnel smoke, and a lot of heat shimmer with it. You could smell it: coal smoke and hot oil. And feel it; she rattled everywhere and vibrated underfoot. You could feel her shudder as she bashed through the little waves rather than her own sweet way, breasting over them. That wasn't just full speed; that was full power; as fast as she could go and pray for the steam-pipe and boilers.

And even that was not enough for Maffit. We had to try and get more sail on her and I was doing my best at hauling just a foot or two from him. I still never worked out exactly what the Captain had in mind. Whether he would have rammed the *USS Oneida* (I know now what her name was) and taken them both down together, if that's what fate decreed. Or whether it was the question of who blinked first.

Then there was a big bang, which was the *Oneida* firing a warning gun. I suppose they still didn't really know who we were, what with the ensign and all. Maybe some 'kick-you-down-stairs' captain in the Royal Navy?

Another big bang and gun smoke from *Onieda* and she was beginning to fill the sky in front of us by now. Captain Maffit stopped whistling, grinned at me, leant over and sung at me. Sung under fire, mark you!

"Missus married Will de weaver. Will'um was a gay deceiver.

"Look away, look away, look away,

"Dixieland!"

I remember fighting a strong urge to turn and run away from the coming collision. Except there was only a few feet to run to. But they blinked first. I saw her waterline as we heaved over a wave and there was white water boiling under her counter as she went full speed astern. Her jib-boom was inches from raking our standing rigging - you could easily see open mouths in white faces - as we raced by. With Maffit waving his hat at them and bawling, "Evenin', George. Lovely weather," or something like that. Of course, we know now that he and Captain Prebble of the *Onieda* were old mates, and were again after the war.

Not that that stopped the *Onieda* and she gave us a broadside, which was the first and last broadside I have experienced - and more than enough at that. I am not saying that it was like the broadside coming from an old ship of the line like HMS Victory, yardarm to yardarm from feet away. Or like being fired on with the huge guns of today. But there was a ragged roar from a couple of eleven-inch pivots as well as the thirty-two-pounders. My ears sang with it, I could not hear properly after, and the smoke was choking. However, the *Onieda* was still running astern and under a lot of helm as she tried to get her guns to bear. It made her roll and it all went high into our masts and rigging. Nevertheless, I found it impressive when it brought down the foretopmast and the gaff. I was glad I was aft looking at the tangle of broken wood and rope all over the forecastle. And amazed that the people crawling out cursing from under the tangle were no worse hurt than they were. There were a lot of main backstays cut so perhaps it was as well that we had not been able to set more sail. I know the Captain sang out to bring down the British ensign and hoist the Confederate Stars and Bars. We got it down all right but the gear and the halliard came down on top of us as well, so we had to do without.

The Yankees got their hand in quickly. I can remember a brown cloud of splinters fly when one of the whalers got hit. I can remember feeling the blow when a big one came in near the waterline and went through a coal bunker without exploding, although it killed Jimmy Duncan and five of the others. Another one came inboard, almost below my feet, smashing the Captain's pantry and galley before it went out through the other side. It must have put the shits up 'Prettyboy' although I think Maffit must have ordered him down into the bread store or spirit room because I did not see him on deck. But then, we didn't need any powder monkeys, did we?

There was the Captain's skill in conning the ship so that the *Onieda* and the others were kept in line astern of us. That way they could not fire properly without hitting each other. But I never really saw it.

And it all went on for about twenty-five minutes, so they tell me.

After the second big one came in that wrecked the pantry, I can remember a wave of heat like from the stokehold came over me. Indeed, I looked round to see if the ship was on fire. And then it was as cold as ice. Much colder than the fire bucket of seawater they'd thrown over me. And that was more or less the end of it for me. I can remember wondering if I had been shot. Everything was dark, although I was aware that I was lying on the deck with my eye close to the pitch and the planking. I can recall hearing distant cheering, which must have been when the *Florida* anchored under the guns of Fort Morgan. It was my turn for the Yellow Jack. Otherwise I really had seen the last of the Confederate States Ship *Florida* forever, and there was no help for it.

I was told that I very nearly died. Accounts that I have read say that the harbour authorities of Mobile moored a smaller ship alongside to accommodate the sick. If that was where I was nursed I have no recollection of it. Nor being transferred thirty miles up harbour to a military hospital in Mobile. All I have is a memory of dreadful pains in my limbs and horrible headache that made me toss and turn in an effort to ease it. The fever caused me to see things. Sometimes I thought I was ill at home and could not understand why they could not take away the pains. At others, I had - of all things - felt that that boy, the Captain's servant, often sat somewhere close by, washed me and sponged my face, gave me drink and the rest of it. Something about the touch, something about the presence, in my deluded mind at times it was as if it was Judith there. Strange, because I do not recollect Judith as being best with sickness. Strange because I knew she was hidden away from me somewhere in this vast New World. Sick as I was, I sometimes craved the petticoat and could not have it. Then after a delay as if someone had been out to the shops, I could have it. It was under the pillow where I could touch it and hold it when I was afraid I might die. If I was on fire, when I held a fold against my cheek it felt of cool silk. And it was smooth and warm when I was shivering. Then sometime later they took it away and I think I wept. And the boy wept with me. Strange to weep, because at that time I began to know I would not die.

Chapter 17

A-roving, A-roving,
since roving's been my ru-i-in,
I'll go no more a-roving,
with you, fair maid.

I cannot tell you anything much about what they call over there 'the Deep South': Alabama and Mobile. Rather, I have only a few fragments of memory of the place. I came to essentially, to that old familiar lift and fall, clink and clank, to discover that I was at sea again in a pretty little runner named the *Coquette*, on her way to Bermuda. With a little luck and a lot of navigational skill, ships could still get in and out of Mobile in 1862. Admiral Farragut changed all that of course in '64 with his 'Damn the torpedoes. Full steam ahead!' and he was almost as bad at going aloft as I. More of that later.

So there I was. Distressed British Seaman (and I was, because there was damn all in my pockets when I searched them, not excepting my watch) and next morning we were going past the green islands and the white roofs of Bermuda and alongside at Hamilton by noon. The place was the same busy bustle as Nassau, making fortunes out of other peoples misfortune. None of the rest of my shipmates was on the *Coquette*. Those that lived served on in the *Florida*, when Captain Maffit made of that little warship a veritable terror of the seas. I wish I could boast of it but my heart was not in it, nor was I there.

Over the years I have had the opportunity of discussing my condition with not only our family physician but with the occasional tolerant medical guest passing through the hotel. It seems that something more than yellow fever is required to explain the long clouding of my mind. Possibly I was simultaneously afflicted with malaria and there may also have been an element of shock to the system, they say. I must be made of tougher stuff than I had thought to have survived. The young find life so exciting that they are often oblivious to danger. Even now, when I consider the undermanning of the *Florida* and what the effect of one of those sudden West Indian squalls might have been, I suddenly feel the need to sit down.

Also, now later in my life, decades later, I must grudgingly concede that more than good fortune was required to have got me passage out of Mobile on that runner. I have hugged to myself for years the belief that it might have been Captain Maffit but, although I'm sure he sanctioned it, what was a cook's mate to him amongst his many cares? And I must admit now that that man, that assistant paymaster, may have had a hand in it. Although why he should bother himself with it still beats me. If one is content to wreck another man's life, why look back? Unless you know you are guilty. And of course it got rid of me. I hate the impression of being given a kindly pat on the head before disposal, like a family pet that has become inconvenient and fortunately is to be re-homed. Well, I shall never see him again.

From Bermuda, I was fortunate enough to get passage in a homeward bound barque out of London River. A rough old trip it was too. Heavy seas and winds from a hurricane far astern. And a damp straw 'donkey's breakfast' in the forecastle to sleep on. I can recall standing near the foot of the mainmast in that ship and looking up. It struck me as being like a gigantic umbrella with some panels full of wind, bulging, and others flogging furiously, as if the whole affair was about to turn inside out. Beautiful they may appear but no more windjammers for me.

Perhaps the grammar school had given me speech that was at odds with my destitute condition and I suppose, as well, I had a tale to tell. As soon as I was able, I had turned to and produced some sort of order out of chaos in the Old Man's cabin. He had collections of newspapers from the fifties! Anyway, when we got in he gave me a few sovereigns for the train home. I don't suppose there was a more surprised man when he was reimbursed, and quickly. Even so, Captain Stevens, whether you are quick or dead by now, my thanks to you once more.

So I trudged into the old town once again, empty handed in every sense of the word. The family knew that I had sailed in the *Florida* by the word of Roderick. They had received my couple of letters from the long impasse at Nassau. They had found, deep in the inside pages, a tale of a clash in the harbour entrance at Mobile involving the *Florida* and of course had heard nothing more, thus greatly fearing my death. Death in Action, eh? That would have been a new one for the Musselwhites.

So, clothed from the 'slops', and shabby and creased, I lifted the knocker on the green front door next to the little shop and listened to it echoing through my parents' house.

Pa, who answered the door, and Ma, who came to see who had come calling, simply goggled at me at first. Ma seized me in a hug whilst I heard my father, obviously groping for reality, observe, "Tom, I think I should give you a key to the door now and not humbug about until your twenty-first," which was obviously designed to deal with all the problems of being delayed by wars between the States, raiding cruisers, battles and all the rest of it.

I went to the Bell next day although I did not relish the idea, coming home forlorn and empty-handed as I was. Strange how, after only a few months, everything looked more dingy and smaller than I remembered, even with the renovations supplied by Confederate gold. I told Job and Rachel how they had been too clever for me in Nassau and though I had kept on the trail of that man, illness had taken me off it. I found it hard to believe my own story, so exactly the same were my surroundings. Judith might have been out at the shops but would be at home for tea. Words were not adequate. I trailed off into silence. Job had aged, I thought. Rachel looked pale and her eyes never seemed to leave my face. Offered tea or brandy at last, I opted for brandy.

It was the theme of those years 1862 to 1864. The sun never shone and if it did it seemed counterfeit. If I drank in the Bell it was in silence, because what was there to say? Rachel would come in the end, take away the bottle and put me to bed on a sofa.

My father could not accept the significance of my malaise. How was one chit of a girl so different from another? Pa helpfully suggested that there were many more fish in the sea and in any case he wished to discuss with me something else, man to man: money. He drove me crazy. I shouted at him that all the thousands of it were useless. It had not moved Judith. Where was Judith? To him who had worked for every coin it was blasphemy I spoke. He thought me mad. I could see his eyes bulge and his lip tremble with the struggle to remain silent. But I felt fame and fortune had utterly failed me and I would have nothing to do with it except to draw my drinking money. Deposit accounts, investments, dividends; for what?

I lived in terror of the night. Of sleep. I might have quite a reasonable day, even a helpful day, taking my turn with the vegetables, helping to carry home Rachel's purchases. How she and Roderick stood for it I shall never know, for with anyone who offered me friendship I could speak of nothing else but Judith. I turned it all over and over again, speculating endlessly in what I had done wrong or failed to do. I recalled endless scenes and conversations and analysed them for clues, for all the good that it did, particularly as I could never touch on the topic that might have been the cardinal one, which now I have revealed to you. Should I have just pushed her down and shagged her? Shagged her and shagged her and shagged her until the tears and the cries ceased and when I pulled up her dress again she would help and then entwine me with her arms and legs. To hell with my superstition, my foolish, distorted ideals. Was that it? All she wanted was to be shagged but she could not say and I would not see? What would it have mattered in St. Michael's Parish? God had to put up with many brides who were with child coming up St. Michael's aisle.

No, my real terror was sleep and dreams. In fact Judy did not visit me often by dream. But the prospect of lying in bed sleepless, thinking about her and dreading her coming, perhaps to punish me by displaying her body, was an ongoing terror. So after possibly quite a civilised evening, come ten o'clock I would begin to throw the drink down until I could hardly speak and hardly walk. The brandy headache and the shakes in the morning seemed to me a small price for the blank, black oblivion all night that went before.

Even in my youthfulness I realised, after a month or so of this, that it could not go on. Since my windfall was so distasteful to me, so tainted now with despair, I went back to sea. That old saw that 'when the gangway is inboard, all debts are paid' still worked to a degree. Now, I would never agree to let a young man in that frame of mind go near a ship. The rail is always too close.

Rachel said nothing but I believed she did not wish me to go. Her eyes spoke of fear. Maybe she intuitively knew of the black night, the darkness in the soul and the black marbled sea passing by. She was ever afraid of the sea.

I did not care: for her, for the watchful sea, for foul liquor in foreign ports, for anything.

I did not sign on again with Royal Mail. I was convinced that the whole fleet would know my story and there would be smiling behind hands, which would be intolerable.

I signed with P&O and sailed on the *Mooltan*. Despite myself she caught my attention, for she was a wonderful ship, quite new, only built in 1861. Screw-driven and with an entirely novel sort of engine, which somehow used the steam twice over and thus only half the coal. But still a looker: long black hull and black funnel. Barque-rigged with topgallants on fore and main. Oh yes, one of the 'other navy' to be sure and rather too many inspections for my taste.

Maybe it was part of the healing process (if it ever has truly healed) but I also remember the *Mooltan* because of the stockpot in the galley. It was stirred with a broken oar. Where it was immersed in the boiling stock the wood was pristine clean, almost white. Above, it was well-nigh black from the greasy hands that did the stirring. My cooks are tired of hearing the story, so they wash their hands.

I also discovered a foundation of professional pride still down there under the wreckage. I would not take so much liquor at night that might make me let my passengers down in the morning.

When I got home and eventually trudged my way to the Bell, I quickly became aware of a tension, particularly between Rachel and myself, but including Uncle Joby. In the end I tackled them and asked them what was wrong. They looked at each other. Job said, no, there was nothing wrong. Rachel said that they thought I ought to be told.

While I was at sea they had received a letter. From Judy.

The atmosphere became as thick as smoke between us. Perhaps I scowled because Rachel rushed it out and said that they had told me because the family thought it would be better, on balance, if I knew she was all right.

I was angry. At first to be treated as though I was a sick child - then that they expected me to give a damn how or where she was. I simply stared ahead, or maybe glared ahead, and gulped my drink. After a while Rachel said in a small voice that Judy had been inquiring after me and was very worried.

That was too much. I sprang to my feet, and stamped and shouted that it was rather late for her to show any concern over me now. I went home.

I did not return next day, or the next. Then I crept back and, after a long silent session at the bar, managed to mutter to Rachel and ask if she would read the letter to me. I did not want to touch it, I remember. As though she could have written it with unwashed hands. But when I had been installed in an armchair in the parlour and Rachel sat down on a stool by my knee, I could see that neat rounded writing on the paper in her hands with a silent shock of recognition. It seemed as though it was from beyond the grave. I could hear the glasses being washed up in the bar below.

The letter commenced with a gush of apologies and excuses for Judith's disappearance and the anguish she knew it had caused. Such effusions are usually measured against what the author intends to do about the hurt and destruction engendered - in this case, nothing. I was included at the end of the paragraph with a clear air of afterthought.

Then followed an excited account of the flight via London and Liverpool. There was no mention of shared or single rooms. I found it hard to apply what I knew of my cousin to the person of that man, without concluding that she wore soiled linen now. I thrust the thought aside. There was a description of horrors on her solo passage to the Bahamas. I guessed - we guessed, Rachel and I - that she had stamped her foot and made a scene in Nassau. The obviously similar second leg in another runner into a Southern port had been rejected. No more travelling without him had been the likely ultimatum. No more arriving in a strange port wondering if he were there. Hence, the uncertain outcome of boarding the *Florida* in disguise, which if things had worked out as planned might have included a world cruise of giving and receiving destruction. A career in which the hull of the vessel glimpsed in the Laird shipyard at Liverpool, now named *Alabama*, was making her notorious reputation as a commerce raider.

My guess is that the proposition amused John Maffit. Indeed with all the other disasters befalling him and his ship, I could visualise him throwing up his arms and saying, "Why not, indeed." Other women famously had concealed their sex and gone to sea. I did not know whether to feel a fool for never trying to see if those vague sensations of recognition were true. Or allow her a little grudging praise for her skill as an actress. Her heart must have been in her mouth at times. And I had to concede, in the right place perhaps, towards the end. Also, I could but wonder whether the excitement of donning a pair of Confederate sailor's trousers had stood up to the experience for her all the way to Mobile Bay! Then I frowned and continued to listen.

It was to be expected that she set down a full account of her marriage. Judith left it out for my benefit. I guessed what she was doing.

There was then a brief account of their journey by railway and carriage across the South into the State of Georgia, to somewhere near the town of Macon, almost in the middle of the State, she said. The Tchocunno Plantation. She had made a little drawing of the house. She was never any good at drawing. There was an oblong box with a shallow, pointed lid. There were two rows of little boxes for windows and four somewhat wavering stripes on the front of the box. It was presumably a Greek revival design like the ones in Cadenas, but little to say how large or small it might be. I thought I would have bet money as well that it was built of wood not marble. And it angered me. I could have bought or built her her grand house. So much for my riches. It could lie there in the bank until it rusted.

The letter ended with the usual little pious platitudes for our welfare. They even included me. I had had enough of it and left. A part of me leaned towards sailing day and Alexandria. Another part sat down in a corner and asked 'Why bother?'

It settled down into a kind of pattern. Every month or so I would be back from sea and, somewhen during the turn-round leave, I would call on Job and Rachel and ask if there was any news. Often I felt distanced, excluded now. They were unfailingly kind but, like it or lump it, a member of their immediate family had taken a different path now and to some extent they must alter course to keep in her wake and at least in sight. Sometimes one of the letters would make me feel worse than before I came. Shamefully, when it carried with it some of the excited babble of a young girl enjoying a new, privileged life, I felt the worst. It was at such times that I felt Rachel's eyes upon me and there always seemed to be a hand on mine or even a kiss on the cheek before I turned away into the darkness. I felt so solitary those days, even in a crowded crew peak or some Maltese grog shop.

Even worse was to come home from sea and discover that she had not written. To face the crew gangway again with that kind of sailing day sadness was hard, hard indeed.

The son-of-a-bitch had married her. Now how do you feel about that? The sea is not a place to contemplate the details, as I am sure I have explained. As time went by, poor Rachel, ever one to forgive and forget and seek harmony, made the mistake of speaking to me of that man by name. I will not have that man's name used in my presence - not then, not now. I will not hear that hated name applied to Judith as a married woman - not then, not now. Then, to hear it come, even from Rachel's lips, was like a blow over the head. I remember my head felt like a bell that had been struck. My vision contracted from the familiar comforts of their parlour until I could see only plate, cup and saucer on the table in front of me. I think I roared out like a wounded animal and I can remember that poor girl's white, terrified face turned up towards me (for I had stood up in my frenzy) even while she still tried to prattle (as it seemed to me) of such sensible, civilised things as 'acceptance' and 'letting go.' Somehow I was got home and the doctor came and dosed me with laudanum. Next morning I found my knuckles raw from beating the table and was told that I had swept away the whole tea service. Well, so it was then, and so it still might be now. We have all of us grown used to the forbidden territory, although it can still cause practical difficulties in my eldest's affairs. I can suggest briefly, but otherwise they must do their best without me. I must be able to turn my mind away quickly. And there is still a faint stain on the private parlour carpet at the Bell, which I look for and contemplate as penance when I must go there.

There was another factor. It grew slowly. That Prussian general might describe what was going on in the States as 'two armed mobs chasing each other round the country' but they were certainly slaughtering each other successfully. The casualty figures when they were published were awesome. And when I am speaking of publishing, there lies the nub of my problem. It was my ship that brought the newspapers to Gibraltar and Malta, and Alexandria. We brought the news. I daresay the high-ups, the ambassadors, the Pasha and so on, were being kept up to date by telegraph, but they were not in the business of disseminating the news. Anything from Bombay surviving across the isthmus was likely to be ill informed and out of date, and used to wrap things in. And you try searching Valletta or Gib for discarded papers that the outward-bound mail steamer had brought out behind us, as we went home.

I had a fragmented picture of their war. There were accounts of battles whose names meant nothing to me: Fredericksburg, Chancellorsville, Gettysburg. There seemed to be a procession of Federal generals who could do nothing right: McClelland, Burnside, Hooker. General Robert E. Lee was the champion of the South and, as things went along, a man called Ulysses S. Grant slowly emerged for the North. There were other names too for the North, like Sheridan and Sherman. Particularly General William Tecumseh Sherman, who, it seems to me, may have been slightly mad.

Back in the Bell, Rachel had bought a big atlas and we pored over this, trying to make sense of the fragments of news. But as often as not battles make famous names of places too small for the map. Gettysburg, for instance, was attractive to Lee because of its boot and shoe factory...

Judith's letters continued to fill out her personal picture. It seemed that there was little or nothing of the man's family nearby. He seems to have been a single son of single sons. She grew fond of the slaves, of the house and the field and told us about them. Rachel could hardly contain her indignation. "She's treating those people as though they were family pets," she raged.

I thought to myself of that place, so far from home and family (not that it was anything but her own fault), and it seemed to me that it was an unexpected benefit that the slaves should grow fond of her and she of them. And a surprise that the selfish little sister should find an unexpected depth in herself for them.

But then I felt angry and said nothing. I put my hand upon Rachel's to calm her, and remember feeling pleased when she did not brush it away. They were as alike, of course, as one would expect of sisters. It was not of face but of body, and a way of carrying themselves. Sometimes, some movement Rachel made would catch my memory and hurt, like a sharp grass stem would catch an imprudent child's finger. I would say if I must, that the beauty of Judith's face was in the bone and those disturbing pale grey eyes. Rachel's' features are regular too, but from her there is an inner warmth like candlelight.

Other letters told of parties and balls she had been invited to and of silks and satins for dresses brought in by blockade-runner. And then of how precious was every pin and needle because they were almost unobtainable. There were but a couple of iron foundries in the whole of the South, and they had much more pressing tasks in those days than supplying ladies' pins. She was encouraged to learn to ride and enjoyed it. And not just ladies' side-saddle, she had added as a sly afterthought.

There was an impression of a country social round that Miss Austen might have written about, diminished by so many men gone to the war, and many fallen, but continuing zealously, in spite of difficulties. Into this she would appear to have been readily accepted, and a little crowing over the success of the 'innkeeper's daughter' was no surprise. She remarked once, in a way that seemed designed for me, that at home, even with all the money in the Bank of England, she would always have been the 'innkeeper's daughter' behind her back, no matter what they might have said to her face. Although I hated it, I had to admit to myself that she was probably right.

This was the pattern life took over most of two years. Unsatisfactory as it may sound, looking at that atlas, meticulously maintained by Rachel, at an interval of weeks or a month when I came home from sea, rather than every day, brought more comprehensible movement to this account of marching armies in an unreal, unknown land. For most of 1863 there appeared no immediate threat in it. Then, in the late autumn, things began to go wrong in the west for the Confederacy. This General Grant broke up a Southern siege on a place with the outlandish name of Chattanooga, in Tennessee. The defeated Southerners reeled back into Georgia. In May, come the end of rain, cold and winter mud, the Northern Army under General Sherman - this strange William Tecumseh Sherman - started out in the direction of Atlanta, an important railway junction that was in Georgia.

Those letters from Judith opened a window on life in the Confederate States as the Civil War entered its final stages. I hope they are in a bundle somewhere near to this account. Perhaps some scholar from the Hartley Institute might find them of value. She did not rave and rant about the right of States to secede from the American Union. You would not have expected her to. She made Rachel drum her fists on the table in frustration with her calm acceptance that the capital asset of the Southern States *was* the slaves. Without them the land could not be worked, the wealth would drain away, and this civilised society would disappear. Which was not to be thought about.

She also chronicled the growing shortages of many necessaries due to the increasingly effective blockade of every Southern port by the US Navy. The sorrow and hardship that the battle casualties were causing, and her fear when that husband, that man, was recalled to duty and sent to join what she called an 'ironclad' back at Mobile, leaving her on her own. I thought that this vessel must owe more to the *Virginia* or *Merrimack*, call her what you will, which had been re-created from a Union frigate burned to the waterline, than our own wonderful ships *HMS Warrior* or *Agincourt*. This thing was called the *Tennessee*.

The *Mooltan* reached Southampton in mid-August. I anticipated trouble when I saw Rachel waiting on the dockside near the P & 0 Steps. As soon as I had got my passengers and their luggage safely away, I slipped ashore myself. I got a hug and we walked a little way from the ship.

"I can't stay for more than a minute. I haven't stripped my cabins and I shall have Chief Steward after me," I said. "It isn't Ma or Pa, is it? Uncle Job's alright, isn't he?"

She put a hand in her basket. The letter had arrived that morning. "I wanted you to see it before you went near home," she said.

"What's in it? You read it," I replied.

He was dead, of course. They'd had a battle at the entrance to Mobile Bay again, and inside as well, it appeared, that made our confrontation there look puny: this was a thing of fleets. You know, this Admiral Farragut and his 'Damn the torpedoes. Full speed ahead' stuff. The *Tennessee* had taken a terrible beating with eleven- and fifteen-inch shells, and one of them had done the job I had failed to do and Jeb's cannon ball had tried to do.

I took the letter from her and skimmed through the rest. It was about what you would expect. I am sure Rachel was somewhat shocked by my apparent calm.

"Hmmm," I said. "I've got to get back aboard. I'll come round to the Bell this evening. Oh, and thanks, Rachel."

Mechanically, I got on with the work in my cabins. After the gales of hatred of that man: airless calm. As though all the portholes in my life were closed. I stripped the berths, took breakfast trays back to the pantry, found somebody's earring on the deck and dropped it in to the purser's office. It was too sudden. It always takes time to sink in with me. What was the significance of this? What was I supposed to do now? I got clean sheets and the rest from the locker and put them ready on the berths. I bundled the dirty linen together and put it in the laundry basket and found myself, almost as an afterthought, taking off my white jacket and throwing it in after them. I knew I was going to have to get off. I went down to my peak. It had been my hidey-hole for a long time, odorous and dark and cramped as it was, but it would not do any longer, so I got out my old grip and shovelled my few odds and sods into it. The ship was emptying rapidly now leaving alleyways deserted. I looked for the chief steward to tell him I wouldn't be back because of family trouble ashore, but I could not find him. And so to the crew's gangway and goodbye to the *Mooltan*. I thought that I would nip back tomorrow and leave a note for the chief steward. Or go to the P and O Office in Canute Road. Yes, that would be better and I could pick up my all-important discharge certificate as well. Or was it important now? It was beginning to rain, which always makes leaving a ship easier.

So to Mount Street and a hundred questions and problems. None of which included the cardinal question. What, if anything, was to be done about Judith, alone now in a foreign country encompassed about with a foreign war. Why should anything be done? Ma would say that she had made her bed and now she could lie on it. True, she had chosen it and had displayed considerable ingenuity getting to it, for a chit of a girl. The very word bed could still enrage me for she must have stripped off her clothes beside it and cavorted in it with that man. And do not shake your head and chide me, saying all marriage is such and one is happy indeed if it is so. I know that. Marriage may be so but not that marriage. My rage was, can be, is, like a half-smothered fire in a coal mine far below.

Leave her to it, then? Joby droops in spite of all his efforts, with two out of his three family women lost. After all these years as publican he is beginning to drink more of his own stock than is good for him.

After supper, during which my parents probably found me rudely preoccupied, I made my way to the Bell. Rachel put the atlas open upon the parlour table. There was a sheaf of newspaper cuttings pinned together. She had been meticulous in gathering whatever she could find of reports from the Civil War and recording them on the map. I was impressed. The map was not that large a scale and the clippings recorded fighting at places that, as usual, the atlas had never heard off but she had done her best with minute ink crosses. They marched roughly southeast from Chattanooga. Resaca. Cassville. Altoona. New Hope Church. The Federal troops had had a reverse after the folly at Kennesaw Mountain on 27 June, twenty miles from Atlanta. Then on 20 July they had beaten off a rebel attack at Peachtree Creek, only five miles north of Atlanta. It was clear where General Sherman was going and why. You could see that Atlanta was an important railway junction.

In early September there were reports that the Confederate Army had abandoned Atlanta, that Sherman had occupied the place on the 2nd and that it was in flames.

It was later that night, lying sleepless in the darkness, that the thought entered my mind that if Judith was left to lie on her bed, she might well die on it. If her nearest town was Macon in the middle of the state, then somewhat closer than we are to London in Southampton, a bloody great army was summoning up its strength and she was right in its path.

No matter what she had done (and what had she done, except in my fevered mind?) we could not abandon her there. But then the flesh quailed. We wrote imploring letters, warning her about what seemed to be approaching, telling her to get out. As if she did not know. And where was she to go? That man had some family still in New Orleans but New Orleans had fallen long ago. Besides, again it was on the other side of battle lines.

God knows if she ever received them, but sometimes it seemed that she could hear us and replied to our letters. She had friendly neighbours but otherwise she knew no one. She had also formed a great attachment to that damned house. She felt it was a kind of memorial to her dead husband and she had some duty to preserve it. I suppose, unless one sees the body, attends the rites of passage, and is consoled by friends and family, there is no true seal on the business of a death. He had left her there to go to his duty and now it seemed she had this crazy inclination to wait for him there. Oh, and one good thing: the slaves were frightened, but loyal.

And the flesh of us all was weak. She was more than four thousand miles away across the stormy Atlantic in a country at war of which we knew nothing. I daresay your airships, if you have them, have brought travel down to a question of days and hours, but for us it was weeks. And then this State of Georgia; how did we get to it with the ports blockaded? How did we get to it from New York or Boston when it was on the other side of the front? How would we get travel documents or guides? Were there hotels or inns? Surely there must be, but we did not know. And so on. And she had brought all this on herself and now on us.

Then several things happened quickly. Firstly, one evening as we endlessly chewed the fat. Uncle Joby suddenly froze in the act of lifting his whisky to his lips and said, "Isn't she still a British citizen?"

Next morning a correspondent reported that General Sherman said that he was going to 'make Georgia howl' and he was going to march to the sea. 'We cannot change the hearts of these people of the South,' he was reported as saying, 'but we can make war so terrible...and make them so sick of war that generations will pass away before they again appeal to it.'

I thought to myself, along the lines of Augustine of Hippo, that we are going to have to go for her, but not yet, not yet; so desperate an expedition it seemed that my heart faltered before its prospect.

Then, in course of the endless discussion of the problem and what we were going to do, Rachel let slip a mention of 'the baby'.

"What baby?" said I.

"What baby?" demanded Job.

She looked at us both with horror and put her hand before her mouth but I think it was deliberate and the rest a little play-acting.

"She wrote some time ago that she might be with child. I did not dare tell Papa, in case I gave you false hopes. Nor you Tommy, for fear it would make you rage."

"You say that I might be a grandfather?" Job asked in a bemused manner.

I said nothing although my thoughts were a tumult. That was *my* baby, my son, my daughter, given away to a stranger. I raged a moment at Judith but then it passed. That which I had longed for, for her, that her lovely beloved face should not disappear from the world for at least another generation, might still come true. My mind became instantly made up. "And I say that I might be a type of uncle, that I might have a niece once removed or whatever." It seemed such a serious and adult thing to be: even a sort of uncle to have a niece. I felt suddenly ridiculously proud of it.

"I'm going to have to go and get them," I said. All eyes turned upon me.

"Then I shall go with you," said Rachel.

Chapter 18

I could write a whole volume more about our journey. Once it was decided that we should go, the explosive release of youthful energy could move mountains. Plenty of money helped. It could not entirely reconcile poor Uncle Joby to the fact that the last female of his family had become totally disobedient and was off on a harebrained scheme. But there was the far-off predicament of his other daughter. We attempted to raise his spirits with the optimism of youth, probably failed, but he let himself be convinced, in public at any rate. I subsidised hired help to run the Bell and look after him. Which would be frequently supplemented with Ma's home cooking, of course.

I filled pocket and purse and Rachel and I went and bought what it was hoped were suitable clothes for the cold of the American winter. I decided that we should be reasonably elegant as well; it carries weight with the functionaries of hotels, and shipping and railway companies. I almost stood over a bespoke tailor until he produced me a respectable suit in thirty-six hours. And we even practised referring to them as 'railroads', although I had an inward reservation about that, in view of the things having been invented here. Rachel believed that it would be foolish to stir up unnecessary antagonism and of course she was right.

We took the London and South Western 'Railroad' to the capital. Trying not to tremble, we walked the marble floors of the Foreign Office in the hope that what we were attempting might permeate upwards through his civil servants to reach the ears of Lord John Russell, if only as an example of the foolhardiness of youth. They were surprisingly amiable and tolerant. We discovered that, officially, we did not require passports to travel in North America but were issued with them anyway in view of the seriousness of the situation there.

We took the new passports to the United States Embassy and left with the appropriate visas, feeling sobered by the gruff warnings of the dangers we might encounter but also with invaluable advice about how, with a lot of luck, we might circumvent them.

Then the turning world brought me again face to face with the Confederate States commissioner in Great Britain, Mr James M. Mason, whom I had last seen as a prisoner being escorted down the ship's side of the *SS Trent*. This produced a letter to be delivered - where else? - to 10 Rumford Place in Liverpool and that *éminence grise* of the Confederate Navy, Commander Bulloch. He recognised Rachel at once, which surprise did nothing to impede the flow of Southern charm, whilst our story raised concern and Southern chivalry about the threatened younger Belle. It also produced names and addresses and invaluable letters of introduction. All of which went on board the *City of Glasgow* for our passage to New York.

Ten months storm and two months fog? With winter upon us, there was no fog in the North Atlantic. A boon for me perhaps, as I have a great dislike of steaming in fog. Speed always seems maniacally fast when you can't see where you're going and know there are no brakes. But even so, how poor Rachel would have blessed that oily calm that goes with fog. She was terribly ill with *mal de mer* and so vehement was her declaration that she would never set foot in a ship ever, ever again that it seemed we should have to become United States citizens ourselves. I felt queasy myself, of which I was ashamed, but which I attributed to being at sea for the first time with little to do but succumb.

To trim the account of our travels to the bare bone, from New York we journeyed more or less west by rail until we reached St. Louis. There, river steamer services on the upper Mississippi were available south to Memphis, Tennessee. From there, it was east by road to this place Chattanooga and after with increasing delay and trepidation, in the direction of Atlanta. All in all, it was not much short of two thousand miles. What is Southampton to the northern coast of Scotland? Five hundred miles? Four times that!

What did we see? A city. New York, built higher, streets jammed with traffic and people, busier even than London. I think people here have little idea of what is being built and settled over there. It is awesome. We were in hot railway carriages, which is to say hot railroad cars, cold railroad cars, cars full of tobacco smoke, spittoons, poker players, conductors not guards, seats that sometimes felt as if they were making permanent impressions on our anatomy, boots on seats, engines that devoured wood and tolled bells when entering settlements where rails frequently share with roads, and a country with woods, mountains, plains, little white farms, where we would have thatches that rolled endlessly past day after day after day. Great platefuls of steak. The smell of wood smoke. Fleas. Deep snows with fir trees. Grimy sheets. The distant other shore across the wide waters of the Mississippi, the 'Father of Waters' himself, rolling once more at peace south to the Gulf of Mexico. Travel-weary, homesick, entranced, fearful; the blasting siren of a stern-wheeler just thrashing her way round the bend, the mournful call of a train - oh, in the night that loneliest of sounds; they are indelible, shared memories for Rachel and me. I knew she must have been often uncomfortable, longing for a bath and to change her clothes, hungry, stiff, cold, hot: I don't remember her ever complaining. I don't remember her ever without a quick smile if I caught her eye or she thought I might be disheartened. The fear of what might lay ahead grew in us both.

The road was rougher. Our stagecoaches crawled behind great columns of covered wagons: the Federal Army supply trains. There were rumours of Confederate cavalry. Worse, rumours of Confederate guerrillas. Our credentials were checked more frequently by suspicious, bearded young men in blue uniforms, wearing those frightful kepis.

Atlanta was never a showpiece. Just a railway town on a junction, sprung up thirty years ago rather like Eastleigh near Southampton, although with more greenery. A third of it had been dynamited and set on fire when the Confederate soldiers abandoned it and destroyed everything that might have been of use to the Union. Then General Sherman had a third burned of what was left, in case it would have been of any use to the Confederacy, when his army marched out towards Savannah and the sea. Atlanta was to be of no strategic use to anyone. We saw railway tracks not simply ripped up but twisted to look like giant hairpins, leaving forlorn locomotives marooned. There were big masonry buildings reduced to a few tottering walls, and wooden ones everywhere, now nothing but ash. Ash still warm. We could see a few furtive people, black and white, scavenging, carting off anything left that might be of value. I found it hard to believe it would ever be rebuilt, although I read that it has and even flourishes.

We made the acquaintance of a journalist, a war correspondent whose advice was invaluable, for just ahead of us then lay 'tiger country'. If our quest were written up as a human-interest story later, we would not begrudge it in return for his cynical common sense and practical tips.

There were many soldiers on the road, some going forward to the front, some coming back. We were passed by jingling cavalry (Americans don't bounce up-and-down on their saddles like we do), field guns, their limbers rattling-clattering, and there were platoons on the march with rifles to shoulders.

The roads had been rough to start with, but with this treatment were puddled and pockmarked with potholes. We lurched and jolted about, knocking into each other until 'Sorry' and 'Pardon me' became worn out and we lapsed into strained, silent endurance. How much worse for the wagons passing us, full of pale, bearded men with bloodstains and bandages. I saw Rachel's eyes follow every one. She never looked away or down as some delicate ladies might. I thought about the soldiers in the High Street that she had wept for when she was a little girl. It seemed to me as though she had had some intuition that they would be as these.

There were columns of prisoners of war. Some of their faces were expressionless, some disconsolate, and a few light-hearted with relief. All were hollow-eyed with the boniness of the half-starved. I heard Rachel's indrawn breath as a group passed by, most of whom were in grey rags supplemented with blankets and any old garments, and the majority barefooted. The Blue and the Grey one had read so effortlessly about in the papers, Johnny Reb and Billy Yank, did nothing to prepare anyone for this threadbare, mud-caked, trampled humanity here. That it always ends like this must be the best kept secret of the Captains and the Kings.

Later, we saw other soldiers too. Some half-in, half-out of trenches or sprawled on their backs, faces to the comfortless winter sky. Some were curled up on the earth as though they slept. Some were alone, some in little groups, some still in their ranks, blue and grey tangled together where they had been trying to kill each other, their weapons still close to hand. War had swept through here so recently that there had been no time to tidy up the truth. Which was awful. And not so far away in front of us came the flat thump of guns.

Rachel at last hid her face in my shoulder but I could not tear my eyes away from it. I heard myself futilely trying to comfort her, saying that this war would be over soon, that nobody could go on long like this. Her muffled reply was to ask, "Where's my sister? Where's my sister?" Oh Lord, how I remember. Where indeed, in the path of this forest fire, where every house and barn was wrecked or smoking. And in my mind I called Judith a silly, silly bitch to have put herself in peril like this because of an infatuation, and then dragged us into it after her. Oh yes, I did.

We found our way into Macon (the locals pronounce it 'Maykin') which appeared to have been a pleasant little town before having a cavalry battle fought in its streets, a day, hours maybe, before. People were still dazedly sweeping up shattered glass and effecting temporary repairs to buildings. We had already seen much worse, but here I kept thinking: that was where she came to buy new gloves, that must be where she bought the groceries - and the damage was more intrusive. Personal.

The people about were so shocked that it was with difficulty we obtained directions to the Tchocanna Plantation. The last of these suddenly emerged from his self-absorption and stared at us.

"You folks ain't from these parts, are you? Asking for the Tchocanna where that young English wife is. Are you English? Are you some of her folk?"

My skin prickled. We must be so close. How would we be received? Was the English lady all right? He did not know.

We discovered an unscathed livery stable, where neither side had apparently had time to steal the horses. So, feeling nervous and out of place, uninvited, we found ourselves walking our hired horse and buggy up a long driveway lined on each side with young trees. About two thirds of the way up we caught again the sudden whiff of burned wood; the horse snorted and tossed his head a little and fear entered our hearts.

It was cold and so quiet. I had somehow expected high walls and a locked wrought iron gate. There was a white painted fence and an unpretentious wooden gate, wide open. There were green lawns planted with many small trees that are no doubt beautiful with blossom in springtime. There was a thin scattering of fallen leaves on the grass. Facing us were half a dozen shallow stone steps leading up to nowhere and nothing, except the now hateful heaps of reeking ash and fallen, blackened beams. Nothing, that is, except three tall surviving brick chimney stacks that only yesterday I had heard bitterly described as 'Sherman's Sentinels'. While we gaped at this freshly born ruin, even as we looked, a tiny flame, almost invisible in the daylight, suddenly sprang up on a charred beam, wavered a moment and went out with a puff of blue smoke. The lawn beneath our feet was pitted with hoof prints.

It seemed so quiet. Perhaps she had gone to neighbours. A wild forlorn hope, perhaps this was not the place at all. Slowly, we began walking round the wreck. It was almost pathetic the way a small orchard and a kitchen garden behind, which would never have been visible to arriving visitors at the house, now just lay there open to view. There were even a few items still fluttering on a clothesline.

About a hundred yards away we could see a row of low log cabins. There was not a soul in sight but I was sure we were being watched and there was a wisp of smoke from a chimney. Uncertainly, we made our way in that direction.

As we approached, we heard a door creak open and a black woman came cautiously out, followed by a youth and a much older man. The cabins must be the slave quarters - and how would the slaves, so recently become freedmen and women in the wake of Sherman's Jubilee, react to strange white people? We walked carefully towards them.

The woman was not in the first flush of youth. Her brown face was becoming lined but she wore a decent brown dress and her mobcap was white and starched. We asked if this was indeed the Tchocanna Plantation and that we were in search of Mrs...

At my question the woman's eyes brimmed over and the boy was knuckling surreptitiously at his. I felt my knees tremble with foreboding.

"Yo' lookin' fo' Miss Judy? Yo' her folks? All the way 'cross the sea from England? Oh, Massa, oh, Massa..." More Negroes were emerging from the cabins, now it was clear we were not soldiers, and many of them were similarly affected. The woman shook her head silently with her lips trembling. At last she managed to quaver "Yo' come. I's got to show you."

They led us to a far corner of the garden. There was a plot surrounded by a white-painted metalwork fence that we had not noticed. To our unbelieving eyes we could see headstones within. The woman opened a gate and led us in.

"We done put her here, Massa..."

There was a new-dug grave in the turf, still raw soil. You could smell the earth. A glass pickle jar with a bunch of chrysanthemums rested on it. It felt quite unreal.

"She got a proper casket, Massa. Ol' Ephraim there, he made it proper, he did. We did it right as we could 'cept we couldn't get no preacher man. There weren't nobody t'ask. Nobody came at all after them horse soldiers gone." She opened her hands helplessly and then let them fall to her sides.

Horse soldiers? Cavalry? The other slaves stood outside the fence with their big straw hats in their hands. It was only just audible but they were humming or singing something. Some strange tune it was, a dirge, a song of mourning, of loss. Some of them rocked to and fro. I had never heard or seen such a thing before, but as I write here I can summon it up still. We were dazed. Rachel and I stood there, staring at the fresh-turned earth. We did not know what to say, what to do or where to go next. It was the end of the road. Nothing but empty-handed return now, after so long a journey.

I put my arm round Rachel's shoulder to try and comfort her. She drew close and leaned on me. We remained dry-eyed; not, I think, from British reserve but from nervous shock.

The coloured folks told us what had happened over a simple meal, although it was hard to swallow a morsel. It took some time because of their unfamiliar dialect and at first we found what they told us difficult to comprehend.

Four days before, a foraging party of Union cavalry had arrived, ostensibly to seize any fodder for their beasts and food for themselves that might have been stored for the winter. Judith, it appeared, jumping to the conclusion that they intended to destroy her precious house, had seized one of her husband's sporting guns and suddenly appeared at the portico from within. Whereupon one of the cavalrymen had shot her dead. Even with the bitterness of a long war and rumours that General Sherman was prepared to look the other way when cases of unnecessary violence and destruction occurred, this seemed a straightforward atrocity.

I felt my heart swell with anger and I began to rehearse to myself my case to deliver to the Federal authorities. It took some time and repetition before I began to understand what had happened. She had learned to ride and enjoyed it, but discarding riding side-saddle as fuddy-duddy around their own land, she had had a pair of trousers made of this material called jean and used a man's saddle. She had been riding so attired that fatal morning and with her hair pushed up into a straw hat and seen in silhouette in the front doorway, they had taken her for a belligerent male and fired at her. It was likely enough, even if there was a passing doubt that these men were spoiling for trouble anyway - trouble that was likely to have followed another road if they had recognised her as an attractive young woman, even if they had murdered her afterwards.

There was nothing to prevent an enormous, crushing conclusion from descending silently upon my spirit. Do you know that feeling you get after swallowing too big a mouthful of something indigestible? How pain grips your chest and you cannot speak? If I went back far enough, I was the root from which had grown up this evil growth, this tragedy befalling my nearest and dearest. It was me; my fault. Oh guilt, guilt, guilt! I wanted to roll on the dirt floor in my agony but dared not move a muscle in case I was looked at.

It was I who had coaxed and encouraged her as a little girl to lift her skirts. It was I who had slavered over the revelation of the private parts of her body. I who addicted her to the opium of the Exquisite Sensations. I had undermined her virginity until it was as empty as a rotten tooth and then denied her relief from the ache of it. For what? For some sort of theory? Some superstitious folk belief in the magic of the maiden, more suited to clodhoppers who begin milking at four in the morning? Just as we were, two generations ago. Now I found my fancy boots still caked with mud.

I loathed the idea of her putting on trousers. Indeed the Bible forbids it somewhere. But because I could watch her strip I had put aside the anathema of the woman in trousers. I remembered at the beginning she had tried to draw up the trousers under the last of her petticoats and I forbade it. It pleasured me to see her stand there in her pants for a moment, trying to hide her groin with a hand. Now wearing trousers had killed her. Had led to that pathetic little oblong of fresh-turned, foreign earth out there and what lay six feet beneath it. There must be a glint in the eye of the God who squatted in St. Michael's tower.

Indeed, suppose her elopement with that man to this far country had been, even in part, to get away from me? I felt I must somehow crack or break, but at last there came relief with the hot guilty tears. Honest Rachel saw, wept with me and held my hand, and made me feel guiltier than ever.

Around us, many of these kindly, simple people wept with us as they spoke. It seemed as though Judy had had a transformation, had blossomed in this place. As they spoke of help and kindness from her in their times of trouble, I became aware of a faint grudging resentment that they should have such memories of her while I had not. All blasted away four days ago. I should never know now.

In this moment of wailing and gnashing of teeth, there was something both of us had forgotten until they came and placed a bundle in Rachel's arms. This baby - a girl - was well into her first year. She looked as if she had just awakened. I remember the small sounds she was making as her mouth moved. Her expression was as if she had not yet made up her mind if it was a good day or a bad day, but then she looked up into her aunt's face and smiled. She was growing sparse black curls on her head already. Was it fancy that those dark eyes now regarding me already had their fairy slant? I can tell you it was not. She sucked her thumb and brought up a little wind as babies do. She was like and she was not, but like enough. It had been, I suppose, a small vain prayer that her mother's face should not yet pass from the world.

"What is her name?" I asked the woman.

"Ain't never bin christened," she said. "What with the war and Massa gittin kilt an' all. Think Miss Judy had Frances in mind cos Massa's family was comin' from New Orleans down the river there. But she try lots of different names different days and the baby don't care."

I had a stroke of genius, I thought. A name had floated into my head, connected with some scandalous duchess I had read about. Genius however, is not always best appreciated by those around one, so I spoke carefully.

"Perhaps we should call her Georgiana," and then hurried on and said, "and Frances too, for ordinary days." So we did eventually, in the old black marble font at St. Michael's.

We walked back with her to the family plot to stand by her mother's grave. I suppose it did her no harm and for us it was a gesture to Judith that we had come and taken up the task that would have been her greatest anxiety. They say that the newly dead are granted forty days and forty nights for a last visit to places and people dear to them before they must away. There was no sudden breath of wind, nor did the sun break through. Poor girl, through what unfamiliar veil would she be looking at us now.

I felt nothing really, except an increasing resolve to go home with Georgiana and bring her up and to hell with this beautiful, poisonous country. It ought to have been a place full of warmth and fun, parasols and pretty dresses and music for Georgiana here - but it was now an ash pile. All gone. Except... except that these coloured people who had been kind to us and who mourned Miss Judy with us were free. No more beasts of burden, heavy or light, dependent on kindness for everything; just free people who knew nothing. God help them.

I was going to attempt to explain what I was feeling to Rachel when a strange thing happened. We heard the sounds of horses approaching up the driveway. Then a single rider walked his horse into the grounds leaving the others behind him, clustered anxiously it seemed. They were US cavalry, we could see. This man was not wearing uniform. He had on an exceedingly creased grey suit and was smoking a slim cigar. His eyes roved about restlessly, lingering with an expression of distaste on the remains of the house. His face was deeply tanned and he had a stubbly beard of the length that leaves you wondering if the owner had had a hard few days outdoors or was growing it. He raised his hat and his hair looked like that of a man who had sat on a bucket and been trimmed by a trooper.

"Good afternoon to you," he said. And then in the way they do, "My name is Sherman, William T. Sherman."

"Good afternoon," I responded automatically. Instantly, as so often on the journey, I received his full attention because of my unfamiliar accent.

"Aren't you British?" he asked sharply. "Do you have business here? With this place?"

I explained that I had and briefly what had happened. His eyes narrowed, and my stomach turned over. It was very different, but there was something reminded me of Captain Maffit. A quick mind. A perceptive glance. In my experience you do not find such men standing behind a shop counter. Yes, I was becoming certain who this man was.

"Then it is true. The woman... the lady they say has been unfortunately killed here, she was English? British? She was related to you?"

But I had a question of my own. "Pray excuse me, sir, if I am jumping to conclusions, but could it possibly be that you are General Sherman. General William Tecumseh Sherman?"

He gave me a sombre look. "I am," he said.

I had never met a general before and my tongue stumbled over introducing Rachel. He tipped his hat to her but she did not smile. He inhaled at length on his cigar and then threw it away, although it was only half smoked. (I must admit here that I still have it preserved in a special tin.)

"I must speak with you," he said. "May I presume on your grief and dismount?" He swung down from his horse, took Rachel's arm and my shoulder and steered us away from the Negroes across the lawn.

"She was your sister?" he asked Rachel, who silently nodded. The baby in her arms cooed and Sherman peered at her and absently twiddled his fingers to try and amuse her.

"And this of course must be her baby. You would not bring one of your own so far." He straightened up. "As it has been reported to me, a considerable error was made here." He fumbled in an inner pocket for his cigar case.

"Firearms were resorted to prematurely, without any attempt to ascertain the situation, which a second or two must surely have made clear. Despite your late and lamented cousin's eccentric, er, costume, her sex should have been clear to all. I cannot expect you to forgive my men. Only remind you that this is the fourth year of a long and bitter war. You must have seen it all around you. And to survive so long is because they have learned to be fastest on the trigger. Unfortunately they have also become callous. What they did subsequently, when they discovered what had happened - to lie that they had been shot at, and to burn down this house as false evidence - was regrettable, most regrettable." He sighed. "Fortunately, conscience was too much for a couple of them. Mr Musselwhite, Miss Day, I have to give the people of this State a rough, bad time to weary them from supporting their mistaken cause and army. But it is not my intention to offer gratuitous violence to these Southern women, no matter how they hate and revile us. As to your sister, ma'am all I can do is express my regret on behalf of the Army of these once United States and cite the war; the damn endless bloody war I told them it would be."

These many years, I have often gone over that meeting in my mind. Were we unduly flattered by such attention from a famous United States general? Was his arrival then merely coincidence? Was there anything in his pocket that conveyed to him that there was an English woman at risk from his forces? That it would be better not to incur the wrath of the British Government on the death of a British subject. And then discovered too late that exactly what he was warned about had come to pass. So back with his staff earlier that day, did he curse a chore that took him aside from more important matters? We went quietly. No fuss with government when we got home. Mission successful? Who knows? These extraordinary personalities can run rings round us lesser mortals when they wish. Who knows? But I will say he proved a friend in need to what was then a very youthful US citizen, later in life.

The pony was put back between the shafts and, distinctly overawed as well as comforted by an escort of two cavalry troopers, the four of us arrived back in Macon. Four? The infant made three. Fourth was Molly, the freed slave woman, who had become distraught at the prospect of separation from her charge, her 'Honeychile'. I had looked at Rachel and Rachel looked back at me and we were both of the same mind. So Molly packed her few possessions and journeyed back across the ocean in a happier direction than her ancestors. How nice to be rich and make youthful, spur-of-the-moment decisions. People collect family photographs today. I am sure that Molly's recollections and stories about Judith kept my uncle alive for many years. Curly white-haired and fragile now, she is still with us, and to her rocking chair is where all the family take their troubles, great and small.

In Macon, recovery was sufficient for us to find lodgings, and next day I found a funeral parlour and paid the director to furnish a headstone for Judith's grave when the time was right. I also visited a lawyer and on his advice swore out an affidavit that put on record everything I knew about that man and his family, the Tchocanna Estate, the child and the circumstances in which we found her. I had a feeling that the baby might one day receive a significant inheritance from Tchocanna. The lawyer also hinted that in less chaotic times there might have been a good deal more to us taking the child away, but as things were he could only advise us to go and go quickly.

Lastly, with some difficulty, I found an Episcopalian clergyman. Next day he accompanied Rachel and myself for a last short vigil by the grave and he read the burial service. If anyone was 'cut down like a flower' it was Judith.

It was strange but although her murder was still only a few days old, it seemed as though it had happened much longer ago to Rachel and me, now we had to a degree got over the shock of the discovery. She had been gone from us more than two years. I looked around me and tried to imagine the place as it might have been in springtime and I daresay it had been beautiful. But it was her place not ours, so let her rest in peace in it now. She was never going to come home.

We started back. The whole State was in the grip of conflict as Sherman marched his terrible way towards the sea at Savannah, so there was no short cut for us. The miles seemed so weary, it had all been in vain and our spirits would have been depressed indeed, if we had been empty-handed. But we had the baby, and caring for her was exhausting enough to keep us from brooding. How much worse we would have managed without Molly's assistance makes me sweat to think about it.

There are travellers' tales enough about our journey but I will keep them for some other volume. I know Rachel could not share it, but for me I remember the bursting relief with which I got my first glimpse of the sea at New York, winter grey and unwelcoming as it was.

We took passage in an Inman liner to Southampton, which was a boon, spending Christmas at sea. We were of course in mourning and took but a quiet part in the jollification but the odd glass of champagne and the occasional sip of port did pass our lips. Come Channel Night, expecting to be home next day, celebrations became even more frenetic and perhaps we took a glass or two more. Rachel said she felt sleepy and went to her cabin. I felt my head go round and decided on some fresh air and took a stroll on deck.

The coastwise lights were flashing and above them the stars were frostily brilliant. Beneath them the sea was like black velvet. It came to me that, as the weather and sea were good, Rachel should see it for one last time before it was time for lights out, unless she was already in bed.

I went down and rapped on her cabin door and explained my suggestion. I was told to come in, so I did. Perhaps her complexion was a little flushed? She was still sitting on the little seat below the porthole in the black velvet evening dress she had bought in New York, but she had drawn it back above her knees. There was a froth of lace from her petticoats and more about her knees from those new short white pantaloons. And her legs were in white silk stockings. Oh, New York, New York! I do not think I had seen more of Rachel than averting my eyes from the occasional glimpse of ankle. I was thunderstruck into banality.

"What are you doing?" I asked.

"Trying to make you really look at me, Tommy. Just for once," she replied. Then she dropped her gaze.

"I know what you and my sister did," she muttered. "I listened at doors and I looked through keyholes. I was so jealous sometimes, I thought I might shrivel up and die." She glared at me defiantly. "So now I don't care. I'm shameless, if that's what it needs. I'm only an innkeeper's daughter too."

She refused to turn away her gaze, lifted her chin, swallowed hard and hitched up her skirt all of an inch more. And I swear you could have cracked walnuts between those knees so hard she was pressing them together. I felt overwhelmed. Then she sagged and her face went so absolutely crimson that I thought for a moment she must have had a seizure.

In the end I found myself on my knees, and not without banging my elbow and head in that cramped little cabin, trying to cover her up, wondering if this was the wrong thing to do and half expecting torrents of tears or raging slaps, remembering the Western Shore at low tide long ago. I would not have believed that a pathetic, whispered 'thank you' could so outweigh the loss of those beautiful, silk-sheathed legs. After that we tried a first awkward, bumpy kiss.

We did go on deck a little later and stayed together leaning on the rail in the dark for a long time. The air was frosty and there was rime forming on the deck planks, but somehow it did not seem to matter. Only a few more nautical miles to go. And then the prospect of another long voyage.

Printed in the United States
64848LVS00001B/53

9 781420 885644